MORE THAN CHARMING

by

JOMARIE DEGIOIA

www.lachesispublishing.com

Published Internationally by Lachesis Publishing Inc.
Rockland, Ontario, Canada

A catalogue record for the print format of this title is available from the National Library of Canada

ISBN 978-1-927555-13-2

A catalogue record for the Ebook is available
from the National Library of Canada
Ebooks are available for purchase from
www.lachesispublishing.com

ISBN 978-1-927555-12-5

Editor: Joanna D'Angelo

Copyeditor: Giovanna Lagana

Dedication

As always, I'm ever grateful to my family for their unfailing support. I also thank my agent, Michelle Grajkowski, and my wonderful editor, Joanna D'Angelo, for helping to bring this story starring my all-time favorite hero to life!

Also Available

More than Passion
Pride and Fire

MORE THAN CHARMING

Chapter 1

England, 1825

"My lord, what a surprise it was to hear you were returning to town after all."

James Bradford, Viscount Roberts, smiled at his elderly butler. "Hello, Giles."

"How was your trip, my lord?"

"The trip from Yorkshire was quite uneventful." James shrugged. "Much like the past year, I'm afraid."

"And how is the earl?"

"Father is as steady as the Thames." James blew out a breath. "Lord, I'm weary."

"From such an uneventful trip?" Giles winked. "Pray tell me the master didn't stop at any nefarious pubs along the way?"

"No." James smiled. "I suppose I'm just a bit out-of-sorts is all, being away from town for the past year. Have you heard any good gossip, Giles?"

"Never let it be said that I carry tales, my lord."

James rolled his eyes.

"Little to report, actually," Giles said. "No young ladies debauched in our parlor, no angry husbands looking for you."

James laughed. "Hardly that when I was in town. I much prefer to charm my way through the ton, Giles, and take my physical pleasures elsewhere."

Giles nodded and followed James into his study. "And aren't we all pleased about that?" The butler indicated a pile of letters and cards on top of the highly polished mahogany desk. "It would appear, my lord, that they have learned of your return to town."

James knew precisely to whom the man was referring. The matrons, with their eyes out for prospective husbands for their daughters, had sent him invitations to teas and dinners and the like.

With a groan, James settled into the chair behind his desk. "And so it begins."

Giles watched him with a wry smile. "If I may speak, my lord."

"Giles, you've been in the service of the Bradford family since my father was a boy. Pray, don't contain your candor now."

"There is a solution."

"Hmm?" James looked at him sharply, a brow arched. "A solution?"

"Take a wife."

James rubbed his hand over his face. "Don't start with that, Giles," he said without anger. "Believe me, it's all I heard in Yorkshire this past year."

"Ah, so the earl is inclined to agree with me?"

"Never mind," James said. "I'm just nine and twenty. Surely I've a few months left before I get leg-shackled."

James saw the butler's smile, but thankfully Giles said no more on the subject. "Would you like something for dinner, my lord?"

"What? Oh, yes," James answered absently, his mind already on the invitations and the possible excuses he could use to extricate himself from the engagements. It wasn't that he didn't want to get married—it was that he hated all of the nonsense that surrounded the Season. All the parading and posturing and matchmaking. He wanted the kind of marriages that his friends had, though. Strong and loving bonds with their wives. And passion. Damn, how he envied Kane and Leed, and now his good friend Chester was finally tying the knot. Soon he would be the only one left standing.

Giles left James to see to his master's meal, but reappeared in the doorway not a scant ten minutes later. "Viscount Leed to see you, my lord."

James felt a genuine smile curve his lips as his good friend Paul Talbot entered the room.

"Roberts!" Paul said. "I heard you were once more here among the living."

"Leed." James stood and extended his hand. "Good to see you, man."

The men exchanged a hearty handshake and Paul took a seat across from James. "And how did you leave Yorkshire?"

"My father isn't much improved, I'm afraid," James answered. "But the doctor assures me he won't worsen."

"Well, that's something," Paul said with a shrug. "Chester will be pleased you're attending the wedding."

James smiled at that. "Yes. About time he quit dancing around that girl and married her."

"Truly."

"And how is your lovely wife, Leed?"

"Michelle is perfection, thank you."

"And Rose?"

A smile spread across Paul's face. "The little imp is just like her mother, I daresay. Strong-willed and into mischief."

"I look forward to seeing Rose," James said. "She was but a babe when I was last in town."

Paul nodded.

"And your sisters?" James asked. "Are they well?"

Something flickered over Paul's face, gone so quickly James dismissed it.

"Yes, the twins are fine," Paul answered. "They'll attend the wedding, of course."

Paul's sisters, Catherine and Elizabeth were a year apart in age, but everyone always referred to them as "the twins" because they looked so much alike.

"Ah. Willing dance partners."

Paul slanted a look at him. "If those papers on your desk are what I think they are, you'll hardly be without willing dance partners. The lovely Catherine and Elizabeth notwithstanding, of course."

"These bloody ridiculous . . ." James picked the invitations up off the desk. "I feel like a prize horse up for auction, for God's sake." Without further hesitation, he swept the letters and cards into the wastebasket.

"Roberts," Paul began, "is something troubling you?"

James let out a loud sigh and raked his fingers through his hair. "I've had quite enough of so-called Society, Leed. Perhaps I'll return to Yorkshire and spend the rest of my days in blessed solitude."

Paul chuckled. "Brooding doesn't suit you, friend."

James couldn't help but laugh. "Brooding is your forte, Lord Leed."

"Chester and I are venturing out to White's this evening. To celebrate his last night of freedom, as it were. What say you, Roberts? Practice your brooding tomorrow and join us tonight?"

James accepted with a grin. "Capital idea."

* * *

Lady Catherine Talbot sat in the parlor of her father's elegant townhouse, perched on an ivory settee with her needlework in her lap. Her head was bent and her eyes were focused on her work. Her sister Elizabeth was chattering on about nothing in particular, as usual. It seemed to Catherine that not very long ago she'd have joined her sister in her silly banter. Oh, but that was before her Great Disgrace.

"Oh, Catherine!" Elizabeth gushed. "I do wonder who will be in attendance at Lord Chester's wedding."

Catherine shrugged. "I admit I don't much care about the guest list, Elizabeth."

Up to this moment she'd given very little thought to the event itself, choosing not to think of anything remotely related to the subject of matrimony. The Earl of Chester was a very great friend of theirs and Catherine was happy for him and Constance, his bride, as they were two of the most wonderful people she'd ever met. But even though she was pleased for them, she couldn't help but be reminded of her own aborted nuptials.

"I just know Constance will make an absolutely beautiful bride," Elizabeth went on, oblivious to Catherine's disinterest. "Her dress sounds breathtaking, though I daresay it won't have as much lace on it as yours did."

Catherine's head shot up at the innocent comment despite herself.

Regret was clear on Elizabeth's face. "Oh, I do apologize, Catherine. It wasn't my intention to remind you."

"Don't fret, Elizabeth. It's been nearly a year now. You may rest assured that I'm no longer put out by such comments."

Elizabeth looked at her with a mixture of doubt and pity, at which Catherine bristled. She gazed at the face so like her own, saw the innocence in Elizabeth's eyes, and couldn't summon anger. She felt as though much more than just one year separated them. Elizabeth seemed so young to her now. So carefree, whereas she felt much older thanks to having had her heart broken. Her heart had mended, thankfully, but she had come out of that ordeal completely changed. Or perhaps she'd just grown up? In any case, she only wanted to get on with her life and forget about the past.

"Do you believe Lord and Lady Kanewood will be there?" Catherine asked, thinking to turn Elizabeth's thoughts. Her question had the desired effect.

"Oh, but of course," Elizabeth answered.

The girl prattled on, oblivious to the look of resignation on her sister's face. Catherine lowered her head and tried to concentrate on her stitches once more, but her heart wasn't in the task at hand. She'd felt out-of-sorts for weeks now, so tired of the forced frivolity associated with attending the whirlwind of balls and parties in town. She'd seen the looks the other women gave her—expressions of smug superiority or, worse, those of pity. Blessedly, she wouldn't have to face such socializing this evening. Despite her younger sister's attempts at persuasion, she declined to attend any of the parties. She looked forward to spending a quiet evening alone after Elizabeth and their father left for the bashes.

"I do believe Lord Chester and Constance are deeply in love." Elizabeth sighed after a while. "Don't you think so, Catherine?"

Catherine was quiet for a moment. She'd thought herself in love with Lord Thomas Waltham, her betrothed. And he with her. She couldn't have been more wrong on that count. Who was she to judge such matters?

"Of course, they are," she said in the end, recalling the sweet looks the bride and groom always seemed to share.

Teatime arrived, much to Catherine's great relief. The maid entered the parlor and served the young ladies their tea and sweet biscuits. Knowing Elizabeth's delight in the fluffy cookies, and well-bred manners that would keep her from talking with her mouth full, Catherine wasn't surprised when the remainder of the afternoon passed in relative silence.

*   *   *

That evening at White's the four gentlemen sat at a table, playing cards and sipping brandy. The Earl of Chester took some good-natured jesting from his friends, with Geoffrey Kane, the Earl of Kanewood, delivering the most barbs.

"My God, Chester," Geoffrey said. "You've known Constance for nearly three years. You've danced with her."

"Charmed her," James put in.

"I believe you take an awfully long time to accomplish your goals, old man," Paul finished.

"It'll make for an interesting wedding night, I daresay." Geoffrey laughed.

Chester reddened. "Never mind. You're the last one to talk of dragging one's feet, Leed."

Paul smiled. "I believe I wished to be quite certain of my feelings before asking the fair Michelle for her hand."

Chester looked at him askance. "You would still be dragging your feet if you hadn't come precariously close to preceding your wedding night."

Leed didn't bat an eyelash. "Too true."

"What was your incentive for matrimony, Kane?" James asked.

"Love, my friend," Geoffrey answered. "It took me a while to recognize it, however."

James was suddenly quiet, but if the others noticed, no remark was made of it. As talk turned bawdier around him, he puzzled over Geoffrey's words.

Nearly three years earlier, James had fancied himself in love with Geoffrey's wife. And while Becca had done nothing to encourage his attentions, he'd foolishly professed his feelings for her. She naturally refused him, but Geoffrey found them together and was furious, innocent though the circumstances. By a twist of fate however, James saved Becca's life and earned Geoffrey's forgiveness and undying gratitude.

James now knew that what he'd felt for Becca was youthful infatuation. But what of love? He had no true notion of that prickly emotion. He wondered if he would even trust himself to recognize it if it did happen. His friends' laughter broke through his reverie.

"Roberts," Chester said. "Where is your head?"

"Hmm?" James answered.

"I believe Roberts is still thinking about all those lovely invitations littering his desk," Paul offered.

"My God," Chester moaned. "Not the matrons."

"Yes," James answered. "Apparently, I'm still very much in demand among the drawing rooms of polite society."

"Better you than me, friend," Chester said. "I'm most pleased my marriage will put an end to that business."

James forced a smile. Marriage. His father had talked of nearly nothing else in Yorkshire. The subject blessedly turned to other topics as the hour grew late.

Paul stood and stretched, laying his cards on the table. "Well, gentlemen. I must be getting home."

Chester and Geoffrey nodded their agreement and made ready to take their leave.

"Riding with me, Roberts?" Chester asked, shrugging into his jacket.

"Thank you, no. I believe I'll set out for the pubs."

The others exchanged a knowing look, which James didn't miss. No matter. At least at the pubs, he'd give no more thought to love or marriage. He'd partake of some stout ale and perhaps a generous serving wench. He could do with some mindless release.

* * *

Long after her sister and father had departed, Catherine sat at the vanity in her pretty bedchamber and absently stared at her reflection in the oval mirror. Her heart-shaped face with its famous Talbot blue-violet eyes stared back at her. Her chestnut hair, so like both Paul's and Elizabeth's, was brushed and fell softly over her shoulders. But Catherine saw resignation in those blue eyes, defeat in the slump of those shoulders. What had she felt for Waltham, both before and after her Great Disgrace? Had she really loved him? She'd been quite pained when she'd learned that he'd eloped to Gretna Green with Lady Joan

Banister. But was it the loss of the man or the loss of a dream that had stung so?

She'd been much like Elizabeth then, flighty and silly with hardly a care in the world. Perhaps Waltham had done her a great service. He could have handled the matter with more care, however. Paul had wanted to kill the man with his bare hands when he'd learned of the betrayal.

Catherine smiled as she thought of her brother, so big and strong and handsome. And loyal. Was there a man like that for her? Someone who would love her and keep her safe?

"Such maudlin thoughts," she berated herself.

With a sigh of irritation, she snuffed out the candle and climbed into bed. She dreamed that night of a man, strong and tall, reaching out to her and whispering love words and promising to be with her always.

* * *

James sat at a table in the corner of the pub, nursing a mug of ale. The place was poorly lit, the patrons alternating between loud and boisterous and sullen and morose. James fit himself into that last category.

Suddenly, a woman filled his field of vision, a serving wench with whose favors he was very well acquainted.

"Lord Roberts!" the girl gushed, a wide smile curving her mouth. "Where have you been keeping yourself?"

James smiled up at her. "Hello, Lizzie."

Lizzie, tall, blonde, and well-endowed, flashed James a saucy grin and sat beside him. "I've missed you sorely, m'lord."

"Have you now?" James let his eyes fall on her bosom as he lightly fingered the handle of his mug of ale. "I'm certain you didn't lack for male attention during my absence."

"Hardly." She leaned toward him as he brought the mug to his lips, and she stroked his cock beneath the table. "But I've sorely missed your particular attention, m'lord."

The months of abstinence while in the country had apparently taken their toll, for he was suddenly as hard as the table beneath his elbow.

James hesitated for the briefest moment. Why ever not? He drained the last of his ale, stood, and tossed several pound notes on the table. Lizzie quickly snatched up the notes and pocketed them. It was understood that the ample tip for service would be rewarded abovestairs.

The room upstairs was as poorly lit as the pub. Lizzie shut the door behind him and removed his jacket and waistcoat. James closed his eyes and permitted her to remove the rest of his clothing. She led him over to the bed.

She pushed him down onto his back and straddled him. She took him in her mouth and her skill brought him to orgasm so quickly, it took him by surprise.

When his breath slowed, he opened his eyes and swore softly. “Forgive me, Lizzie.”

“Nonsense, m’lord.” Lizzie grinned as she came to her feet and stripped off her gown. She crawled over him on the bed. “Now we can take our time.”

His laughter soon grew into groans of pleasure.

Much later, in his bedchamber at his townhouse, James stripped off his own clothes. Despite the lateness of the hour, he ordered a bath and some brandy. He’d need help getting to sleep tonight.

As he sank into the steaming water, he thought about his encounter with Lizzie. He’d assured her pleasure before taking his own that second time, but he’d felt empty afterward. As usual, no tenderness or emotions were exchanged, implied, or expected. But for the first time in his adult life, James gained no real satisfaction from the act.

He got out of the bath and readied for bed. The bath had soothed him, body and mind, and after he drained his glass of brandy, he felt he could finally get some sleep. He got into the enormous four-poster and let sleep claim him. He dreamed of a girl, whose face he couldn’t see clearly. She pledged him her love and sweetly asked for his in return.

A smile curved his lips as his breathing grew deep and even.

Chapter 2

James awoke the next morning and stretched, ignoring the slight headache rapping in his head. His dream came back to him, the sweet girl reaching out to him once more.

He shook his head at his foolishness. "Of course, James. She's merely waiting for you to sweep her off her feet." If he hadn't found such a girl in all his years in society, he wouldn't find her now.

As he stood beside the bed, his mind went back to his vague dissatisfaction at the pub. Perhaps he should take a mistress. No. Although many gentlemen kept women tucked away for the sole purpose of seeing to their pleasure, James had no desire to use a woman in such a way.

"Better to take my pleasure with the wenches at the pubs," he muttered as he went into his dressing room to ready for the day. At least no lasting attachment was expected or desired on either party's behalf.

Once dressed, he went down to the breakfast room and helped himself to a hearty meal from the sideboard. Despite his overindulgence of the previous evening, he was ravenously hungry. He thought ahead to Chester's wedding and smiled. He set upon his meal with relish, his mind on the pleasant time he was certain to have with his good friends if not with a girl who couldn't possibly exist.

* * *

Catherine opened her eyes to find her sister flitting about her chamber. It was the day of Lord Chester's wedding, and obviously the girl was in a fit about something. What now?

"Elizabeth." She rubbed her eyes. "What on earth are you about?"

"Oh, good morning, Catherine," her sister said. "I need to borrow something of yours, something that will complement my gown for the wedding celebration."

Catherine sat up in her bed and yawned. "What is it you need?"

"Where are your ribbons?" Elizabeth asked, rifling through the drawers of Catherine's vanity.

"Come away from there," Catherine said without anger.

She rose and padded over to the vanity. She pulled open a drawer on the right and waved her hand. "The ribbons," she said, turning toward the dressing room.

Elizabeth gave an exaggerated sigh of relief and picked out two long peach ribbons. She fairly skipped from the room, her mind certainly focused on her attire for that evening's bash.

Catherine emerged from the dressing room, wearing a day dress of light rose. Unlike Elizabeth, she didn't give much thought to the coming festivities. She'd set aside a gown of deep blue, the cut quite daring. It was part of the wardrobe that was created for her after her engagement, and made her appear quite worldly. But seeing as she was no longer a young girl in her first Season, the gown was appropriate for her use now. As she glanced into the drawer that Elizabeth had left open, she spied ribbons of precisely the same shade of blue. She suddenly remembered her dream, the mystery lover speaking his wonderful promises.

Wouldn't it be marvelous if she actually met such a man? Surely she wouldn't tonight, not at an event attended by so many people already of her acquaintance. Nevertheless, she felt a tingle of excitement for the coming evening and smiled as she set the ribbons aside for her lady's maid to later twine in her hair

The day passed predictably if not quickly, and the time soon arrived for Catherine to ready for the party. Elizabeth had driven her mad with her impatience and Catherine was glad to retire to her room to make her own preparations. After her lady's maid Annie dressed her upswept, glossy brown curls with the blue ribbons, she gazed into the mirror. The style served to make Catherine's eyes appear larger, the lashes framing them long and thick. She could almost see a flicker of anticipation in their bright blue depths. Hmm.

She stood, clad in her chemise, petticoat, and stays as Annie stepped out of the dressing room with the lovely blue gown. The maid assisted her into the gown and deftly fastened the hooks in the back.

Catherine gasped as she looked into the cheval mirror. “Oh, my. This dress is quite revealing.”

Annie shook her head. “Nay, my lady. Ya’ look absolutely splendid.”

Catherine’s eyes fell on her bosom, a large portion of which was visible above the bodice of the gown. She tried to tug the gown upward to no avail. She pulled on her long satin gloves and sighed, prepared to wait for her sister to join her.

* * *

James dressed himself with care for the coming evening. After shaving, he donned the crisp white shirt left out by his valet and tied his cravat precisely. He pulled on black breeches, shining boots, and a waistcoat of silver-gray. A well-fitting jacket of black finished his dress. He checked his appearance in the mirror atop his washstand, raked his fingers through his black hair. Satisfied, he took himself downstairs and called for his carriage.

The party was a huge affair, as the Earl of Chester boasted many friends. He and Constance, his wife of but a few hours, greeted the guests as they entered the salon. The main salon served as a grand ballroom this evening, its polished floor gleaming in the light of hundreds of candles.

James entered the home and sought out the couple. “Lady Chester,” he greeted Constance, The new bride was a picture, her golden hair upswept and her gray eyes sparkling. “May I say that you make an exceptionally beautiful bride.”

Constance accepted his compliment with a blush, at which her husband placed a tender kiss on her temple. James watched the simple exchange with a twinge of envy. Obviously, Chester had made a love match.

His charm reasserted itself as he shook his friend’s hand with warm regard and bowed to the new bride. “Pray do me the honor of a dance this evening, Lady Chester?”

"Of course," she said with a shy smile.

James stepped into the ballroom. An orchestra was at one end of the space, and there were chairs set up around the perimeter. He spied Paul and his wife, Michelle, well away from the orchestra. Paul saw him as well, and waved in greeting.

James joined them. "Leed," he said in greeting. He turned to Paul's wife, a beauty with hair of golden red. "Michelle," he said, grasping her hand and bringing it to his lips.

Michelle curtsied as James bowed to her.

James turned to find that Paul's father, the Earl of Talbot had joined them, along with Elizabeth. James favored the girl with a smile and turned to greet her father. "Lord Talbot."

"Hello, Roberts," Talbot said in his booming voice. "How's your father?"

"Still ailing, I'm afraid, sir."

"Pity," Talbot said. "Do give him my best?"

"Certainly," James said. He turned to the earl's youngest child. "How are you, Elizabeth?"

The girl curtsied quickly and smiled up at him. "Very well thank you, Lord Roberts," she gushed. "Isn't the wedding just splendid? The music is lovely and I believe I've never seen so many happy people in one place."

James chuckled at the girl's exuberance. "But what of Catherine's wedding? Surely it was as lovely as this affair."

Elizabeth paled and lost her smile. "Oh, you don't know! Catherine never married."

"What?" James asked in confusion.

"Lord Waltham eloped with Lady Joan Banister scarcely one week before the wedding."

James turned to Paul. "Leed?"

"Elizabeth," Paul scolded. "I've told you repeatedly not to speak of it."

Elizabeth blushed. "I'm sorry, Paul."

The Earl of Talbot shot his youngest daughter a look of vexation, at which Elizabeth lowered her eyes in acute embarrassment.

Michelle apparently took pity on the girl. "It's all right, Elizabeth. Thankfully, Catherine didn't hear you."

"Oh, yes." Elizabeth nodded vigorously, her brown curls bouncing. "Thank goodness!"

"Is this true, Leed?" James asked Paul.

"Yes," Paul said, his voice clipped. "I apologize for not telling you last year, but I thought it best to keep the matter as quiet as possible."

"Understandable." James shook his head. "What Catherine must have gone through."

Paul simply nodded.

James had always thought Catherine a sweet girl, with never a bad word to say of anyone. She giggled as freely as Elizabeth did, finding something pleasant in everything. And to think that Waltham could treat her so shabbily? Bastard. If Waltham had been there just now, he'd have happily throttled him.

He turned to Elizabeth once more. "And where is Catherine, Elizabeth?"

"Why, she was just speaking with a friend," she answered. "She should join us momentarily, I imagine."

James heard only half of what Elizabeth said to him, for over her shoulder he spied the most beautiful young woman he'd ever seen. Her glossy brown curls were upswept, several tendrils left free to fall about her shoulders and frame her face. She was dressed in a gown of deep blue, the color complementing her striking eyes. The cut of the gown accentuated her lovely figure; her full breasts and slender waist drew his appreciative glance. My God. Surely this beautiful creature couldn't be Catherine Talbot!

James watched her approach, noting that she carried herself regally, her hips swaying gently. She no longer flitted about the room like her sister. He'd always thought her pretty, but the past year had matured her looks. She'd lost her girlish countenance, but it was replaced with breathtaking beauty. If Waltham's betrayal had this effect on her, perhaps he should thank the man before he throttled him.

He glanced at Elizabeth, then back at Catherine. They were no longer twins.

Catherine came to a stop in front of him, a small smile on her face. "Lord Roberts," she said softly, curtsying.

James blinked. Even her voice held a sultry note he'd never heard in it before.

He bowed to her. "Lady Catherine," he said, using her formal address for the first time.

She cocked her head to the side and smiled widely, the effect startling him. The dimple in her cheek only added to her appeal.

James recovered himself and took her gloved hand in his. "You look very much the lady this evening, Catherine."

She stared up at him for a moment, and when her pupils dilated, he felt it like a caress.

"Oh, Catherine," Elizabeth gushed. "There you are."

Catherine turned her head and smiled at her sister, and James released her hand with regret. Geoffrey and Becca soon joined them, and talk became quite animated. James returned his friends' comments absently, his eyes continually settling on Catherine. What was the matter with him? She was his friend's little sister, and he'd never thought of her in any other way. But she was a woman now. As desirable as any he'd ever known.

As they all took themselves into the supper room, he vowed to put her, and his troubling reaction to her, out of his mind.

* * *

Catherine returned to the ballroom after supper, with Elizabeth in tow. The younger girl was chatting about how lovely all the ladies' dresses were, at which Catherine nodded absently. She tried to put her strange reaction to Lord Roberts out of her mind. Not likely. He looked incredible this evening. His breeches hugged his long muscular legs, his black jacket made his shoulders impossibly wide. His silver waistcoat nearly matched his incredible eyes. How could he have grown even more handsome since she'd seen him last?

When he'd taken her hand in his, she'd felt a spark shoot through her fingers and down to her toes. She'd stared into his eyes for the longest moment, seeing affection in their silver depths as she always had in the past. But had there been something else there, as well? It was something she'd never seen before. An awareness, as though he were seeing her for the first time.

She declined an offer to dance given by an awkward young

gentleman and chose to sit in one of the gilded chairs lining the walls of the wide room. Michelle joined her there after Elizabeth ran off to speak to a friend.

"Catherine," Michelle said with a smile. "That dress is simply stunning."

"Thank you," Catherine said. "I daresay Paul would never have let me wear such a thing when he was escorting me to the bashes."

"He does still tend to be a bit overprotective of his sisters."

"Something you chide him about constantly, I'm sure," Catherine said.

Michelle laughed. "I fear Rose will have quite a time of it when she comes out."

"Indeed. Poor girl. But I'm sure Rose will be just as strong as her mama when it comes time for her debut."

Michelle reached out and squeezed her hand, smiling warmly at her. "I have faith that Rose will be just as strong as her beautiful aunt, Catherine."

Catherine's eyes filled with tears. She was so lucky to have such a loving and supportive family through last year's ordeal. And she was truly happy to have Michelle as her sister-in-law. She couldn't have chosen a better bride for her only brother.

Catherine turned her gaze back to the ballroom and saw Lord Roberts step out of the supper room and approach Elizabeth, his hand outstretched. As Catherine watched, Elizabeth put her gloved hand in his. He twirled her out onto the dance floor, nodding at whatever Elizabeth said.

As they made their way across the floor, Lord Roberts spied her. His silvery eyes met hers for the briefest moment, sending a pleasurable shiver through her. She composed herself and returned her attention to Michelle.

The number ended and he escorted Elizabeth to join Catherine and Michelle. He smiled at Michelle and turned to face Catherine. "Catherine, I would be honored if you would join me for a dance."

She stared up at him for a long moment. She'd danced with him so often in the past, and she shouldn't have hesitated. But he evoked such strange feelings in her this evening.

With both Michelle and Elizabeth watching her, she set aside her reservations and put her gloved hand in his. "I'd love to, Lord Roberts."

He led her out onto the floor. She matched him step for step and had never enjoyed a dance as much. It was over too soon in her opinion. He must have been of the same mind, for when the dance ended he held on to her hand a bit longer.

He released her at last and smiled. "Why don't we go out onto the terrace?"

Catherine, still flushed from their ease and comfort on the dance floor, nodded. "Oh, yes. That would be lovely."

He waved at her to take the lead and followed her out the open doors. She came to a stop at the railing, staring out at the starry sky. He stepped behind her, joining her in her reverie.

They stood quietly for a long while, until Catherine finally broke the silence. "Beautiful, isn't it?"

"Incredible," he answered, his voice low.

Catherine could sense him so close behind her, could feel his heat. She was certain that if she simply leaned back, her shoulders would come into contact with the hard wall of his chest. She was unable to resist the notion and gave in to her fancy, leaning back to brush against him. He wrapped his arms around her, cradling her as he exhaled. She felt his breath tickling her ear and it felt so wonderful. She closed her eyes and relaxed against him, relishing the sweet comfort of the moment.

After too short a while, he dropped his arms from her. Catherine was shocked back to her senses. She straightened and gripped the railing tightly with both of her gloved hands. What was wrong with her? Her behavior was quite improper.

Lord Roberts took a step forward to stand beside her at the railing. Fortunately, his easy charm saved her and the moment. "I very much enjoyed our dance, Catherine."

"I managed to keep off your toes." She laughed, trying to calm her nerves.

He smiled down at her. "I did think for a while there that I had gone quite deaf."

"Deaf?" she asked. "Why would you think that?"

"After my dance with Elizabeth, my ears were fairly ringing."

Catherine laughed again. He smiled in response and brushed a stray curl away from her cheek. At his touch, she froze. He stared down at her, losing his smile.

"Catherine," he whispered.

She stared up at him, her heart racing. His gaze settled on her mouth. He bent his head and brushed her lips with his. She stiffened for a moment. In the next she rubbed her lips against his and was rewarded as a delightful tingling spread from their point of contact. Suddenly, he pulled back.

Catherine opened her eyes and blinked up at him. She brought her fingers to her lips and felt them quiver. Waltham had kissed her. Proper kisses that were pleasant. But this kiss . . . It was so warm and sensual. And was that his tongue that had brushed across her lips before he pulled away?

"Forgive me, Catherine," he said.

She said nothing to that. What could she say? That their kiss was the single most wondrous thing she'd ever experienced? He'd surely think her a wanton if she uttered such words. Instead, she simply nodded her acceptance of his apology. He gently took her hand in his and escorted her back into the ballroom.

Lord Roberts left her alone for the rest of the evening. Catherine sat beside Michelle, smiling as her sister-in-law told another story of little Rose's escapades. Her brother, Paul, soon joined them, flanked by Geoffrey and Becca.

"Roberts is back in his element," Geoffrey said, flicking his head in Lord Roberts's direction. "A year rusticating in the country hasn't changed him."

"He certainly is charming," Becca added. "And apparently all the ladies think so."

Catherine tried not to notice that he danced with every girl present. Why should she? His popularity had never bothered her before. She caught a bit of what Geoffrey and Paul were saying as they lowered their voices.

"I wonder how he fared at the pubs," Geoffrey said.

"I daresay he fared as well as he usually does," Paul joked.

Catherine knew by their hushed tones and knowing glances that the gentlemen were discussing something quite provocative.

She flushed as she pictured Lord Roberts in the arms of some faceless woman. A flash of jealousy quickly replaced her embarrassment. What was wrong with her?

She stood. “Excuse me.” The gentlemen nodded, but Michelle and Becca both blinked at her. “Headache.”

She sought out her father and, perpetuating the fictitious headache, persuaded him to take her home.

As Catherine readied herself for bed a while later, her mind was still on Lord Roberts and his wonderful kiss. From the moment their eyes had met that evening, she’d felt something she’d never felt before with him or any other gentleman. He appeared unaffected, however. His usual charming self. Surely he was far too worldly and experienced to let one dance, one brief kiss, affect him.

Too weary to puzzle it through, she climbed into her bed and fell into a fitful sleep. She met her dream lover once more, a tall man with black hair and startling silver eyes, whispering love words in her ear.

* * *

James was disappointed when he noticed Catherine’s absence. It was probably for the best, though. He went on as usual, making certain not to dance with any one girl more than twice lest she get the idea he was interested in a more permanent pairing.

Much later, in the solitude of his bedchamber, James stripped out of his finery and stretched out on the bed. He stared up at the ceiling, his hands behind his head, and puzzled over his reaction to Catherine. She’d grown into a beautiful woman. Had he never noticed how pure her skin was, how full her lips? It wasn’t only her beauty that captivated him now. His esteem increased after he’d learned of Waltham’s betrayal. The regal way in which she carried herself proved she could handle an unbearable situation with grace and maturity. Even her laugh, no longer a girlish giggle, now had a soft and husky note that spoke of secret pleasures.

He was sexually experienced, yet tonight he’d felt desire like never before. That it was the result of an innocent girl’s brief kiss was absurd. She was Catherine Talbot! He'd known her since she was a child, and always thought of her as a little sister, but the thoughts going through his mind at present were anything but brotherly.

He'd been stunned by their sudden closeness out on the terrace. As he'd held her for that too-brief moment, her smooth white shoulder had beckoned his touch and he'd been unable to resist bending his head closer to breathe in her sweet scent. With his lips a mere breath away from her skin, he'd caught himself. He'd had to grip the railing to keep his hands from shaking with the effort to keep from touching her.

James swore out loud. He never should have touched her. But she'd felt so right in his arms, as if she belonged there.

He let out a ragged sigh, the sound loud in the quiet of the chamber. He closed his eyes and immediately thought back to their encounter on the terrace. That brief moment of contentment as he'd held her in his arms had startled him. But their kiss . . . Her lips had been so soft, so sweet, his body had reacted swiftly with desire. Even now, his blood warmed as he thought of her lovely mouth and the way it had welcomed him.

When sleep finally claimed him, he dreamed of the girl once more. Only this night he could see she had glossy brown hair, stunning violet eyes, and a soft husky voice that promised to love him forever.

Chapter 3

A few days later James stood in front of his washstand, readying himself for the coming evening's festivities. He finished shaving and wiped a cloth over his face, stopping to stare at his reflection. Catherine would be in attendance tonight. Gorgeous, available Catherine Talbot. Sister to his very good friend. God help him.

He'd been successful thus far in his efforts to avoid her, staying away from the parties and even declining an invitation to dine at Paul and Michelle's townhouse two days prior. Paul had looked at him slyly and James had easily guessed what he'd been thinking—another trip to the pubs. How wrong he was. Ever since holding a certain girl in his arms, he couldn't arouse much desire for the experienced wenches at the public houses.

Sighing in irritation, he donned his shirt and tied the neck cloth his valet had set out. He shrugged into a waistcoat of deep blue, and the color immediately brought to mind Catherine's beautiful eyes.

"I'm a fool," he grumbled.

Later, James stood with some acquaintances at the Markham's bash when he spied Catherine in the doorway. The dress she wore, so dark a pink it was nearly red, hugged her luscious figure. Her hair was piled in an artful mass atop her head and curls framed her face. He watched as she looked about, her beautiful eyes opened wide as she listened to something her sister said. A smile spread across her face and James mirrored the motion. The widow commanding his attention must have seen where his was focused for she harrumphed beside him.

Priscilla Brooks, Lady Brookdale, shot a glance at Catherine, her eyes narrowed. "Oh, there is Catherine Talbot. Quite a shame, that."

"What?" James said absently, turning to face her fully.

"Ah, to think she let Waltham get away."

He frowned slightly. "I believe Catherine was quite fortunate to let him 'get away,' as you put it."

Priscilla hid her vexation but barely. James knew she wanted an assignation—she'd been after him for some time. He doubted she'd lacked for lovers over the past year he'd been in the country, or even since the night three years ago when he'd grappled with her lover John on the stairwell of his best friend Kane's London townhouse. John, Kane's brother, had tried to kidnap Kane's wife Becca, but James managed to wrestle him away from her. John was killed when they both toppled over the banister, but Priscilla didn't appear to miss him overmuch.

"I daresay the scandal has aged the poor thing," Priscilla said, placing her hand on James's arm.

His brows shot up. "Aged her?" He turned back to run his eyes over Catherine once more. "She has matured, that's certain."

Priscilla clutched his arm a bit too tightly. "Roberts," she purred, leaning a bit closer than was proper. "I would so enjoy a stroll on the terrace with you."

James still stared at Catherine, but he hadn't missed the carnal invitation in Priscilla's voice. While he wouldn't accept her advances, he didn't want her to feel slighted. She was a viper of the first order and he wouldn't want to turn her venom in Catherine's direction. It turned out that Priscilla and John had been well suited.

James, Leed, and Chester had been assisting Kane with an investigation over some missing funds from his estate when they uncovered it was John who had been stealing from his own brother. John had seduced the newly-widowed Priscilla and used her carriage to make an attempt on Kane's life, which had very nearly cost him his young bride, Becca.

He turned and forced a smile. "Perhaps after supper, Priscilla," he said, patting her hand as he would a child's. When he turned back to the entrance, he noticed Catherine was gone. As he searched the room for her slender form, he could feel Priscilla tugging on his arm.

"Oh, Roberts," she whined. "I demand you dance with me this very moment!"

He relented and led her out onto the dance floor. As he twirled her about the room, his eyes fell on Catherine where she sat delicately sipping a glass of punch. Their eyes locked. He heard Priscilla's voice calling to him in irritation and forced his attention back to his dance partner.

"Roberts," she said. "You didn't answer me."

"I'm sorry, Priscilla. I was momentarily distracted."

"I offered you a ride in my carriage this evening." She leaned closer. "I brought the barouche."

Her intentions were clear to James. He stiffened and held her away from him without losing a step. "No thank you, Lady Brookdale."

Priscilla gave an unladylike snort and took herself off the dance floor just as the number was ending. James watched her go with a flash of anger. What did she think he was? He stalked off the floor, shaking his head. Did she truly think he'd dally with her? She would no doubt want an extended liaison and he was in no mind to make such an unspoken promise. He'd be lucky to escape with his manly parts intact.

This was worse than the matrons trying to catch him for their daughters. He took himself out onto the terrace.

* * *

Catherine stood at one end of the room, admiring the arrangements. A talented orchestra played tunefully, and snatches of conversation and laughter could be heard above the music. Perhaps, then, the evening wouldn't be so very terrible.

She'd seen Lord Roberts soon after she'd arrived, with Lady Brookdale draped over him. She hadn't expected him to be here. He hadn't attended any of the parties of late, and she'd been certain tonight would be no different. The parties weren't all he'd avoided, either. She'd felt keen disappointment when she'd arrived at her brother's house two nights past and found he'd declined an invitation to dine. Surely that was due to her improper behavior at Lord Chester's wedding.

When Lady Brookdale approached her, she realized she'd been looking for another glimpse of Lord Roberts. Foolish girl.

"Ah, that Roberts is a scoundrel," Lady Brookdale said with a gleam in her eye.

Catherine nodded absently, her eyes still searching the room for a glimpse of him.

The woman settled herself beside Catherine and leaned closer to her. "Though not quite as delicious as Waltham, I would imagine. Eh, Catherine?"

Catherine stiffened at the mention of her ex-fiancé. The look on the lady's face, her lips curved in a sly grin, sent warning bells ringing in her head. "W-why do you say that?"

"He and Lady Joan have only just arrived. Lord, he's a handsome man, is he not?"

Catherine saw Waltham poised in the entry to the ballroom then, his wife on his arm. Her shock gave way to contemplation. She'd thought him quite handsome, with his lean regal bearing and fair looks. But with Lord Roberts ever present in her mind, Waltham paled by comparison. Had she never noticed how slender Waltham was? How thin his fair hair? She wondered what she'd ever seen in him.

Lady Joan, a friend of Catherine's before her elopement, was a plain young woman with quite a large fortune. Catherine bore her no ill will at present, for judging by the discomfort evident on her pale face, she wasn't enjoying her husband's company this evening.

"Hmm. Would you please excuse me, Lady Brookdale?"

"Certainly, dear." Lady Brookdale clicked her tongue. "No doubt you're upset."

Catherine didn't disagree with her, not aloud. How could she say she felt nothing but regret for wasting the past year mourning Lord Waltham's loss?

* * *

James reentered the ballroom just after that bastard Waltham arrived. His eyes settled on Catherine, seated next to Lady Brookdale, and watched as Priscilla whispered something to her.

Catherine had paled slightly then stood, obviously thinking to lose herself in the crowd. James, his hands in fists, strode purposefully toward her.

"Catherine," he said when he reached her side.

She turned and gazed up at him in surprise. "Lord Roberts! I didn't realize you were here." She seemed to collect herself. "How nice to see you."

James felt that now-familiar spark pass between them and sought to keep it contained. He nodded curtly and attempted to keep his demeanor pleasant yet impersonal.

He failed miserably when she arched a graceful brow at him.

"I daresay you've nearly mastered that," she teased, her eyes sparkling.

"Mastered what?" he couldn't help asking, feigning innocence.

Catherine simply laughed, that husky sound he'd heard in his mind over the past few days.

He returned her smile with one of his own. "I've known you too long to stand on ceremony, Catherine."

Her smile dimmed. "Lord Roberts, I—"

"Perhaps you'll honor me with a dance?" Before she could deny or acquiesce, the party began to adjourn to the supper room. "Let me escort you into supper, at least."

After a brief pause, she inclined her head and he took the opportunity to hold her elbow and escort her into the room. As they took their meal together, they fell back into the pleasant conversations they used to share. He soon realized that her mind had matured along with her face and body. Gone was the flighty girl he'd known. She eloquently expressed opinions on everything from law to politics. Obviously, she paid close attention to her brother's speeches in Parliament. It was one more quality of Catherine's that he admired. He relished being in the company of a woman who was intelligent as well as beautiful.

Buoyed by their easy exchange in the supper room, James once again asked Catherine to dance with him. She agreed and put her hand in his. But when she looked up at him, he felt desire lick through him again. *Careful, old boy.*

He held her a bit farther away than he wished to as they twirled about the room. Catherine's face showed her puzzlement over his abrupt change in demeanor, so he offered her one of his smiles and she gave the slightest shrug before following him through the dance.

Her hand, which she'd placed on his shoulder, slowly worked its way upward to his neck. With delicate fingers, she stroked the hair at the nape of his neck, sending a thrill though him. He tried to ignore the action, but it proved impossible. She was driving him mad, the little caresses making him want her. He looked down at her. She caught the motion and stared up at him, her eyes dark. His gaze fell on her parted lips and he pulled her closer. He lowered his head to hers, eager to kiss her, before finally remembering where they were.

As the music ceased, he held her away from him. "No."

Catherine blinked up at him.

"No," he said again, more to himself than to her.

He took her hand and quickly strode with her to where her sister sat. With a curt nod, he left her there.

James found himself out on the terrace once more. He was the worst kind of rake, first for wanting Catherine and then for treating her so coldly after their dance. No doubt he'd carry her look of hurt and confusion in his mind for some time.

"It's better this way," he told himself. He was a fool if he believed that. When she'd touched him so innocently, he'd wanted to hold her tight, to strip off her lovely gown and run his hands over her smooth skin. What was the matter with him? One would think he hadn't been with a woman in months instead of days.

A man's voice reached him from the far corner of the terrace then, one he didn't recognize.

"I don't know if you were wise, Waltham," the man said, laughter in his voice.

"Wise?" Waltham returned. "In what way, friend?"

Waltham. The bastard who'd disgraced Catherine. James held himself still and listened.

"Didn't you see her?" the first man said. "My God, man! She's astonishing."

"Perhaps I was too hasty," Waltham allowed. "Who knew Catherine Talbot would turn into such a hot piece?"

James's stomach clenched. How dare he say such things?

"Quite tasty," his friend said. "I wonder if she's still fond of you."

"I'm quite certain I can make her recall her feelings for me. God knows I've got to assuage my lust somewhere. Perhaps if I offer her an arrangement, we can—"

His words were cut off in mid-sentence as James barreled up to him and grabbed him by the lapels of his jacket. "You bastard. Don't ever speak of Catherine in that manner again!"

Waltham blinked in surprise, his hands working to pry James from him. "Roberts," he sputtered. "What the devil?"

"What you did to her was despicable." He brought his face close to Waltham's. "But she's most fortunate to be rid of you."

James released him and straightened his own clothing. He fixed a sharp look on Catherine's ex-fiancé. "Don't let me hear you speak her name again, Waltham," he warned, turning on his heel.

"I wonder what that was all about," he heard Waltham's companion ask.

"Quite interesting," Waltham answered.

"How so?" the other man asked.

James turned to stare at Waltham from his vantage point near the doors to the ballroom.

"Never mind," Waltham sketched him a bow. "Good evening, Roberts."

James stalked back into the ballroom. *How dare Waltham think to dally with Catherine? She deserves more than that. She deserves someone to cherish her, to keep her safe. She deserves someone like . . . Someone like me.*

He shook his head at that fanciful thought and strode back into the ballroom. He saw Catherine. Lord, he wanted to go to her. No. She didn't deserve his awkward attempt at charm, either.

Giles met James at the door of his townhouse. "Home so early, my lord?"

"Yes," James answered curtly.

Giles arched a silver brow. “Has something happened?”

“What? No, nothing,” James muttered.

“If I didn’t know better, I would think a young lady was involved.”

James shot Giles a look of irritation the butler didn’t miss.

“No.” Giles laughed. “It can’t be true. One of the young society ladies has captivated you at long last?”

“Let it go, Giles.”

James went up to his chamber and changed out of his formal attire. It was far too early for him to retire, so he donned his burgundy dressing gown. He belted the quilted satin around his waist and went down to the parlor.

His brow arched as he spotted the tray Giles had thoughtfully left for him. On it sat a bottle of brandy and a glass. He smiled. *Wise old fellow, that Giles.*

He poured a generous amount into his glass and settled himself on an oversized wing chair. He couldn’t get the image of Catherine out of his mind. Her scent, her touch. Waltham’s insinuations still burned. Bastard. James stared into the cold fireplace and let the brandy warm him.

Sometime later, an hour or maybe more, he heard a light rapping at the door.

“Come in,” he called.

The door opened and there Catherine stood, framed in the doorway.

“Catherine?” He came to his feet. “What are you doing here?”

“I wished to thank you for this evening,” she said softly.

James stared at her for a beat, unable to believe she was standing there in his parlor. “But who answered the door?” he heard himself ask. “Didn’t Giles—?”

“He told me to come right in,” she told him.

James shook his head, his lip curled slightly. That old man was too sharp for his own good.

He smiled at Catherine, suddenly remembering his casual attire. “I’m sorry to receive you this way.”

She waved her hand dismissively and took a seat on the chair he’d just vacated. He found her incredibly tempting in the pretty pink gown, even more so than when they'd danced together at the night's bash.

He took a step back. "Now, exactly why is it you wish to thank me?"

Catherine cleared her throat. "Lady Brookdale told me what happened on the terrace," she said in a small voice.

His lips thinned. What was Priscilla's game now? He took Catherine's hand in his. "I'm sorry you had to hear of that, Catherine."

As he watched, her eyes filled with tears.

"I'm so ashamed," she sobbed.

He sat beside her in the big chair. "Catherine, you have no reason to be ashamed."

She shook her head. "Lady Brookdale said that everyone assumes I'll be open to such an arrangement with Waltham."

Anger burned in his gut. "Why that vindictive little—"

He managed to keep his anger in check and looked at Catherine once more. She gazed up at him, vulnerability clear in her brilliant eyes, her trembling mouth.

"Catherine, Lady Brookdale is mistaken." He reached out to stroke her cheek. "No one who knows you would ever believe that."

Catherine closed her eyes and leaned into his hand. A surge of affection struck him. She was incredible, the way she'd endured the horrible gossip that evening. He was suddenly very aware of their position. She was a young woman alone with him, a man clad in only a thin dressing gown.

He tried to do the right thing. He truly did.

"Catherine," he whispered.

She opened her eyes and stared up at him. "Yes?"

"You shouldn't be here."

She gave a small nod and started to stand.

He held her hand, unwilling to let her go. "But I'm so glad you are."

He brought his lips to hers and kissed her with all the tenderness she aroused. She leaned into him and he cupped her face in his hands, flicking his tongue over her lips. She opened her mouth instinctively, welcoming him. He moaned softly and took what she offered, stroking her tongue with his.

Catherine twined her fingers in the hair at the nape of his neck as she'd done earlier that evening on the dance floor, and it set him on fire again. His fingers tunneled through her hair, letting her curls loose from their pins. She gasped and he dragged his mouth from hers.

James ran his gaze over her. Her eyes had darkened to a deep violet and her lips were swollen. He kissed her again, hungrily. She whimpered, the sound soft in her throat. Her hands caressed him, stroking his neck, his shoulders.

He grabbed her to him, pressing his lips to the soft skin on her neck. "Catherine . . ."

He ran his hands over her flesh and his mouth followed. His lips brushed over the swell of her breast. He breathed her in. God, she smelled so sweet. He pressed her back against the arm of the chair, eager to take all she had to offer.

"Lord Roberts." She sighed.

The sound of her voice, husky with wanting, stopped him.

He sat upright and held her away from him. "This isn't right," he said, his voice hoarse.

She shook her head in disagreement and reached for him once more.

"No," he said.

The hurt in her beautiful eyes nearly broke his heart.

"I . . . I'm sorry," she whispered.

Before he could stop her, she ran from the room.

He stood. "Catherine, wait!"

He heard the front door slam, heard her carriage pull away, and sank back into the chair. He raked his fingers through his hair. "Ah, hell."

What was he going to do? He wanted her like he'd never wanted any other woman. And judging from the way she kissed him just now, she wanted him, too. But what could he do about it? She was his friend's little sister. She was off-limits to him . . . Or was she?

Lord, he was weary. He poured more of the fine brandy into his glass and took a long swallow.

"Has Lady Catherine left?" Giles asked from the doorway.

"You know damn well she left," James grumbled. "What were you thinking, sending her in here?"

Giles raised his eyebrows. "She said she needed to speak to you, so I simply—"

"It won't serve, Giles," James cut in. "You put an innocent girl in a compromising situation."

"I wasn't the one who compromised her." Giles slanted him a look. "And here I believed I was jesting when I mentioned debauching young ladies in the parlor."

James was too tired to argue with the old man, not that he'd any hope of winning. He rubbed his hand over his face. "What am I going to do?"

Giles said nothing, but James saw the smug expression on the butler's face.

"Good night, Giles," he said pointedly.

"Good night, my lord."

James would have sworn he could hear the man whistling as he took himself off to the servants' quarters.

Chapter 4

Catherine sobbed all the way home. After Lady Brookdale told her what had happened, Catherine asked her father to take her home. But Elizabeth had balked at such an early end to the evening, so Paul and Michelle offered to take her and the earl home later, leaving Catherine the use of the carriage on her own. On an impulse she'd instructed the driver to Lord Roberts's townhouse. What a disastrous decision that turned out to be.

She threw herself at him! He'd looked incredible in his satin dressing gown, the fabric draping elegantly over his body, dark hairs visible at the base of his strong throat. She'd wondered if the silky-looking hairs covered his chest. But it was the concern in his silvery eyes that had been her undoing.

She never should have gone to him. Surely he thought her a wanton. But his kisses made her feel so wonderful, like nothing in the world could ever hurt her. What was she going to do?

Catherine arrived home and hurried up to her bedchamber. When she saw her tear-stained face in her vanity mirror, she was thankful she had told her maid not to wait up. She quickly washed all traces of those shameful tears and got ready for bed. She planned to be fast asleep by the time her father and sister returned.

Catherine stayed away from the parties for the last week of the Season. It wasn't only Lord Roberts she was avoiding. She had no desire to see Waltham again and, with the terrible rumors of which Lady Brookdale had spoken, the bashes held no attraction for her. She spent her nights alone in her father's townhouse and her days at Paul and Michelle's. They were quite busy writing speeches, what with Parliament set to adjourn shortly. Catherine was only too happy to help, watching little Rose so the child didn't have to spend her days shut in her nursery.

One such afternoon she sat crossed-legged on the floor of

the parlor, playing with the toddler. Rose had golden-red curls, big blue eyes, and a charming personality. She was also willful and very vocal. Catherine smiled as her niece told her dolls precisely what she wished them to do. The little girl's chatter sent any dark thoughts fleeing from her mind, and Catherine hugged Rose to her and cradled her in her lap.

She caught a glimpse of movement out of the corner of her eye and lifted her head to see Lord Roberts standing in the doorway. Her silly heart skipped a beat and she swallowed.

"Hello, Catherine," he said stiffly.

She winced at his chilly tone. "Hello, Lord Roberts."

The silence between them was deafening as they stared into each other's eyes. Paul's voice broke through.

"Roberts," Catherine's brother called. "There you are."

James bowed to Catherine and left her to follow Paul into his study.

Catherine's shoulders slumped a bit. Rose apparently sensed the change in her and turned in her lap. She reached up and brushed her hand over Catherine's cheek. Catherine kissed the chubby little hand and smiled once more. Forcing Lord Roberts from her mind, she returned her attention to her little charge.

* * *

James tried to concentrate on what Paul was saying, but thoughts of Catherine intruded. Had he known she was here, he never would have come. He was struck by the pleasing picture Catherine made in the parlor, her head bent to Rose's as she listened raptly while the tot told a story in baby talk. God, the hurt on her face after his cold greeting had been palpable.

He forced his attention back to his friend. "I wished to tell you I'm leaving for Yorkshire, Leed," he told Paul. "I realize your work will keep you in town for a while yet."

Paul nodded. "Michelle and I are merely finishing a few speeches, but we don't expect to get to Leed Manor for at least a fortnight."

James cleared his throat. "I see Catherine is minding Rose," he said, keeping his voice even. "How has she been?"

"She's been well." Paul's brow furrowed at Roberts's concern. "Why do you ask?"

James thought of the last time he saw her in his townhouse, both the desire on her face and the hurt in her eyes. He could say nothing of it to her brother, however. He couldn't compromise her reputation. Not after Priscilla's spiteful words.

"I'd heard of the vicious rumors circulating," James said.

"Oh, that." Paul grinned. "Michelle told Lady Brookdale in no uncertain terms that Catherine was a lady of virtue, something of which she'd have no knowledge."

James blinked. "She didn't."

"You know my wife. Lady Brookdale has ceased spreading her lies, I'm happy to say."

"Good."

"You must come to stay at the manor, Roberts. Michelle will send out the invitations when we're more firm in our plans."

James could only nod. No doubt Catherine would be in attendance, but to refuse his friend would seem strange in the least and rude in the worst.

"I'll try my best to get away." He rose. "I'll leave you to your speeches."

"Good day, Roberts."

James took his leave. He peeked cautiously into the parlor as he made his way to the front door, but he didn't find Catherine within. Relieved and disappointed, he headed out into the August sunshine.

* * *

Two weeks later James sat in the parlor of his family estate, passing teatime with his father. James had access to all the holdings that went along with his title, but he preferred spending time at Bradford Hall. It was a grand home, but it was also full of warm memories for him. He looked over at his father, a still-handsome man in his early sixties. The Earl of Bradford coughed, causing James to jump to his feet.

The earl caught the motion and smiled. "Easy, my boy. I merely felt a tickle, is all."

"You're feeling better these days, Father. Aren't you?"

The earl nodded, adjusting the wool blanket that lay across his lap. "Yes, son. I must say that having you here is quite a tonic for me."

James smiled and sipped his tea.

"And how did you leave London?" his father asked.

"Hmm?" James started. "Fine. Why do you ask?"

The earl got a gleam in his eye. "Did you enjoy the company of any particular lady while in town?"

James's eyes widened, a reaction his father didn't miss.

"I knew it," the earl said.

"And what is it you believe you know?"

"You've been brooding quite a bit of late, James." He grinned. "Not like you in the least."

A smile teased the corner of James's mouth. "Never mind."

"Who is she, son?"

James stood and crossed to the window. Catherine's image floated before him, not as he'd seen her at Paul's home but as she'd left him at his own. The pain visible in her violet eyes . . .

"Well?" the earl prodded. "Do I hear wedding bells?"

"What?" James said, turning to face his father. "No, no."

"Are you not fond of her?"

"Of course I'm fond of her. But she won't suit."

"Whyever not?"

James stared out the window once more, quiet.

"Is she married?" his father asked.

"No."

"A commoner?"

"No."

"Too young?"

James shook his head.

"Too old, then?"

"No, no," James said in irritation. "She's none of those."

"Son, if she's none of those, what's stopping you from pursuing her?"

James let out a long sigh, sitting down once more. "It's impossible."

"I've never seen you like this." His father shook his head.

"You need to listen to your heart."

"How on earth can I trust my heart to tell me what to do?" James frowned. "I thought myself in love before and nearly ruined two people's lives because of my ridiculous declaration."

"You weren't in love with Kane's wife, James."

"I know. Thank God they know, as well. But how do I know what I feel for this girl isn't infatuation?"

His father didn't answer, but James knew it didn't feel the same. He wanted Catherine with a passion he hadn't felt for Becca. He also wanted to protect her and keep her safe. But did he love her? And if he thought he might—how could he be sure? On the other hand, did it matter? Love was the last requirement in a ton marriage. His friends had made love matches, but he was a fool to expect to have their good fortune. Worse, if he openly courted Catherine and it didn't work out, then he wouldn't be any better than that scoundrel Waltham. Not to mention she was his dear friend's little sister. He'd lose Paul as a friend, as well.

"I fell in love with your mother at first glance, James."

James faced him. "Mother was beautiful, inside and out."

"Everyone told me she was wrong for me, that I should marry much higher than a baronet's daughter," the earl said. "And I almost allowed them to persuade me to let her go."

"I never heard of this. Mother might be gone these past ten years, but even as a boy, I was aware of the affection between you."

"Ah, she was wonderful. So sweet and kind," the earl said, his eyes shining. "And beautiful. Lord, I'd never seen such beauty."

James smiled. His mother was all of those things and more—always full of laughter and hugs and kisses for her only child.

"She was a strong woman, your mother," his father went on. "She refused to let the hateful comments affect her, you know. She always kept her grace about her."

James started. His father could have been describing Catherine.

"I trusted my heart, son. And I never regretted it."

James stood and began to pace. "I'm not at all certain that what I feel is akin to what you and Mother shared."

The earl shrugged his shoulders. "You never know for certain." He winked. "That's where the trust comes in."

James nodded and let his mind work. Whatever he felt for Catherine, he'd never puzzle it through by avoiding her. When he looked back at his father, he saw the man had dozed off, a common occurrence in the late afternoons. A smile was on the older man's face. No doubt he was wrapped comfortably in his memories. James pulled a blanket over his father, tucked it into place, and took himself upstairs to his chamber.

He crossed to the small writing desk in the corner of the room and picked up the letter still sitting atop as it had for the past two days. It was the invitation to Leed Manor, and James had met its arrival with a mixture of impatience and dread. He knew his course of action now.

He sat down and opened the drawer, withdrew a sheet of paper, and penned his response in the affirmative. He sealed the missive and went downstairs to see it delivered without delay.

* * *

Catherine strolled through the courtyard at Leed Manor, her brother's magnificent estate. The home had been built nearly three centuries earlier and had always resembled a medieval fortress. Michelle had performed a wondrous transformation on the house, warming the spaces inside and softening the edges outside. The courtyard where Catherine strolled was enclosed by high stone walls, but alive with color. Surprising, given that Yorkshire was in the north and it was the middle of September. Catherine sat on one of the stone benches placed about the garden and sighed.

She'd come to Leed Manor a few days earlier, preceding the guests Paul and Michelle had invited. She knew Lord Roberts would be included in the party, for Paul was very fond of him. Happily, Chester and Constance had responded and would attend. With Geoffrey and Becca sure to come, it promised to be a very pleasant time indeed.

Would Lord Roberts attend? Or had her shameful behavior destroyed the friendship they'd shared for so many years? She recalled his demeanor when last she saw him at Paul's townhouse. His eyes had held a coldness she hadn't seen before, and his voice possessed a clipped quality that pierced her heart. She sighed again and took herself back into the house.

* * *

At teatime the family and guests sat in the great hall, a cavernous space made to seem less so by the strategic placement of furniture and decorations. A huge fireplace dominated the space designated as the parlor, and Catherine sat across from it on a rose-colored settee. Though the room was full of warmth and animated conversation, James kept his place at the entry.

He watched as Catherine took a bite of a lemon tart. She apparently didn't notice that a biscuit had fallen onto the hem of her pale green tea gown. But Geoffrey and Becca's son Michael spied it and ran up to her, grabbing the biscuit and popping it into his mouth. He laughed at his victory and spit crumbs all over the front of his new suit—much to his father's delight and his mother's consternation. James smiled at his antics. The little boy was almost three years old and full of laughter and mischief. He possessed his mother's big green eyes, and knew precisely how to use them to his advantage. Geoffrey's niece, Ann, who had just turned six, sat quietly beside Rebecca.

James guessed that the pretty blonde-haired girl was shy around the guests as she sat quite closely to Becca, holding fast to her hand. Ann was Patricia's child with Geoffrey's late brother John. After the terrible ordeal with John several years ago, Geoffrey and Becca insisted that Patricia leave the child with them. The woman held little affection for her own daughter, having always been more concerned with her own frivolities. Her name was never mentioned in company. Without Geoffrey and Becca's love and guidance, James was certain that Ann would have been a little girl lost.

Paul and Michelle's daughter, Rose, eyed Michael closely as she toddled about the space, a much-loved rag doll clutched in her arms. She made her way toward Catherine and held her arms high in the air. "Up!"

Catherine set her teacup aside and lifted the little girl onto her lap. Rose immediately began to play with Catherine's skirts, twisting them in her chubby little hands. Her gown was soon pulled up to mid-calf, giving James a delightful glimpse of shapely legs and ankles. He lifted his eyes to her face and found her regarding him closely. He started to smile, at which she lowered her eyes. She was still hurt, then.

He turned and joined his friends where they stood by the mantle.

"Roberts," Paul said in greeting. "We wondered if you would show yourself."

James held up his hands in a show of defeat. "I couldn't stay away."

"It does promise to be most enjoyable," Chester put in. "It's all Constance has been talking about."

"And Rebecca," Geoffrey said. "Although I daresay after a week or so of my son's running about, we may find the manor in crumbled ruins around us."

James chuckled. "Where is the little mite?"

Geoffrey flicked his head in Catherine's direction. James's eyes followed, widening as they found her once more. He watched as the little boy sat himself down at her feet and wrapped his arms around one of her bared legs.

"It seems he's jealous of little Rose's monopolizing Catherine's attention." Geoffrey chuckled.

"I don't blame him," James found himself saying. He flushed hotly. "It's obvious she's wonderful with the children."

Geoffrey nodded and turned back to the other gentlemen. James, however, couldn't drag his eyes from Catherine.

Becca stood then, announcing the child's naptime.

"Oh," Michelle added. "I should put Rose down, as well."

"Let me do it?" Catherine offered, standing up with the little girl perched on her hip.

Michelle smiled gratefully and nodded her assent. Not to be left out, Michael grabbed on to Catherine's skirt. James watched her as she smiled down at the little boy.

"You may come, too, Michael," she soothed, taking the child's hand. "Ann, I could use your help."

Ann hopped off the settee, taking measured steps toward Catherine. With a shy smile on her fair little face, she stepped close to Catherine and matched her steps with hers.

James caught Catherine's eye as she passed him. She nodded to him stiffly and walked quickly toward the stairs, bound for the nursery. He bit back a groan. He had a feeling he was in for a challenging time.

* * *

The next morning, all in attendance at the manor fell into the routine of a long country visit. The gentlemen left early to go hunting, leaving the ladies to sit and chat as they sipped tea or worked on their needlepoint. Talk soon turned to the past Season, and specifically, the Markham's ball. Catherine felt her cheeks burning as Lady Brookdale's name was mentioned.

"To think she uttered such hateful comments about Catherine," Elizabeth said.

Catherine feigned intense interest in her needlework.

"Hush, Elizabeth," Michelle said.

Elizabeth giggled. "I could scarcely believe it when you put that awful woman in her place."

Catherine picked her head up. "Michelle did what?"

Michelle flashed a look of irritation at Elizabeth, at which the girl looked down at her lap.

"It wasn't anything at all," Michelle told Catherine.

Catherine saw the looks being exchanged among the women present and knew that Michelle was making light of it. "What precisely did you do, Michelle?"

Michelle set her needlework aside. "I merely told Lady Brookdale that she was mistaken in her appraisal of you."

"Hardly!" Elizabeth cut in. "You told her she had no virtue."

"What?" Catherine came to her feet.

"No, not you." Elizabeth giggled again. "Lady Brookdale."

Catherine closed her eyes. How could she bring her sister-in-law into such an ugly business? She sat back down and said no more, letting the conversation lead itself away from the topic and toward more mundane subjects.

Long after dinner, which the ladies took without the men present, Catherine went up to her guestroom. The gentlemen had taken their midday meal in the field as expected, and Catherine was glad to pass the day without Lord Roberts's handsome visage intruding upon her. Not that she didn't see him constantly in her mind, as dashing as he'd been the previous evening. She caught his gaze but once, and it was enough to set her pulse racing.

Thinking to put both him and the unpleasant conversation of the morning out of her mind, she ordered a bath and stripped out of her day dress.

* * *

James spent the morning and early afternoon in pursuit of partridge, as its season opened September first. The true pleasure of the outing was, of course, camaraderie. The Earl of Talbot was quite pleased to hunt with the younger men in attendance, expressing to James his regret that his father couldn't join them. James sorely wished his father was as hale and hearty as Paul's.

Despite the exhilarating pastime, James found his mind occupied with images of Catherine: as she sat in the parlor with her lovely legs in plain view; as she appeared at dinner looking incredible in her elegant gown. The one and only time he'd managed to meet her violet gaze during the previous evening, the passion clear in her eyes had shaken him. He tried to put her out of his mind as he and the other gentlemen returned to the manor.

Chapter 5

Catherine stepped out of her bath and picked up a fluffy towel to dry herself, inadvertently tipping over the pitcher of clean rinsing water. Thankfully, there wasn't much left to spread across the floor. She quickly donned her chemise and petticoat and proceeded to rub the towel over her hair. After a few moments, she set the towel aside and ran her fingers through her dark curls, spreading them to dry more quickly. The spilled water forgotten, she studied her reflection in the mirror atop the washstand.

Her cheeks were rosy from the steamy bath water and her hair was curled about her face. Did Lord Roberts find her pretty? The look he'd given her last evening told her that it might be so. But then again, she'd thought Waltham quite taken with her and he obviously hadn't been since he ended up marrying another woman. Tired of the endless circles in which her mind was running, she turned and hurried across the room to finish getting dressed.

She stepped into the spilled water and lost her footing. Letting out a yelp of surprise, she crashed to the floor.

Suddenly, Lord Roberts opened her door and rushed inside. "Catherine?" he called. "Catherine! Are you all right?"

He helped her to her feet and Catherine laughed shakily, clinging to him. She quickly recovered her footing and held herself away from him, heat creeping up her cheeks. "Thank you, yes. I spilled some water, is all."

She finally looked at him. He was magnificent in his hunting clothes, masculine and virile. And mmm, he smelled of the outdoors.

He ran his gaze over her and she flushed hotter. No doubt she looked like a hoyden, her hair a tangle, her chemise soaking wet.

His eyes settled on her face, intensity in their glare. “Catherine,” he whispered.

She gasped at the heat in his gaze. “Lord Roberts, I . . .”

“Catherine,” he said again, his voice lowered to a husky rasp.

He pulled her to him, sealing his mouth to hers. Catherine opened her mouth for him, timidly rubbing her tongue against his. He groaned and wrapped his arms around her, slanting his mouth over hers again and again.

She reached up, her fingers running through his hair, and pressed herself against him. How wonderful his hard body felt against her soft one! His hands were everywhere, in her hair, on her waist, cupping her bottom. She gasped as she felt the hardness of his arousal pressed against her belly, feelings she couldn’t name pulsing through her. He started to lift her petticoat, his fingertips stroking the backs of her knees, her thighs, as he reached higher toward her—

“What’s going on here!?” Paul roared from the doorway.

Lord Roberts froze. He lifted his head and glanced over at her brother. Catherine followed his gaze. Oh, the look in Paul’s eyes was chilling.

“Leed,” Lord Roberts said hoarsely.

Catherine’s arms were still up around his neck, her head resting against his chest. She sighed, taking much longer to recover than he apparently had. Lord Roberts stroked her back as if pleased to have her draped all over him. Oh, his hands felt wonderful on her, warm and strong.

“I want an answer,” Paul growled.

Lord Roberts dropped his hands to his sides and faced her brother once more. “Leed, I . . . That is . . .”

“Downstairs in my study, Roberts. Now.”

Catherine recovered herself and hid behind Lord Roberts. Paul scowled at her and turned on his heel, knowing full well Lord Roberts would soon follow. She watched as her brother stomped from the room.

“Ah, hell,” Lord Roberts muttered. He turned to her. “Catherine, I’m so sorry . . . We’ll talk later.”

She gazed up at him, her lips parted. He managed a smile,

gave her a quick kiss, and hurried to catch up with her brother.

* * *

James found Paul pacing in his study, obviously still quite furious. He squared his shoulders and stepped inside, pulling the door closed.

Paul turned and fixed piercing blue eyes on him. "What were you thinking, compromising my sister?"

"Leed, It's not what you think—"

"This is not the first time you've compromised a lady. If you recall, your infatuation with Becca almost got you called out by Kane! Has it been so long since you've had female companionship, Roberts, that you thought to ruin an innocent girl?"

James's hands were fists at his side, anger causing him to shake. "This has nothing to do with what happened with Becca. It's completely different. And I haven't ruined your sister. We were merely, um . . ."

Paul crossed his arms over his chest. "Pray tell me, Roberts. I know full well what you appeared to be doing."

James laughed, the situation suddenly ridiculous to him. "Leed, you don't believe I would ever take advantage of Catherine, do you?"

Paul scowled at him. "Don't attempt to charm your way out of this. If I hadn't come upon you when I did, you surely would have—"

"No!" James cut in. "I would never treat Catherine in so deplorable a manner. She deserves much better."

Paul got a gleam in his eye then. James pulled back, a warning bell trilling through his mind.

"Prove it," Paul dared.

James blinked. "But how do you propose that I—?"

"Marry her."

James balked. Marry her! "You can't be serious. Simply because I was—"

"Found in a compromising situation with my innocent sister?"

James narrowed his gaze. "I won't be forced into a marriage, Leed."

Paul's frown cleared. "Catherine has had enough pain this past year, Roberts. I won't see her hurt again by an experienced rogue like yourself."

"I would never hurt Catherine. I'm very fond of her."

Paul arched a brow at him. "Yes. That is quite evident."

James grunted in frustration. "That's not what I mean."

Paul crossed to the door and pulled it open. "Think about what I said, Roberts."

He was dismissed, then? Fine. Without another word, James left the study.

* * *

Catherine dressed quickly, thinking to take herself downstairs to tea before Paul returned. She had no doubt that he would, knowing her brother as she did. To think that he'd discovered her in such a situation! It was disgraceful. And what of Lord Roberts? Paul had looked ready to throttle him.

She refused to think of how absolutely wonderful Lord Roberts's kisses and caresses had made her feel. She hastily finished dressing and pulled open the chamber door. A tall figure filled the doorway.

"Paul!" she exclaimed, her hand frozen on the knob.

Her brother stepped into the room. "Close the door, Catherine."

She did so and turned slowly to face him. His scowl was ferocious. She held her hands in front of herself in a placating manner. "Paul, I realize you're angry, and—"

"What were you thinking, being alone with a man in your room?"

"I didn't . . ." she began. "That is to say, it was an accident."

Paul snorted. "An accident? Pray tell me, sister, how such an 'accident' occurred."

"Very well," she said, wringing her hands. "I slipped in a bit of water on the floor and fell. Apparently, Lord Roberts heard me cry out and came in to help and—"

"Enough," Paul said, holding up his hand. "How many times, Catherine?"

Catherine blinked up at him. "How many times?" she murmured. "What do you—?"

"How many times have you been alone with him?"

Catherine gasped at what he was intimating. "Paul, I've never! . . . Well, there was that one time at his townhouse, but that was—"

"What!?" he roared.

"It wasn't as you presume," she rushed out. "I merely went there to give him my thanks when he defended me to Waltham—"

Paul groaned and raked his fingers through his hair. "You need to think about this, Catherine. Your carelessness could have caused this family a huge scandal had someone other than I discovered your indiscretion."

Her mouth gaped open at his low opinion of her. "Paul, you don't think that I would ever do anything to disgrace myself or our family . . . Do you?" she said in a hurt voice.

He pulled open her chamber door and cast a measuring glance over her. "I only know what I saw, sister." He closed the door and left her there.

Shame washed over her. What had she been thinking, throwing herself at Lord Roberts? And now her own brother believed her a loose woman! She collapsed on the bed and cried, burying her face in the pillow lest one of the other guests hear her.

* * *

James paced the floor of his guestroom, his mind working. What Leed had presumed enraged him. He'd never do anything to hurt Catherine! But marry her?

He'd foolishly thought to take Becca from Geoffrey all those years ago, when his fevered young mind had seen her as the only woman for him. What a bloody fool he'd been. He sent up another silent prayer for his coming to his senses and regaining the friendship of both Geoffrey and his wife and forced his mind back to the present.

Ah, Catherine. The way she'd sweetly responded to his kisses and caresses was still fresh in his mind. She'd been all but naked in her wet chemise, her pebbled nipples visible through the lawn. And when he'd brushed his fingers over the smooth skin at the back of her thighs . . . The stark desire she'd aroused in him was unlike anything he'd ever felt for any woman. Although he'd denied it to her brother, James was honest enough to admit to himself that he might indeed have thrown caution to the wind and taken her there in her guest chamber, making her his in every way. "God bless Leed."

Suddenly, a grin spread across his face. Of course! It was all so clear to him now. Why not marry her? Catherine was sweet and beautiful and intelligent. They'd known each other for so very long, and got along quite famously. He wanted her more than he'd ever wanted any other woman.

Yes. He would marry her.

But would she have him?

"She damned well better have me."

He walked into the small sitting room adjoining his bedchamber. Taking a sheet of paper from the writing desk, he set about penning a note to his intended.

* * *

Catherine stared up at the ceiling, her tears dry on her cheeks. Her shame was now complete. First, she behaved wantonly with Lord Roberts and then her brother had all but called her a trollop. She glanced at the clock on the bed stand and was startled to see it was nearly the dinner hour. Rousing herself, she changed out of her crumpled tea gown and rang for Annie.

Twenty minutes later, Catherine stood in front of the cheval mirror, clad in a gown of silver-blue. Annie had left her curls upswept and unadorned. Catherine pulled on her gloves and studied her face in the mirror. Her nose was a bit red, her eyes shiny with the tears that threatened to spill over her lashes. However was she going to face her brother? And Lord Roberts! Blinking rapidly to keep back her tears, she turned to join the other guests in the great hall to await the dinner hour.

Something caught her eye as she approached the door. Someone had apparently slipped a note underneath it while she was dressing. She picked it up gingerly, soon recognizing Lord Roberts's masculine hand. She'd intercepted his response several days earlier, tracing her fingertips over the ink until she'd finally replaced it in the salver. But to see her name written in his hand? Oh!

She opened the note and read it, her mouth agape. He requested a secret meeting with her after dinner, she read, when the gentlemen and ladies would be separated. He asked her to meet him in the courtyard garden. How could she? She smiled, a thrill going down her spine. How could she not?

Slipping the piece of paper into her reticule, she looped the ties of the little purse over her wrist and went down to the great hall.

* * *

The ladies adjourned to the parlor after dinner as the gentlemen took themselves into the library for brandy and cigars. Catherine frantically sought to think of an excuse to leave their company. She was eager to get to Lord Roberts, his note fairly burning her through the fabric of her reticule. Much to her chagrin, her attempt to extricate herself from the parlor was waylaid by her sister.

"Catherine," Elizabeth began, "hasn't our visit been ever so pleasant thus far?"

"Yes," Catherine said absently, looking toward the door with longing.

Elizabeth chattered on for ten minutes, driving Catherine quite mad. Thankfully, Constance joined them just then. A thought immediately came to Catherine's mind, one which caused her lips to curve into a sly smile.

"Oh, Constance," Catherine began. "Elizabeth was just telling me that she so wishes to visit you at Chesterfield."

"But, Catherine, I wasn't . . . Ooh, Chesterfield! Why, yes. That would be ever the thing."

With Elizabeth's attention successfully diverted, Catherine

quickly slipped from the room. She hurried to the back of the house where a row of windows looked out into the courtyard. She froze as she spied the romantic figure before her.

Lord Roberts was turned slightly away from her, his face set as he gazed out over the darkened garden. The moonlight glinted off his jet-black hair and outlined his dashing form. She took a deep breath, opened the glass door, and stepped out onto the stone path.

He turned, a beautiful smile spreading across his face. "It felt like an eternity to me, Catherine. Waiting, hoping you would appear."

"Lord Roberts." She breathed.

"You look like a vision, draped in the moonlight."

She crossed to him. "That sounds very romantic."

He shrugged and took her hands in his. "I'm so pleased you came."

She shivered as she felt his warmth through her gloves. "How could I stay away?"

He pulled her to him, sealing his mouth to hers. She caught his passion and brought her hands up behind his neck, bringing her body so close to his. Moaning softly, he turned and pinned her against the stone wall, pressing intimately against her. She felt him again, felt that insistent hardness against her belly as she had that afternoon. She reached inside of his jacket to stroke his back. He made the most intriguing sound, something between a growl and a moan. Her caresses became bolder and her hands moved lower.

"Ah, Catherine," he groaned, burying his face in the crook of her neck.

He placed teasing kisses on her throat. She leaned her head back and sighed.

"Lord Roberts . . ."

He froze, then his shoulders shook with suppressed laughter. Catherine opened her eyes and gazed at him.

He smiled down at her. "Considering where your hands are, love, I believe you may call me 'James.'"

Catherine realized then that her hands were on his firm buttocks. She flushed. "All right," she said softly. "James."

"God, the sound of my name on those rosy lips." He kissed her again, his tongue sweeping through her mouth. "I want to touch all of you."

"Like at your townhouse?"

"Yes." His teeth tugged at her bottom lip. "But more."

She couldn't know what he meant, but he sounded almost frantic. "M-more?"

"I have to stop myself before I pull up the skirt of this beautiful gown and take you on one of these unforgiving stone benches."

His words, his hands, his kisses . . . "Oh!"

He took in a deep, shuddering breath. "Catherine."

She opened her eyes and stared up at him, her breath coming fast. "Yes, James?"

"Your brother is quite angry with me." He placed little kisses on her nose, her brow. "He believes that I dishonored you."

She gasped. "But you didn't! We've never—"

"Shh," he soothed, kissing her lightly on her lips.

"How can Paul think that I would ever do anything to dishonor the family—?"

"Catherine," he said again.

James smiled at her, stopping her tears before they started. She smiled in return.

She gazed into his beautiful gray eyes, their silver flecks sparkling at her. "Yes, James?"

"Marry me."

She blinked in surprise. "M-marry you?"

He nodded. "We get along so well. I want you. And I can tell you want me, too."

She stiffened. "I don't know." She thought of something, something abhorrent, and looked at him sharply. "Did Paul tell you to do this?"

He shook his head. "I do what I wish to, Catherine." He stroked her cheek with his finger. "And I want to marry you. Very much."

Her heart pounded. She'd nearly married before, and it had turned out badly. How could she risk going through such a debacle again? Her family couldn't withstand another scandal. Another disgrace. Then again, it was no fault of her own that Waltham had jilted her. But she couldn't bear it if it happened again. It would mean disaster for her and her family, not to mention that James and her brother would no longer be friends.

She suddenly felt trapped in his embrace. She couldn't think about this now, not with him pressed so closely to her. Not with her heart still racing from his kisses, his touch.

He seemed to sense her reticence, for a flicker of disappointment appeared in his gaze. "It's all right, love. Please promise me you'll give it some thought?"

She stood perfectly still for a long moment. Finally, she nodded.

"Yes, I promise I will think about it," she said in a shaky voice.

He let out a breath. "Take all the time you need. I want you to be as certain as I."

As if to prove his point, he captured her lips once more. His kiss was tender, teasing, and she felt her knees go weak.

He pulled back and took a few steps away from her. "Why don't you go back inside, Catherine? Surely you'll be missed by the others."

She nodded and brushed her hands over her gown. She walked over to the glass doors and stopped, turning back to him. "Aren't you coming?"

James shook his head and adjusted his jacket in front of him. Maybe he was chilled? "I need a few moments to, um, collect my thoughts."

She nodded once more and left him there. As she pulled the doors shut, she thought she heard him utter a prayer.

Chapter 6

His body at last under control, James returned to the house. Would Catherine accept his proposal? Until the moment he'd asked her, he hadn't realized how much he wanted to make her his wife. He joined the gentlemen in the library and settled himself in a large wing chair, avoiding Paul's gaze.

He quickly saw that his friends hadn't missed his arrival. Chester elbowed Paul to gain his attention. Paul turned from his conversation with Geoffrey and arched a brow in question.

"What is it, Chester?" James heard Paul ask.

"It seems Roberts has acquired your habit of brooding, Leed." Chester laughed.

Paul glanced over at James and lost his smile, a dark scowl taking its place. James hid his reaction. If Paul knew what James and Catherine had been doing in the garden, he'd do more than scowl.

"My God, Leed," Geoffrey said at last. "I daresay Roberts will never master it to your ability."

Chester laughed again and loudly. James turned his head, not surprised to find himself the subject of close scrutiny from all three gentlemen.

Paul stalked over to where James sat and glared down at him. "I'm well aware of what you were about during dinner, Roberts."

James came to his feet. "I can't begin to guess your meaning."

"Staring at Catherine. Sitting too close for my sanity. Pray tell me, what are your intentions?"

James bristled. "It's out of my hands, Leed."

"What the devil does that mean?"

James looked around the room for a moment. His other

friends wore matching looks of interest on their faces. Thankfully, Catherine's father apparently sensed nothing amiss. James stood and crossed the room to the bookshelves, waiting for Catherine's brother to join him. Paul shot a glance at Chester and Geoffrey, who hid their grins and turned from them. He joined James, arching a brow in question.

"I asked Catherine to marry me," James said in a low voice.

Paul began to smile.

"Don't look so smug, Leed," James said in irritation. "She has yet to give me her answer."

"But how can she refuse you? You were in her room."

James turned to leave. "I won't discuss this with you."

Paul caught him by the arm. "I'm sorry to force this on you, Roberts."

James fixed his eyes on his friend. "I didn't propose to her because of you. I asked Catherine to marry me because I wish it."

Paul blinked. A wide smile spread across his face. "Then surely you must—"

"Never mind," James cut in with a wave of his hand. "I want her for my wife, Leed. That's all you need to know."

Paul simply nodded and left James then. James returned to the wing chair and sat. He recalled the look in Catherine's beautiful eyes when he'd asked her to marry him. Her fear had been palpable. It galled him to think that her experience with Waltham could ruin their chance at happiness.

His thoughts went to his conversation with her brother. Surely Paul was under the impression that James loved Catherine. He wouldn't give thought to that prickly emotion. But what if Catherine's thoughts were of her brother's bent? He was startled out of his reverie to find Chester suddenly standing over him, a glass of brandy in his hand.

"Roberts," Chester said, holding the glass out to James.

James thanked him and took the glass. He took a long swallow of the liquor. He closed his eyes and sighed, resting his head on the back of the chair.

"What the devil is ailing you, man?" Chester asked.

"Ah, Chester. It's out of my hands."

"What's this? I never thought you'd give up so easily."

James opened his eyes and looked up at him. "What are you saying?"

"I've seen that look before," Chester said. "Only a woman can cause that kind of discomfort."

James said nothing as he took another long swallow of brandy.

"And given Leed's behavior," Chester finished, "I can only assume that Catherine is the lady in question."

James felt his lips curve in a smile.

Chester chuckled. "You're in a bad way, friend."

"What?" James asked. "Oh, no. I'm fond of Catherine, but . . ."

Chester shook his head and grinned. James opened his mouth to respond as Paul announced that it was time to rejoin the ladies in the parlor. James followed the gentlemen into the great hall.

* * *

Catherine froze when James walked into the room. His eyes, steady in their gaze, met hers. She couldn't face the questions she saw there. Not yet. She had no notion of what her answer would be and, despite his assurance that she may take as long as she liked to give him an answer, she had the distinct impression he wouldn't be put off for long.

She murmured an excuse to Michelle and arose from her seat. As she hurried toward the doorway, James stepped into her path, but she skirted around him with her eyes downcast. She was such a coward. Where was the girl who bravely went to his townhouse alone one night?

In the quiet of her guest chamber much later that night, Catherine stared once more at the ceiling. What was she going to tell James? Should she marry him? She'd always thought him handsome and charming, even when she was but a girl. And now, whenever he looked at her, her pulse raced. His kisses set her on fire. His caresses made her feel wanted. But did she love him? And what of his feelings? With a sob of frustration, she closed her eyes and tried to will herself to sleep.

A few minutes later, Catherine sensed rather than heard him enter her room. She opened her eyes and stared up into his beautiful gray ones. “James,” she whispered.

James smiled down at her, his eyes glittering. She ran her eyes over him. He wore only breeches topped by his fine white shirt, open at the neck to reveal dark hairs. “Hello, love.”

Catherine smiled at the sweetly-spoken endearment. Her eyes widened as she realized their position. Not only was she alone with a man in her room—again!—but that man was leaning over her in bed.

“James, you shouldn’t be here.”

He placed a hand on either side of her head on the pillow and leaned closer. “I need an answer, Catherine.”

She gave a frantic shake of her head. “But you assured me that I could take as much time as I needed.”

James struck a thoughtful pose, then gave a small shrug. “I lied.”

He kissed her tenderly, letting his tongue slowly caress her lips. Catherine instinctively opened her mouth, welcoming him. The kiss deepened, their tongues touching.

He finally pulled back and sat beside her on the bed. He reached out to stroke her cheek. “Marry me, Catherine.”

“James, I don’t know if we suit each other.”

He arched a brow at that. He looked down at her, at the sheet down around her waist. Her nightgown of thin lawn must hide virtually nothing from him. She could feel his gaze as if it touched her skin and her nipples tightened.

“You suit me,” he said, his voice husky. He brought his eyes back up to her face. His gaze was tender, compelling. “I’ll be a good husband, Catherine. I’ll never hurt you.”

She blinked up at him, her mind muddled from his closeness, his sweet words. “James, I don’t know.”

“Do you care for me?”

“Yes,” she said without hesitation. “Very much.”

He kissed her again, slowly pushing the sheets aside. He ran his hands over her, brushing his palm over her breast. She gasped at the thrill that bit of contact gave her. His mouth left hers to nuzzle the soft skin on her neck.

"Marry me, Catherine," he whispered raggedly against her ear. "Please say you'll be mine."

She heard it in his voice, the emotion she so wished to believe he felt for her. She couldn't find it in her heart to refuse him. "Yes." She breathed.

He lifted his head, hope clear on his face. "What did you say?"

She brought her hand to his cheek. "Yes. I'll marry you."

He grinned at her. He kissed her once more, slowly easing her nightgown off her shoulders. He trailed kisses over her throat, her breasts. He stared down at her. "God, you're beautiful," he rasped.

James bent his head and placed a tender kiss on her nipple. Catherine arched in response and he closed his mouth over the sensitive bud. She moaned softly as he caressed her other breast. His hand stole under her nightgown, over her leg, her thigh, finally seeking the curls that shielded her womanhood. He stroked her gently, urging her legs apart.

"Oh, my goodness!" She gasped as his fingers delved inside her.

Catherine moaned as his mouth laved one nipple, then the other. His fingers stroked her delicate folds—gently at first and then with more pressure. She reached up and held him tightly to her, her legs moving restlessly on the bed. She lifted her pelvis toward him, riding his fingers with her moist heat.

"God, I want to give you more," he said. "So much more . . ."

She was close to . . . something. Her wetness drenched his fingers now and her breath came in quick gasps as she trembled beneath his expert attention. James brought his mouth to hers, catching her cries as she suddenly climaxed.

He placed little kisses on her face. "My God, Catherine."

Her eyes fluttered open. "Wh-what just happened?"

He smiled down at her. "That was proof you're as passionate as I, love. Tell me now we don't suit."

She blushed and threw her arms around him. "You do suit me, James."

James breathed in sharply, then quickly pulled away. "I'd

best return to my chamber, bride," he said hoarsely. "If I stay, I'll have to take you."

Her brow furrowed. "But didn't you just do that?"

He shook his head, a wicked smile on his face. "That was merely a glimpse of what we'll share, Catherine." He kissed her quickly and stood beside the bed. "Good night, love."

"Good night," she answered with a small smile.

James left her then, first making certain that no one was about to spy his sneaking out of her room. He paused in the doorway and turned to her, a tender look in his eyes. "Until the morrow," he whispered.

She nodded and snuggled into her pillow, a sigh escaping her lips. Her body still tingled where he'd touched her. What he'd done to her! She felt right about accepting his proposal. In the back of her mind, however, she couldn't help but think that he'd never said he loved her.

She refused to let one little word, or the absence of it, detract from the wonderful feelings he evoked in her. She fell into an easy sleep.

* * *

James tossed and turned in the bed in his guestroom. Just the thought of Catherine and the way she'd responded to him had his cock hard and throbbing. Her flesh against his fingers . . . She was so hot, so tight. Lord, but he wanted to make her his! He took a deep shuddering breath and tried to cool his blood. After her climax, he'd been nearly mad with desire to be inside her. Her nightgown gathered around her waist, her lovely legs open on the bed. Her silky curls had been sweetly damp from his attentions. If he'd unbuttoned his breeches and driven into her, taken her maidenhead and stroked deep inside her . . .

He'd speak to Catherine's father tomorrow. As soon as he rose. Certainly, the Earl of Talbot would have no objections to their union. Her brother would certainly be pleased.

Catherine cared for him. She told him so and she was an open, honest girl. He'd made no declaration of love, and felt guilty about that, but he wouldn't say those words to her unless he was certain. And he wasn't.

He closed his eyes and once more pictured her as he'd left her, all soft and welcoming. He breathed out another ragged sigh and prayed for sleep to take him.

The next morning James awoke early and with determination. He must approach the Earl of Talbot directly, as the gentlemen were planning to hunt quite early this morning. He rushed through his morning toilette and dressed with care. Black boots, buff-colored breeches, stark white shirt and cravat, green waistcoat. At last he donned his brown hunting jacket and went downstairs to the breakfast room.

James entered the breakfast room, pleased to find it nearly empty. Chester and Geoffrey were the only others present. His mind fully occupied on his coming conversation with Catherine's father, he served himself a small portion of eggs and ham from the sideboard.

"Good morning, Roberts," Chester said.

"Good morning," James returned absently.

Chester sipped his tea, a thoughtful look on his face. "How does this morning find you?"

James looked up and read the concern on Chester's face. He gave a short laugh. "A far sight better than last evening, I assure you."

"All is settled, then?"

He shook his head. "Not quite yet."

"What's this?" Geoffrey cut in. "This has something to do with all the brooding going on last evening, I would imagine."

James shot him a look of mild irritation at which Geoffrey laughed.

"I daresay the atmosphere was positively Gothic," Chester added.

Just then, Paul and his father joined them. Paul looked closely at James. "Roberts."

James nodded, watching as Paul served himself. When the earl stood alone at the sideboard, James rose to his feet. He crossed to Lord Talbot, ignoring the speculative glances he received from his friends. "If I may have a word with you, sir. It's of the utmost importance."

Talbot smiled. "Certainly, my boy. What is this regarding?"

James threw a glance at the table. He turned back to the older gentleman. "If you would, sir, I'd prefer to speak with you in private."

The earl nodded, his brows raised. James suggested the library and waved the man ahead of him. He closed the door and faced Catherine's father, suddenly very nervous.

"You've certainly piqued my interest, son," the earl said. "Do tell me what has you so intent."

James clasped his hands behind his back. He cleared his throat and began. "Sir, it would do me a great honor if you would give me your daughter's hand in marriage."

The Earl of Talbot blinked at him. "What's this? You wish to marry my daughter?"

James gave a firm nod.

The earl furrowed his brow in thought. He looked at James closely. "Catherine?"

James chuckled. "Yes, sir. Catherine."

A smile spread across the older man's face. "Of course, my boy!" He gave James a hearty slap on the back.

James felt as if a weight had been lifted off his shoulders. He offered his hand to the earl, at which he was pulled into a rough embrace. The man strode back to the breakfast room, James in tow. The other men looked up from their plates, puzzlement clear on their faces.

"It seems, gentlemen," Catherine's father boomed, "I'm soon to have another son."

Paul grinned. Chester and Geoffrey blinked. James breathed a sigh of relief.

Chapter 7

James left his breakfast untouched and hurried up the stairs to Catherine's chamber. He rapped on the door, stepping impatiently from one foot to the other. Catherine opened her door and gave him a secret smile. As he opened his mouth to speak, Elizabeth walked out of her guestroom next door. With a swish, Catherine closed her door as James turned on his heel to face her sister.

"Lord Roberts!" Elizabeth said in surprise. "I thought you would have joined the gentlemen on their hunt this morning."

"Good morning, Elizabeth. I most certainly will be joining the men. I . . . I forgot something in my room."

Elizabeth nodded and headed down the hall to the grand staircase. James let out a breath and turned just as Catherine opened her door once more.

"James, what are you doing here?"

She gasped as he swept into the room and closed the door. He leaned against the door and studied her for a moment. Her hair was upswept in a simple style, glossy curls teasing her cheeks. She wore a day dress of violet, the color lovely against her skin.

Catherine's brow furrowed as she looked down and brushed her hands over her skirt. "What is it?"

"You're so beautiful, Catherine." He grabbed her and held her to him, raining kisses on her face until she laughed. "And you're mine."

"What—" she said, out of breath. "What do you mean?"

He set her down, his hands still on her waist. "You're my bride. Your father has given me your hand."

"Oh, James!" she happily exclaimed.

She caught his enthusiasm and threw her arms around him. James hugged her, breathing in her intoxicating scent. "Of course," he whispered, nibbling on her ear. "I'll have the rest of you, as well."

"Mmm." She leaned her head to the side. "All of me."

James pulled back and stared at her. "Catherine, I . . . I care for you very much."

"Thank you," she said softly, reaching up to touch his face. "I'm so happy."

He flashed her a smile and hugged her once more. At last he released her. "I must go join the others, love." He was pleased to see a flash of disappointment in her eyes. "I will, however, take tea with you this afternoon."

Catherine smiled then, clasping her hands. "Do you think Father will announce our engagement then?"

James nodded. He gave her a sweet kiss and left to join the gentlemen in time to follow them out to the stables.

"Son," Catherine's father said to James as they rode out. "I must say you took me completely by surprise. I didn't realize you had feelings for my oldest girl."

"It happened rather suddenly, sir."

Paul snorted, drawing James and the earl's attention.

"Was there something you wished to say, Leed?" James asked.

"Quite suddenly indeed, Roberts," Paul said. "I believe it was precisely upon our return from the hunt yesterday."

"Never mind," James said.

The gentlemen's attentions soon turned to the pleasant task at hand, enjoying each other's company and the glorious fall morning.

* * *

Catherine served herself from the sideboard and sat at the table in the breakfast room. Did James feel more for her than he said? The look in his beautiful gray eyes had been most tender. He cared for her. It would have to suffice.

"I nearly bumped into Lord Roberts this morning,

Catherine," Elizabeth said as she entered the room. "He looked frightfully handsome in his hunting clothes."

"Indeed," Catherine agreed, sipping her tea.

Elizabeth blinked. "You saw him, as well?"

Catherine opened her mouth to respond, stopping herself at the last moment. If she were to tell Elizabeth about James's proposal and her acceptance, the news would travel through the manor in mere moments.

"Yes," she said at last. "I saw him."

Elizabeth sighed. "I do wish there were more young men here visiting."

Catherine set her cup down and fixed a look of curiosity on her sister. "Why do you say that?"

Elizabeth shrugged. "I'm nearly eighteen, Catherine. By the time you were my age, you were betrothed and jilted." Elizabeth's mouth was an O of surprise. "I didn't intend that the way it sounded, Catherine!"

"Don't fret so, Elizabeth," Catherine soothed. "I daresay future mention of my failed wedding will cause me no more discomfort."

Elizabeth let out an exaggerated sigh of relief. "Thank goodness I'll no longer have to school my words."

"Yes," Catherine said drily, sipping from her cup once more. "You did do an admirable job of it."

Elizabeth nodded and turned her attention back to her plate as Catherine hid her smile.

That afternoon, as Catherine went up to her guestroom to ready herself for tea, she was waylaid in the hall by her father. Lord Talbot's big frame nearly filled the passageway.

She blinked up at him in surprise. "Hello, Father."

"Daughter," he said in his deep voice, "I'd like a word with you."

Catherine nodded, unable to keep the smile off her face. Would he now speak of James's offer? The earl waved her ahead of him and followed her into her chamber. She sat on the edge of the bed and looked up at her father expectantly.

"Catherine," he began, his hands behind his back. "I believe you well know what this is regarding."

She gave a small nod.

The Earl of Talbot returned the gesture. "Roberts spoke to me this morning, daughter. I've agreed to give him your hand in marriage."

"I know," she said. "James told me so."

"Did he now? You seem pleased by all of this."

She smiled her agreement to that assessment.

"You're receptive to the match, I take it?"

"Oh, yes!" She calmed herself. "I—I'm very fond of him, Father."

"As he is of you, my dear," the man said. "That much was evident to me. I believe you've made an excellent match."

Catherine stood and hugged her father.

"I'm pleased to see you happy again." He placed his hands on her shoulders and looked down at her. "So you see now, Catherine? That nasty business with Waltham was for the best."

"I think so too, Father," she said with a sigh. "I believe James and I will be very happy."

He studied her a bit longer, obvious moisture gathering in his eyes, then nodded. "I'll make the announcement over tea, daughter."

"Thank you so much, Father."

He hugged her once more and left her to her preparations. She quickly changed into a tea gown of pale blue and ran her fingers through the curls framing her face. As she pulled her door open, she nearly ran into James where he stood, poised to knock on the wood panel.

"James!" She gasped. "You keep surprising me."

"Well, you better get used to me. You'll be seeing a lot more of me from now on," he said with a wicked grin.

Her cheeks flamed.

James smiled down at her. "I thought to escort you to tea, Catherine."

Catherine beamed a smile at him and placed her hand on his arm. As they descended the staircase, she watched him out of the corner of her eye. He'd changed as well, and now wore a dark blue jacket over gray breeches. He'd washed after the hunt, but Catherine could still detect the scent of the outdoors on him.

Mmm, that scent had been so delectable yesterday. She sighed, drawing his attention.

"What is it, love?" James asked.

"I can scarcely believe I'm betrothed to the most charming man I've ever known."

He leaned closer. "That man is very pleased with his choice, as well." They reached the bottom of the stairs. "Yes, very pleased, indeed. Why, only last evening—"

"James!"

"You're so pretty when you blush, Catherine."

She couldn't help herself and her cheeks flushed hotter. Chuckling, James led her into the great room.

As anticipated, Catherine's father announced their engagement over tea. Catherine found herself enveloped in warm embraces from the ladies present. The surprise on Elizabeth's face was comical. Her big grin was proof, however, that she was very pleased with her sister's news.

"Dinner tonight shall be in the couple's honor," Paul announced.

"I believe I can express my betrothed's thanks as well as my own," James said.

Catherine nodded, then soon found herself drawn into the ladies' conversations while the gentlemen monopolized James' attention.

James did manage, however, to catch her eye one time. He slowly winked, causing Catherine to flush. She saw the glint in his eye and felt deliciously warm. Michelle's voice dragged her attention back to the discussion of dresses and flowers and the like.

Dinner was a loud, boisterous affair. Catherine sat beside James, who fairly beamed as the congratulations of the afternoon were repeated. After the meal was concluded, the sexes separated as usual. Catherine wondered if they would once again meet in the courtyard, but it seemed James was waylaid by her brother. He cast a look of regret over his shoulder, which Catherine caught and returned. By the time the gentlemen joined the ladies in the parlor, any chance for a secret meeting had passed.

* * *

Much later, after most of the guests had retired to their chambers, James couldn't get the image of his beautiful bride out of his head. He would stop by her room this evening to wish her good night. He pictured her in one of her delicate nightgowns and knew that he'd be hard-pressed to leave her alone. Perhaps he shouldn't go to her room. Her pleasured cries of last night echoed through his mind. To hell with that!

He made his way down the hallway to Catherine's guestroom, glancing back over his shoulder. He turned just as he reached her door and stopped dead in his tracks.

"Going somewhere, Roberts?" Paul drawled. He leaned against the wall beside Catherine's door, his arms crossed in front of him.

James swore softly. "Good evening, Leed. I was merely coming to wish Catherine a good night."

Paul nodded and rapped his knuckles on the door.

"Yes?" Catherine said breathlessly from behind the wood panel, excitement clear in her voice.

James smiled at the sound and opened his mouth to respond.

Her brother held up a hand to still him. "Catherine."

A gasp was heard from within, followed by a long pause. "Yes, Paul?"

Paul stared at James, a crooked smile on his face. "Roberts wishes to bid you good night."

"Oh, I um . . . Good night, James."

James fixed a scowl at his friend and turned to the door. "Good night, Catherine."

Paul arched a brow at him. "Was there something else, Roberts?"

Her brother was obviously going to stand there until James was well away from her room. With a sigh of irritation, James turned on his heel and returned to his chamber.

In his guestroom James removed his jacket and threw it on the bed in a fit of pique. Laughter suddenly burst out of him. He should be grateful to Paul for keeping him from Catherine this evening. No doubt he'd have been unable to keep his hands off her. Any chance of taking a virgin bride would have surely been dashed. Shaking his head at the absolute absurdity of his situation, he readied for bed. He stretched out on the bed and let his mind work.

Lord, he wanted Catherine. His thoughts went back to last night, to their encounter in her chamber. No other woman responded to him the way she did. Her heat had stunned him. The memories flashing through his mind fueled his anticipation of their wedding night, of her spread beneath him, of her heat holding his cock as tightly as it had his fingers. He closed his eyes with a groan and sought to block that provocative image from his mind. It proved impossible. He knew with absolute certainty that it would be a long time before sleep claimed him that night.

"Ah, hell."

He punched his pillow and waited for his discomfort to ease enough to let him get to sleep.

* * *

Inside her chamber Catherine breathed a sigh, one mixed with relief and regret. What if James had gotten to her room first? What would Paul have done then?

She shook her head. It was a good thing James hadn't come into her room. Although if he had, he no doubt would have performed more of those delicious deeds upon her person. Catherine flushed at that. No matter. She and James were to be married, and shouldn't she want her husband to please her? She wished to please him, although she didn't know how to go about it. Perhaps her groom would be obliged to instruct her. She fairly tingled as she imagined what were certain to be the most delightful lessons she'd ever known.

She climbed into her bed and closed her eyes, her handsome groom clear in her mind.

* * *

James left for Bradford Hall early the next morning, wishing to give his father the news of his betrothal directly. He found the man ensconced in the parlor, in front of a glowing fire in deference to the autumn afternoon's chill.

"Hello, Father," James said in greeting.

The Earl of Bradford looked up in surprise. "James, whatever are you doing here? I believed you would remain at Leed's for a fortnight at the very least."

James patted his father on the shoulder and sat across from him, suddenly at a loss for the right words.

A smile teased the corner of the earl's mouth. "What happened?"

"I've asked her to marry me, Father. And I am pleased to tell you that she has consented."

His father blinked, then a slow smile spread across his face. "Well, well. Pray, what has changed?"

James shrugged, his own grin matching his father's. "I realized that fighting our match would be impossible."

"You love her, then?"

It was James's turn to be taken aback. He shifted in his chair. "I . . . I'm not certain. I care for her more than I've ever cared for another."

The earl folded his hands in his lap and fixed a curious look on his son. "And who is this fair young lady who has so captivated you?"

James's grin widened. "Catherine Talbot."

"What?" his father asked in surprise. "Leed's little sister? She's but a child, no?"

James smiled wryly. "She's nineteen, Father. Hardly a child."

"Nineteen? Where does the time go? And how long have you had such feelings for her?"

"Nearly two months, I imagine. I admit I was quite drawn to her when I saw her at Chester's wedding. I hadn't seen her for nearly a year prior. She's matured considerably since Waltham's betrayal of her."

"What's this? A betrayal?"

James then told his father of Catherine's betrothal and the

wedding that never took place. Anger at the scoundrel's ill-use of her caused his fists to clench. "The bloody fool hurt her."

"Yes, I imagine that would mature the girl," the earl stated. "Unfortunate business, that."

"Most fortunate for me, however."

"I've never before seen you so happy, son. Most fortunate, indeed." The older man studied him for a long moment. "Perhaps some brandy to celebrate?"

James stood and rang for the servant.

* * *

It was decided that Catherine would be married at Talbot Hall, her father's grand estate, in two weeks' time. Once James procured a special license, there would be no reason to wait any longer. Her aborted wedding to Waltham had been set to take place in the church nearest the hall, but Catherine wanted no reminders of that folly.

The estate was also situated in Yorkshire, farther to the north. After her father had regained his fortune, lost mainly to a bout of gambling two years past, much was spent on reparations to the main house. As a result the estate was well-suited to host as lavish a celebration as the wedding promised to be. Elizabeth threw herself into the wedding preparations and Catherine was only too pleased to permit her and Michelle free rein to plan the event. She herself had done most of the planning for her ill-fated wedding to Waltham and had no desire to do so again. She wished only to marry James. What color flowers and how large the orchestra? Those were details that didn't interest her.

When James returned to Leed Manor late that evening, Catherine greeted the carriage in the drive.

He stepped down and placed his hands on her shoulders. "What are you doing out here, Catherine? It's far too chilly."

Catherine clicked her tongue at him. "I wished to give you a proper greeting, groom," she said sweetly.

She stood on tiptoe and kissed him lightly, pulling back to smile up at him.

He flashed a wicked smile. "That isn't a proper greeting, bride," he said in a low voice.

He grabbed her to him and kissed her soundly, his tongue sweeping into her mouth. "Now, that's a proper greeting."

She gasped, but kissed him back, much to his obvious delight. He pulled back and winking, took her hand. "Let us go inside, love."

In the drawing room, as the guests awaited the dinner bell, they were surrounded by the ladies. As talk of flowers and orchestras and banquets floated about him, James's eyes settled on her. Catherine shrugged and smiled at him, forcing her attention to the discussion. She was unable to deny the passion in her fiancé's smoldering gray eyes, however. Oh, she was a lucky bride.

Long after dinner, James stood to accompany Catherine to her chamber. Apparently ignoring her brother's piercing gaze, he nodded a good evening to all assembled and led her from the room.

When they reached her chamber door, Catherine looked up at him expectantly. He leaned close to her, placing his mouth on hers. Sighing, she opened to him. James took her mouth, tasting his fill as she began to press against him. He finally lifted his head.

"James," she whispered as his mouth left hers.

James groaned softly and placed his hands on her shoulders. "I must bid you good night here in the hall, Catherine."

"But why?"

He reluctantly pulled away from her. "Your brother will have me drawn and quartered, Catherine."

Catherine gazed up at him and smiled a siren's smile at him. "Good night then, James."

"Good night, love. I believe I'll join your brother for a brandy." He turned away and started down the hall. She could hear his frustrated mutterings and knew he gave voice to everything she was feeling. She entered her chamber with a longing sigh.

Chapter 8

The next two weeks passed much too slowly for James's sanity. He breathed a sigh of relief when, two days before the wedding, Catherine left for Talbot Hall. Being so close to her and unable to touch her was slowly driving him mad. No doubt her brother seemed to find that fact quite amusing.

James took himself off to Bradford Hall to determine if his father would be able to attend the wedding. The weather had turned chilly, it being the start of October, but the ride to Talbot Hall was only a few hours. The earl wouldn't permit his son to dissuade him from attending the celebration. Acquiescing to his father's wishes, James spoke with his father's manservant and made certain that the older gentleman would be comfortable on the journey.

Taking himself into his study, James worked a bit on his ledgers, his mind constantly coming back to Catherine. Lord, how he missed her. How he wanted her. He refused to puzzle through his feelings for her. Catherine hadn't asked for those words he was so reluctant to give, thank God. If she wasn't troubled by that pesky emotion, he most certainly wouldn't bring it to her attention.

He completed his work and closed his ledgers with satisfaction. The year he'd spent with his father, in exile as it were, had given him the opportunity to see his matters straightened. His holdings, not far from Bradford Hall, were well-managed by his steward and quite profitable. The leased properties were on prime farmland and brought in a handsome sum each quarter. He prayed it would be a very long time before he added his father's properties to his own, and was quite content to share Bradford Hall with the earl.

James suddenly straightened. He'd need to prepare his suite of rooms for his new bride. He strode from the room, intent on speaking with the staff and putting all in order for Catherine's arrival. He stilled. Lady Roberts. His wife.

He'd known he would marry some day. He never would have guessed Catherine Talbot would be the one. Now he was hard pressed to picture any other woman filling that role.

"Amazing."

He shook his head and continued toward the back of the house.

* * *

It was the evening before their nuptials were to take place and Catherine paced the floor of her room at Talbot Hall. Her wedding dress, a magnificent confection of white satin, hung at the ready in her dressing room. She crossed to it, a small smile on her face. Michelle assisted her in the selection of the gown and assured her that the cut was well suited to her figure. The dress was quite elegant, trimmed with wide piping and graceful bows. Catherine's heart did a little flip as she imagined James's face when he saw her in the dress. And wouldn't he look absolutely splendid in his formal black? Lord, he was a handsome man.

She missed his kisses, his caresses, these past two days. While they had never been alone for any length of time, they'd managed to steal kisses now and again. James had told her in hushed tones of all the wonderful things he wished to do with her, his eyes glittering. Were such deeds possible? She was breathless with anticipation.

A maid knocked on her door and handed a missive to Catherine, leaving with a curtsy. Catherine turned the paper over, a thrill going through her when she once more recognized James's hand. She closed the chamber door and sat at her vanity, breaking the seal on the letter. She gasped as she read his message, the passionate words affecting her nearly as much as if he stood before her reciting them.

My Dearest Catherine,
I'm counting the hours until you are mine. I picture you at Talbot, tucked cozily in your bed, and my pulse races. Tomorrow, love, we will be one. I promise to make you happy, bride. To the fullest of my ability. Think of me as you drift off to sleep tonight, knowing I lay in the bed we will share as man and wife. Sleep well.
Until tomorrow,
James

Catherine sighed, pressing the paper to her breast. She'd saved his note from Leed Manor, the one in which he asked to meet her in the courtyard. She opened the drawer and placed this note on top of it. Withdrawing a length of violet ribbon from a box atop the vanity, she secured the papers with a pretty bow. How utterly romantic and silly. No matter. Even if James didn't love her, there was no denying the passion in his letters.

She felt her heart clench as the realization struck her that she might very well be falling in love with her groom. And while James was always sweet and tender, she wouldn't fool herself into thinking he felt that incredible emotion for her. Sighing once more, she closed the drawer, James's romantic words still ringing through her mind. She changed into her nightgown and climbed into bed, finding it quite easy to follow James's instructions. She drifted off to sleep, dreaming of her groom.

In her dreams, however, James promised to love her forever.

* * *

The next day, their wedding day, dawned crisp and sunny. James left Bradford Hall with his father, the older man dressed for the chill of the morning. They had a thirty-mile ride to Talbot Hall, a manageable feat to be sure as the roads appeared to be dry and relatively smooth in that part of Yorkshire. The gentlemen sat across from each other inside the carriage. The Earl of Bradford settled himself comfortably against the cushioned seat. James fidgeted, his mind on the coming ceremony.

"James, do sit still. You're fairly rocking the carriage." The earl smiled broadly at him. "You'll spook the horses."

James smiled, losing a bit of his nervousness. He reviewed the plans that had been discussed over the past few days, most pleased with the developments. His father was to remain at Talbot Hall after the celebration, at the happy insistence of Catherine's father, for nearly a fortnight. James and Catherine would adjourn to Bradford Hall that very evening after the ceremony, affording the newlyweds a bit of solitude. His lips curved into a smile at that thought. Lord, he could scarcely wait to bring her back with him. To make her his. But he had yet to get through the bloody ceremony. He straightened his clothes and sat stiffly in the cozy carriage.

His father chuckled at his obvious agitation. "Relax, boy," the earl said. "Catherine Talbot is a lovely girl. You've made a sound match."

James felt a rightness, a certainty, seize him as he thought of Catherine as his wife. Her beauty, her sweetness, her passion, pleased him greatly.

"I concur, Father," James allowed with a grin. "Quite a sound match indeed."

When they arrived at Talbot Hall, Catherine's father and brother greeted them. The wedding guests would arrive that afternoon to join in the celebration, but only their close relatives would witness the ceremony itself, much to the groom's great relief. His nerves were fairly humming. Strange, as social engagements never caused him anything but ease. And yet he stood in the drawing room of the great house, his hands clenching and unclenching.

Paul smiled wryly. "A bit nervous, Roberts?"

James fixed a look of exasperation at his future brother-in-law, not dignifying his jibe with a verbal response. Paul barked out a laugh, but before James could think to reply, he stiffened and turned toward the doorway.

Michelle and Elizabeth entered the drawing room, looking very lovely in gowns of rose. They crossed to join Paul and James's father and turned to face the doorway. James followed their gaze, drawing in a breath at the sight before him.

There stood the Earl of Talbot with his eldest daughter on his arm. Catherine took James's breath away, resplendent in white satin. Her hair was upswept, glossy brown tendrils brushing her slight shoulders. Her gown hugged her curves, giving James a provocative glimpse of perfect creamy skin above the bodice. He brought his eyes to her face. Her eyes sparkled; a smile curved her full lips. He could hardly believe she was soon to be his.

Catherine ran her gaze over him. Her eyes darkened and James felt that spark of connection when her father placed her hand in his. He turned to face the minister.

The ceremony was concluded with much haste, almost before he realized it. James kissed her soundly, sealing their union. Suddenly, everyone was talking at once, offering the couple their congratulations. Michelle left to see to the final preparations for the celebration, dragging Elizabeth along with her. She shot a meaningful glance at her husband, who took her cue and invited the older gentlemen to join him in the library. James watched them go, holding tightly to Catherine's hand.

When they were at last alone, he turned to face her. "God, you look incredible, bride."

Catherine smiled up at him. "Thank you," she said softly.

He bent his head to hers and kissed her tenderly. Catherine opened for him, placing her gloved hands on his chest and rising up on tiptoe. James wrapped his arms around her and deepened the kiss, letting his tongue stroke and tease hers.

He pulled back, gazing deeply into her violet eyes. "Tonight, Catherine," he promised in a husky voice.

Catherine simply nodded. "I don't know what will happen, James. But I'm so happy to be with you."

He nearly grabbed her and ran from the room. God, she was made for him. Just him.

The orchestra music reached him, signaling the arrival of the wedding guests. Taking her hand in his once more, he led his wife into the grand ballroom.

* * *

After bidding farewell to her family, Catherine joined James in his carriage. He waited for her to sit and lowered himself beside her. Settling back against the cushioned seat, he grasped her hand in his, twining their fingers together. Catherine stared down at their hands, clasped so intimately, and felt warmth spread through her. They were married!

"Did you enjoy the celebration, wife?"

Catherine smiled at his easy use of the endearment. "Yes, husband," she returned. "Everything was lovely."

"I've a wedding supper planned for us at Bradford."

It struck her then. They would be alone at Bradford, away from her family and all she'd known before. And what about the coming evening? What of the wedding night?

"A wedding supper?" she asked, striving to keep her nervousness out of her voice. "For just the two of us?"

James quirked a half-smile at her. "Is there someone you wish to have join us?"

"Oh, no," she answered quickly. "It'll be wonderful, I'm certain."

"Catherine," he whispered, drawing her to his side.

She stared up at him. "Yes, James?" she asked, breathless.

"Kiss me," he gently instructed.

She closed her eyes and gently placed her lips on his. At the feel of his warm breath on her skin, she grew bolder and licked his lips with her tongue. He growled in response and she giggled, then began moving her lips against his. He kissed her back, their lips beginning that sensual dance that made her knees weak.

They spent the remainder of the carriage ride kissing and cuddling, Catherine's nervousness all but disappearing in the cozy interior of the carriage.

When they arrived at Bradford Hall, James assisted Catherine down from the carriage. He waved her ahead of him and followed her up the wide stone steps to the large entryway. Just as a servant was opening the door, he swept Catherine up into his arms.

She grabbed on to his shoulders for support. "James!"

James laughed as he twirled her in his arms, the sound

echoing throughout the marble-tiled entry. He placed her back on her feet and kissed her. "Welcome home, Lady Roberts."

She lowered her lashes, embarrassed by his display.

He leaned closer. "Is everything all right, love?"

"James," she whispered. "The servants will see."

He led her into the formal dining room. "Catherine, we're married. I will no longer resist the urge to touch you whenever and wherever I wish." He stopped and shot her a look of worry. "Unless you don't wish me to?"

"Oh, no, James! That is," she recovered, "I want you to touch me."

"Ah, I'll touch you, wife," he whispered. "Until you sigh with pleasure."

His words caused a flush to spread over her body. As if he hadn't just said the most outrageous and provocative thing, he rang for their supper and held out Catherine's chair for her.

The meal was magnificent, the pheasant done to perfection. They chatted easily over their meal, but when his hand brushed hers, she suddenly grew quiet. She studied her husband in the candlelight, pondering her feelings for the very handsome man seated across from her. His touch made her feel so happy. Was it the norm to feel such things for one's spouse? Surely her brother and his wife were quite pleased with one another. But then, they were in love.

As if James noticed the small change in her demeanor, he arched a brow at her. "You don't think that I'll devour you before we sample the magnificent dessert the cook has prepared, do you?"

Catherine laughed and shook herself out of her reverie. "I was merely marveling that we are even seated here, James. Why only a year ago, I—"

"Don't speak of him, love," James cut in. "That fool's betrayal led to my making you my own."

Catherine felt her heart flutter at that statement. "Am I truly your own, James?" she couldn't help but ask.

He lost his smile as he gazed at her. He stood suddenly and pulled her to her feet and Catherine let out a yelp of surprise.

"Dessert can wait," he murmured, pulling her close.

He kissed her fiercely. Before she could catch her breath, he swept her into his arms once more and carried her up the grand staircase to his chamber.

Not until they were inside the bedroom did James let her go, and then only to close the door. He leaned against the wood panel and ran his eyes over her from head to toe. Catherine turned from his close scrutiny and looked about the room.

The chamber was quite grand, decorated in shades of blue. A sitting area was at one end of the space and a fire blazed brightly in the fireplace situated between two plump upholstered chairs. The other furniture filling the space was of dark wood and intricately carved, glowing from frequent polishing. She gasped as her eyes settled on the largest bed she'd ever seen.

She squared her shoulders and turned back to James. She'd regained her earlier composure, and her nervousness along with it. "I suppose you wish to go to bed now."

James nearly choked at that ridiculous understatement. If he told her precisely what it was he wanted just now, his innocent bride would undoubtedly faint dead away.

"Why don't you ready for bed?"

Catherine nodded and all but ran into the dressing room.

He stripped out of his finery, deciding at the last moment to leave on his breeches. He started to sit on the edge of the bed to await his bride's appearance when he realized that the huge four-poster might be intimidating to her. Crossing over to the sitting area of the room, he settled himself on the arm of one of the well-stuffed chairs that flanked the fireplace.

At last she emerged. My God, she was worth the wait. Catherine walked toward him, a smile curving her lips. Her eyes ran over him, making him grateful that he'd kept on his breeches.

She quickly lowered her eyes to the floor. "I'm ready for bed, husband."

He rose to his feet and crossed to her. Her thin gown caressed her curves, giving his eyes a tantalizing preview of what awaited him.

"My God, Catherine. You take my breath away."

She brought her gaze to his and reached up to touch his face.

He pulled her close to him, their foreheads touching. “I want you so much, Catherine.”

“I’m yours, James.”

He kissed her gently and pulled back to cup her face with his hand. “I’ve never wanted a woman the way I want you. I’m afraid I’ll hurt you.”

“You’ll never hurt me, James.” Catherine smiled up at him. “You promised.”

He was confused for a moment, until he remembered the promise he gave her the night he asked her to marry him. He shook his head. “There will be a little pain, love,” he said. “It’ll be over quickly, I promise.”

She furrowed her brow. *Ah, hell.* He thought to turn her attention and pulled her close, running his hands over her back.

She placed her hands on his bare chest. “You’re beautifully made, James.”

He chuckled and captured her lips. His tongue teased her, drawing a reaction from her. She whimpered as his hands caressed her breasts through her thin nightgown. He brought his lips to her neck, to her silken skin. She purred against him, the sound driving him mad.

He unbuttoned her gown, placing kisses on the skin he was revealing. He cupped her breasts once more.

She grabbed his wrists and strained toward him, closing her eyes. “James . . .”

He bent his head and flicked his tongue over one nipple, delighting in the tiny shudder she gave. He closed his mouth over it, sucking until it was a hard nub, then lavished attention on the other breast. So sweet. When he lifted his head, he saw the passion etched on Catherine’s face. She opened her eyes, their irises darkened to violet.

He removed her nightgown and lifted her in his arms. He placed her in the middle of the big bed, peeled off his breeches and joined her. He stretched out on top of her, supporting part of his weight with his elbows.

“Ah, Catherine,” he murmured, reveling in the feel of her body beneath his.

She gasped as his chest brushed against her breasts. He

kissed her deeply, his tongue thrusting slowly in and out of her mouth. Catherine twined her fingers through his hair as his mouth claimed her breast once more. Her body arched upward and he kissed and licked her sweet flesh, wanting to taste all of her. He stopped at her waist. Best to wait for another time to put his mouth on her most private place.

He brought his face to hers and kissed her gently. "Catherine, I'll try not to hurt you."

"You can't hurt me, James," she said breathlessly. "You can't."

How could she have such faith in him? His fingers shook as he caressed her and found her already wet for him. He could wait no longer to be inside her. He settled himself between her thighs and eased into her, letting out a groan of intense pleasure as he felt her warmth welcome him. The thin barrier of her virginity momentarily blocked his entrance.

He held himself still and stared down at her. "Catherine," he ground out. "Hold on to me."

Catherine reached up to grab his shoulders as he entered her fully. He caught her cry in his mouth and steeled himself not to move for a few moments. He continued to caress her with his hands and mouth and then slipped his fingers between them and stroked her clitoris until she was writhing beneath him.

"James, I need you," she moaned and shuddered as his fingers continued to play with her. Finally, until he could stand it no more, he began to move inside her gently as he let her get accustomed to him. She lifted her hips and took in more of him, a sigh escaping her lips. His thrusts became more forceful. He was soon driving into her, his control quickly vanishing. Catherine caught his passion, her legs squeezing to draw him even deeper.

"Oh, James." She gasped. "Oh, yes . . ."

She tightened around him as she neared her release. As she cried out his name, he gave in to his own climax, shouting as he poured himself into her. He rested his head in the crook of her neck, his heartbeat slowly resuming its normal pace. He breathed in deeply, liking his scent mingling with her sweetness.

"Catherine," he said when he found his voice.

She opened her eyes and gazed up at him. “Yes, James?” she asked, her voice husky.

“I . . .” He couldn’t put into words what he was feeling. Never before had he felt such release, such a sense of completion. He turned his thoughts instead to her virgin’s pain. “I’m sorry I hurt you, love.”

“You didn’t hurt me, James. Merely a twinge. It’s forgotten.”

He smiled his relief at that and rolled over, drawing her to his side. Catherine rested her head on his chest, her fingers curling in the dark hairs.

“James,” she whispered. “Did I . . . please you?”

He heard the doubt in her voice and dropped a kiss on her tousled curls. “Sweetheart, you were perfect.”

Catherine sighed and cuddled closer. James knew by her soft, even breathing that she’d fallen asleep. He thought of the incredible passion they’d just shared. He’d never felt that way before, his release never that explosive. It was as if she was made for his loving, and he for hers. And to think he’d very nearly lost her to that bastard Waltham! His heart clenched at the thought of her with any other man. She was his, body and soul.

He kissed his wife once more and sighed, joining her in slumber.

Chapter 9

Catherine was slow to awaken the next morning. She stretched languorously, shocked when she bumped into James's fit body. Her eyes snapped open in surprise. She found him leaning above her, smiling broadly.

"Good morning."

She clutched the sheets to her bosom and James chuckled.

"Catherine, we were completely intimate last night. There's no part of you I haven't seen."

"I didn't see all of you, James."

He grinned and threw the sheets off of himself. She gasped and shut her eyes tight. He laughed again and kissed her.

"Come, wife," he gently chided. "You don't wish to stay in bed all day, do you?"

She opened her eyes and shrugged.

"Catherine, is everything all right?"

She was embarrassed, but not enough to keep her thoughts from her husband. "I want you to make love to me again, James," she whispered shyly.

He sharply drew in a breath. He gently ran his finger across her cheek, down her neck. "Aren't you sore this morning?"

She shook her head and smiled. "I told you, you can't hurt me, husband. Did you forget?"

"But, I thought that after we—"

"James?"

"Yes, Catherine?"

"Kiss me," she instructed.

He honored his wife's request. He took her again, slowly, gently, and when they came together, their climax was shattering. Afterward, he cradled her in his arms.

“That was wonderful.” Catherine sighed, rubbing her face against his chest.

James held her closer then abruptly sat up in the bed. “We should get dressed.”

“James, is something wrong?”

“What? No, nothing.” He flashed her his charming smile. “I’ll order a bath for you if you like.”

She stared at him for a long moment, finally accepting his offer with a small nod. He went into the dressing room. When he emerged, dressed in gray breeches topped with a white shirt and dark blue jacket, he crossed to her.

“I’ll see you downstairs in the breakfast room, love,” he said, kissing her lightly.

She nodded and watched him go, admiring his long, easy stride. The servants left her to her bath shortly thereafter, leaving her in total privacy. She removed her gown and wrapper and stepped into the tub, letting the warm water soothe her spirits.

Her mind found its way back to the subject of her husband and his very confusing behavior of the morning. James had seemed strange to her for that brief moment in their bed. Why, it seemed as though the incredible way in which they fit each other was troubling to him. Was he somehow displeased with her performance? He’d seemed more than pleased, but perhaps she was incapable of judging such matters. Surely her mind was muddled from the intense pleasure she felt when they came together. She set about bathing herself, clearing her mind of everything but the feel of the water and the scent of the soap.

* * *

James sat at the table in the breakfast room, awaiting Catherine’s arrival. He thought to wait for his wife to choose his meal from the sideboard, content to sip his tea until she came downstairs. After their lovemaking this morning, he needed time to gather his wits. The way Catherine made him feel . . . He couldn’t put a name to it, or, rather, was reluctant to. Their lovemaking was incredible, that was certain. But he wondered what Catherine felt for him.

James looked up as she stopped in the doorway, lowering her lashes in obvious shyness. He took in her appearance. She wore a lovely day dress of white, dotted with tiny blue flowers. Her hair shone, graceful curls framing her face. He flashed her a smile, which she returned, her dimple making its appearance.

"Good morning, James."

She walked to the sideboard and he stood to join her. "Good morning, love," he said, placing a kiss on her cheek.

They helped themselves to some eggs and ham and sat at the table.

James spread his napkin on his lap, eyeing her appreciatively. "You look lovely this morning, Catherine."

"Thank you."

"Did you enjoy your bath?"

"Very much so." She sipped her tea. "It was delightful."

James finished his meal and waited for her to do the same. "What would you like to do this day?"

She shrugged. "Whatever you wish."

"Perhaps a stroll about the grounds?" he suggested. "You haven't seen the gardens for quite some time, I daresay."

She set her cup down. "I would like that very much. Your gardens were always so beautiful."

"Our gardens," he corrected her with a smile.

She nodded enthusiastically. "Our gardens," she repeated, her eyes sparkling. "I wonder if the roses are still in bloom?"

"I believe they've gone to sleep, wife."

"No matter." She shrugged. "I'll enjoy our walk nevertheless."

They finished their tea and Catherine went upstairs to dress for their stroll. When she rejoined him, she wore a dark blue spencer, the little velvet jacket coming just to her waist. She pulled on kid gloves of soft gray leather and placed her hand on his arm. James led her out the back of the house and into the glorious fall sunshine.

The garden was formally arranged, with graceful statues placed about the area. While no flowers were in bloom this late in the season, the hedgerows were still a vibrant green, thick and squat, dividing the garden into geometric shapes. Marble benches were placed strategically about to allow for the rest and reflection of the visitors. In the center of the garden there was a large reflecting pool, the surface barely rippled in the still morning.

"Oh." Catherine sighed with pleasure. "It's as I remembered."

"What's that?" he asked, intrigued.

She crossed to the pool to gaze into her reflection. "Elizabeth and I used to sneak out here when visiting," she confided. "I used to gaze into this pool and let my mind drift."

He watched her sweet smile as she faced the water, lost in her memories, and smiled in response.

"And where did your mind go then, Catherine?" he couldn't help asking.

"You'll think me silly," she said softly.

He stood beside her and turned her to face him. "Catherine, I would never find you silly."

She smiled at that. "I used to dream of my future," she admitted. "Of my husband."

He smiled widely. "You dreamed of me, did you?" he teased.

She arched a brow at him. "I didn't know whom I was to marry then, James."

Did she think of that bloody fool Waltham? He shook his head at his quick flare of anger. What the devil ailed him this morning?

"Well, you're quite stuck with me, I'm afraid," he said in more of a serious tone than he'd intended. He led her over to one of the marble benches and sat, pulling her down onto his lap. "Are you happy, Catherine?"

She sighed and wrapped her arms around him. "Yes, I'm very happy."

He knew her mind was filled with the intimacies they so recently shared when she lowered her lashes and blushed.

He reached out to stroke her cheek. "Is something troubling you?"

"James, when we . . . ?" she began. "Never mind."

"Catherine," he said gently. "Last night was incredible." He smiled wickedly. "And this morning—"

Her gasp stopped him in mid-sentence. He kissed her open mouth. She kissed him back, wrapping her arms tightly around him. Their tongues mated, making him want more. He pulled back, surprised at the passion she could arouse so quickly.

"Catherine." He breathed. "Let's go inside."

She shook her head. "It's too beautiful out here, James."

He ran his gaze over her, his eyes settling on her mouth. He lightly nipped her lower lip. "Mmm," he murmured, rubbing her lips with his. "I could kiss you all day."

She wriggled in his lap as he devoured her mouth, the motion driving him mad. He placed his hands on her hips to still her.

"Catherine," he said hoarsely. "If you keep moving like that, I'll lay you down across this bench and take you right here."

Her pupils dilated and he hardened.

"Oh, James." She sighed into his mouth.

"God," he groaned as she pressed herself to him. He stood quickly, cradling her in his arms. "I don't care how beautiful it is out here. We're going inside."

Catherine nodded, her eyes dark. They spent the remainder of the morning tucked cozily in the big bed in their chamber.

Later on, they took their dinner downstairs in the dining room. They dined on simple fare, sliced roast beef and fresh bread and salads. Catherine eyed James's plate, piled high with the tender meat.

He caught her eye and shrugged his shoulders. "I need to keep up my strength," he teased.

She blushed and returned her eyes to the tabletop. He chuckled over her shyness, finding it interesting considering her total lack of that trait in their bed. He said nothing of it to her, however. He took a big bite of bread, content to watch her as she ate daintily from her own plate.

* * *

When they finished their meal, James escorted her to the parlor.

It was as she remembered, a beautiful room decorated in yellow and ivory. He looked at her with obvious regret and she swallowed her disappointment.

"I have some estate business to attend to, Catherine," he informed her. "I expect to be back by tea time."

The kiss he gave her before he left was sweet. Catherine crossed to the window seat, pleased to find a few books resting there. She chose one and settled herself on the yellow-striped cushion. Looking out the window, she spied James leading his horse from the stable. She watched him, admiring the graceful way he moved. He mounted his horse and rode off toward the cottages that dotted the estate, no doubt to see to his father's tenants.

Catherine sighed and opened the book, trying to lose herself in the simple story. She couldn't. Thoughts of her husband intruded quite naturally, since she'd given herself to him less than two hours earlier. When he made love to her, she felt incredible, cherished and loved. James never told her he loved her, not even as he held her afterward. She knew that he cared for her. He'd told her as much. And there hadn't been a repeat of his strange behavior of the morning after their visit to the gardens.

A dark thought flitted through her mind. She remembered hearing of James's feelings toward Lady Kanewood a few years ago. Had he loved her? Did he love her still? She'd seen them together many times, and nothing was evident to suggest he'd renewed his attentions. She knew Lord Kanewood counted James as a friend. Would that be so if James still had feelings for the man's wife?

James was friendly toward Becca, but he was so to everyone. He was the most charming man Catherine had ever known. No. She didn't think he harbored any deep affection for Becca.

But did James love her? He was so attentive to her, so tender. Perhaps that was simply the way it was between a man and a woman who shared intimacies. She squared her shoulders and focused once more on the book in her lap.

* * *

James rode the estate, making mental note of such matters as what lengths of fencing needed repair, what trails needed grooming. He paid his respects to his father's tenants, informing them of his marriage. Without exception, they expressed delight over his news. Apparently, the Earl of Bradford had often shared his wishes to see his son settled down. James accepted their kind words and made note of any repairs that needed to be done to the various cottages.

He left the last cottage and turned his mount toward the main house, eager to see Catherine. On the ride back, the strange feelings that had assailed him that morning surfaced anew. He didn't much favor such vulnerability. Not one bit. Surely he could charm his way through such feelings. He wouldn't puzzle through them now. Catherine had made no declaration of love to him, and asked for none from him. Did she love him?

"She damn well better," he grumbled. He shook his head at that. What place did that prickly emotion have in their marriage? He and Catherine were well-suited to each other. God, how she fit him . . . "Very well-suited." He chuckled.

And if she came to feel love for him? He'd accept it. As long as she didn't expect it from him. He'd be damned if he behaved foolishly over a woman again. He almost lost a lifelong friendship the last time he "fell in love". No, that messy emotion had no place in his life. After the disaster with Geoffrey's wife, Becca, he'd decided he would keep a tight rein on those sorts of feelings and not allow himself to lose all reason.

He dismounted in front of the stables, handed the reins to the groom and strode purposefully toward the house.

* * *

Stepping out of their dressing room that evening before dinner, his muddled thoughts of the morning fled as he spied the stunning beauty before him. Catherine stood in front of the cheval mirror, a lovely gown of deep green wrapping her slender form. Her hair was upswept, teasing curls framing her face. She smiled widely at him, that adorable dimple showing in her cheek.

"Good evening, James," she said, crossing to him.

"Hello, love." He held out his arm to her. "Shall we go down to dinner?"

She nodded and placed her hand on his arm.

After dinner, James and Catherine adjourned to the parlor for some cards. They decided to play a game of Commerce, a kind of poker game. Three cards were dealt face down on the table, which the players could discard if they wished. The object was to make pairs, flushes, threes of a kind, and so on.

James dealt the first hand and settled back in his chair. "Do you wish to discard, Catherine?"

Catherine smiled cheekily at him. "Oh, no, James."

He arched a brow at her. He discarded and took new cards. They turned their cards over and he let out a low whistle. Her hand showed three tens.

"You've luck on your side, wife," he teased.

She grinned and shrugged her shoulders. Play continued.

Catherine won almost every hand, much to his chagrin. After nearly an hour of play, she stilled. James held his cards, puzzling over them as he felt Catherine's regard like a caress. He looked up as her gaze fell on his mouth. Heat filled him.

"Catherine," James said in a low voice.

She lifted her gaze a fraction to meet his gaze. "Yes, James?"

"If you continue to look at me in that manner, I'll have to kiss you," he told her. "And if I start kissing you, I won't be able to stop."

Her breath caught and she licked those luscious lips. "But I don't want you to stop. Ever."

He placed his cards deliberately on the table. Standing, he took her hand in his and pulled her to her feet. "Upstairs."

She nodded and preceded him out of the parlor and up the grand staircase. When they reached the chamber, James pulled her close, his eyes settling on her rosy lips. He bent his head and gently captured her lips in a kiss.

He pulled back to smile down at her. "Why don't we get ready for bed, love?"

She nodded and crossed to the dressing room. He removed his jacket and waistcoat, laying both across one of the overstuffed chairs. He sat down and pulled off his boots, his eyes continually settling on the closed door of the dressing room. God, how he wanted her! With barely a kiss, she could set his pulse to pounding. He stood and tugged his shirt out of his waistband and froze, stunned as two slender arms hugged him from behind. "Catherine, you gave me quite a start."

She moved her hands slowly up inside his shirt, trailing her fingers over his stomach, his chest. James sucked in a breath and turned to face her.

"Hello, husband," she said softly, smiling up at him.

He stared down at her. She wore only her thin nightgown, her hair a wild tumble of curls. But the invitation in her gorgeous violet eyes? "Your boldness pleases me, love."

She tilted her head to one side. "Hmm."

"Just what are you about, wife?" he asked, the delicious possibilities running through his mind.

She shrugged her slight shoulders. "I thought I'd help you undress," she said, a trace of shyness in her voice.

He grinned and dropped his hands to his sides. She untied his cravat, slowly pulling the neck cloth free. She placed the length of silk around her own neck and he laughed softly. She worked the buttons of his shirt free, caressing his chest with her palms flat, her fingers splayed. James couldn't be still any longer. He unbuttoned and opened her nightgown, feasting his eyes on her exquisite form. Such full breasts, pert rosy nipples. His mouth went dry.

His shirt fell to the floor only moments before her nightgown. Catherine began to unbutton his breeches, her fingers a bit clumsy. Many women had undressed him, but never before had he felt such desire as when his sweet wife ran her fingers over him, gently stroking him through his breeches. She reached inside to grasp him.

"My God, Catherine," he moaned, stilling her hand with his own.

She looked up at him, confusion clear on her face.

“If you continue, love,” he told her, bringing her fingers to his lips, “I fear I won’t make it to the bed.”

He grabbed the ends of the cravat, twisting the silk in his fists, and pulled her closer, capturing her lips in a searing kiss. She whimpered and leaned into him, rubbing her breasts against his chest. He pulled back and scooped her up in his arms. When she was cradled in the center of the big bed, James removed his breeches and lay down beside her. She gazed up at him, her eyes dark. He bent his head to kiss her, when something else caught his attention.

His cravat was still around her neck, only now it lay tantalizingly over one breast. James could see her nipple through the silk, the sight arousing him even more. He reached out and brushed his hand over it, the fabric gently caressing her. Catherine gasped at the gentle contact. James tugged on the neck cloth, slowly removing it. When she closed her eyes as it trailed over her skin, a delicious notion came to him.

Taking the length of silk, James wrapped it loosely around his hand. He brushed the silk over her face, her lips. Catherine sighed and kissed his fingers. He moved lower, letting the soft fabric run over her neck, her breasts.

She arched in response. “James, please . . .”

He stared down at her. Her eyes were closed, her lips parted. Her body was flushed, her nipples erect. He passed the cloth over her once more, thrilled with her response.

“Catherine,” he whispered, leaning down to brush his lips across her breast.

He paused for a long moment, finally closing his mouth over her nipple. She let out a sigh. He kissed the valley between her breasts.

“Do you like this, love?” he asked, his breath hot on her skin. “Do you like my mouth on you?”

“Mmm, yes . . .”

He ran his lips over her, down to the curls that shielded her womanhood. When he gently parted her legs, she held herself still, no doubt thinking he’d enter her. James waited for her to open her eyes. She did, puzzlement cutting through her passionate gaze.

"James." She breathed. "What are you—?"

"You'll like this, Catherine," he told her. "I promise."

He lowered his head to place his mouth on her very center.

"James, you can't—!"

His lips caressed her, his tongue teased her. She grabbed the sheets and cried out. He found the extra-sensitive nub hidden in the folds of her, rubbing the tip of his tongue over it again and again. Her taste was incredibly sweet and tart. His cock swelled as he felt her shudder against his tongue. She cried out as her climax took her.

James came over her then and entered her with one smooth thrust. He could feel her quivering, still in the throes of her orgasm. He drove into her, eager to join her in fulfillment. Catherine reached up and grabbed his shoulders, pulling him down for a hot, wet kiss. James thrust his tongue into her mouth, lost to everything but the taste of her, the feel of her. He felt her tighten around him, close to her second release, and came with one final deep thrust. She joined him, holding tightly to him as her body shook.

He whispered her name as he kissed her, waiting for her to come back down to earth.

She opened her eyes and gazed up at him. "James, that was . . ."

"Did you like that?"

She lowered her lashes. "Very much."

He hugged her to him. Maybe it wasn't love, but what they'd just shared brought him more pleasure than he'd ever felt. Damn, he was a lucky man.

Chapter 10

The next morning, James was the first to awaken. Catherine rested beside him, her arm thrown over his chest. He saw the cravat beside her and grinned, his blood warming as he remembered all that had happened last evening. He shifted in the bed and gently rolled with her until she was beneath him on her back.

He nuzzled the soft skin of her neck, nibbling her ear. She shifted beneath him and let out a sigh. He placed light kisses over her throat, her breasts, drawing a response from her even though she was still half-asleep. His fingers moved between their bodies, caressing the folds of her.

"James," she whispered, parting her legs for him.

James proceeded to make slow, sweet love to his wife. What a bloody wonderful way to start the day.

Afterward, Catherine cuddled into the pillows. James kissed her tenderly and swung his legs over the side of the bed. He had a busy day ahead of him, with many repairs to see to, and wished to get an early start. He hurried through his morning toilette and dressed.

When he emerged from the dressing room, he wasn't surprised to see that Catherine was once more sleeping soundly. Little wonder his sweet wife was so tired. After dropping a kiss on her tousled head, he stepped into the sitting room adjoining their chamber. He crossed to the writing desk near the window, sat down, and withdrew paper and pen. In the note he wrote to Catherine, he explained his absence and his duties of the day. And he couldn't resist making mention of the wonderful night of passion they'd shared, imagining the pretty blush covering her cheeks when she read his words. He folded the missive and wrote her name on the outside.

Smiling broadly, he strode into their chamber and placed the note beside her head on the pillow. He stared down at her for a long moment, an emotion he dared not name bubbling up inside of him. He cared deeply for Catherine. He desired her like no other woman. Could he? . . . No! He wasn't the young fop he'd been with Becca. He wouldn't make that mistake again.

Turning on his heel, he strode from the room.

* * *

Catherine awoke and stretched languorously, a smile curving her lips. Reaching over to James's side of the bed, her hands came into contact with nothing but sheets and pillow. She opened her eyes and sat up in confusion. "James?"

When no answer came, she turned to climb out of bed. She stopped when she saw the note resting on her pillow. Her heart gave a tiny flip. She snatched it up and opened it, wildly curious. She read his words, feeling a touch of regret when she realized she in all likelihood wouldn't see her husband until late that afternoon. Her breath caught as she read what was penned next. "Last night was incredible, sweetheart," he wrote. "You pleased me greatly." Catherine sighed. The words were not flowery but incredibly provocative. He even made mention of the cravat.

She read the note again. No mention was made of his feelings for her. No matter. He desired her and she pleased him. That would have to suffice.

Catherine rose and padded over to the vanity. Annie had seen to all of her mistress's belongings, the previous notes from James included. Catherine pulled open the drawer and added this note to the others, letting her fingers trail over her name on the smooth paper.

"He must care a bit for me to be considerate enough to write before leaving for the day," she told herself. "So what if he doesn't love me?"

Her heart clenched and she knew in that moment that she loved him. Should she tell him? He'd feel obligated to return the sentiment. She closed the drawer firmly and forced the issue from her mind. "I won't put that pressure on him. Not now."

She set the notes and his heated words out of her mind and set about readying for her day.

* * *

Their days fell into a pattern. Nearly each morning James woke his wife with kisses and, sometimes, more. He was a busy man, with both his father's and his own holdings to oversee. While he had work to attend to on the estate, Catherine occupied herself in the main house. There was much correspondence to be seen to, invitations requiring responses and notes of thanks for wedding gifts received. When she wasn't working at the writing desk in the very large, very impressive library, she tucked herself into the window seat of the parlor, a book or a little piece of needlework in her lap. The spot soon became a favorite of hers.

Catherine was surprised to find another of his notes to her on the window seat one morning, one that simply stated that he missed her and couldn't wait to hold her, wearing nothing between the two of them. His words never ceased to cause her to blush, and she added this heated note to the growing stack in her vanity.

The next afternoon, nearly two weeks after their wedding, the Earl of Bradford returned to the hall. James headed to the parlor when he overheard his father addressing Catherine with obvious fondness.

"Daughter, how has my son been treating you?"

"James has been wonderful to me, sir."

James felt a smile curve his lips.

"Is that so?" the earl went on. "You're happy, I take it?"

"She's very happy, Father," James said from the doorway.

"James!" the older man exclaimed, coming to his feet.

The earl gave his son a firm embrace and sat back down on one of the settees. James sat down beside Catherine, taking her hand in his. His father apparently didn't miss the gesture.

"It appears that marriage agrees with you, my boy," he said, helping himself to the sweet biscuits accompanying the hot tea.

James simply nodded, letting his thumb caress Catherine's palm.

"I had been telling him that for months," the earl added.

"Months?" Catherine asked in obvious confusion.

"Never mind," James said with a grin.

Catherine stood, causing the men to follow suit. "I'm certain you and your father have estate concerns to discuss, James. I'll be abovestairs."

James's father kissed her cheek, then watched his son's exchange with Catherine very closely.

"I'll soon be upstairs to ready for dinner, Catherine," James told her.

She nodded to him. He couldn't resist the lure of her perfect mouth, and kissed her tenderly. Catherine left the parlor and James watched her go, that odd, soft sensation filling his breast. He turned back to find his father regarding him closely and arched a brow.

"Was there something you wished to say, Father?" he asked, sitting once more.

"You love that girl," the earl stated simply.

"What? Why, that's . . . I don't think . . ."

"Don't fight it, my boy." The earl laughed.

James's befuddlement turned to pique. "Pray, don't tell me of my feelings."

His father blinked. "I didn't mean to upset you, son. I merely thought that—"

James let out a loud sigh, raking his fingers through his hair. "No, Father," he cut in. "It is I who should apologize. I shouldn't have lost my temper."

The earl apparently accepted James's apology, and thankfully said nothing more of love. What James felt for Catherine . . . He'd puzzle it through some day. He didn't need anyone, even his well-meaning father, to tell him his feelings.

* * *

One week after the earl's return to the hall, Catherine tore into the pile of correspondence awaiting her attention. An invitation to Chesterfield caught her eye. The Earl of Chester and his wife wanted them to come for an extended visit and Catherine was quite happy to be included in the party. It was the first such invitation she and James had received as husband and wife and it was sure to be a pleasant time. She set the missive aside, planning to show it to James when he returned to the house. The small clock on the desk showed her it was time to ready for tea. She turned quickly to leave the room and bumped into James in the doorway.

"James!" she exclaimed.

"Hello, love," James said. "Did I surprise you?"

She recovered and took in his bedraggled appearance, smiling up at him. "You look a fright, husband."

James nodded his agreement, brushing the dust from his jacket. Catherine reached up and pulled a piece of straw from his dark hair. He looked at the offending article and shrugged his broad shoulders, grinning sheepishly. He appeared boyish and carefree and utterly adorable. She threw her arms around him. "I missed you, James."

James hugged her back. "Come, wife. You're getting your dress dirty."

She pulled back to look up at him. "You should get out of these clothes," she said, caressing his neck.

He'd removed his cravat at some point, and his shirt was open at the collar. Catherine's fingers brushed the hairs curling into the V of his shirt. He placed his hands on her bottom and pressed her against him, making her aware of just how she was affecting him. *Oh, my.*

"Catherine," he whispered, "why don't you accompany me upstairs to our chamber?"

She flushed and James lowered his head to hers, placing his lips against her ear. "I don't understand how you can blush so prettily even as you're making me so hard I can't think straight."

She had no answer to that outrageous statement. Instead, she reached up and placed her lips on his, heedless of the dirt he was getting all over her yellow day dress. When he finally released her, she was nearly as filthy as he was. He laughed softly and grabbed her hand, leading her from the room. His father came upon them as they turned to climb the staircase.

"I daresay my son has gotten your pretty dress quite dirty, Catherine," he teased as he passed them.

James laughed and she swatted him as he all but pulled her up the stairs behind him.

They were late for tea, but if the earl noticed, he made no mention of it. They talked of the repairs James had seen to and those still needing his attention. Catherine recalled the invitation to Chesterfield and told James of it, at which he expressed his agreement to her immediate response. The earl managed to doze off in the comfortable chair after a while.

"Do you think we should leave him, James?"

"My father usually naps at this time of the day, love," he told her. "That's one of his favorite spots. No doubt he'll wake in time for dinner."

That brought another matter to Catherine's attention. She lowered her eyes to the folds of her skirt, twisting the fabric nervously in her hands. "Does he take dinner in his room because of me?"

"What? No, no," James assured her. "He goes to sleep quite early, and we don't take our supper until a much later hour."

Catherine nodded, relieved. She'd wanted to ask him that question for the last few days, but was sorely afraid of the answer. It was enough that James didn't love her. She was loath to come between him and his father.

"Catherine?" he asked. "Is something wrong?"

She smiled at him in answer and shook her head. He offered her a sweet biscuit and turned the conversation back to the coming visit to Chesterfield. She hoped it would keep her brooding thoughts about James at bay.

Chapter 11

Chester and Constance met their carriage when they arrived at Chesterfield. James assisted Catherine from the vehicle as they faced their good friends.

"Roberts!" Chester said, grabbing James's hand and giving it a firm shake. "So glad you could make it."

James smiled. "Thank you for having us, Chester." He turned to Constance. "Hello, Constance."

"Hello, Lord Roberts," she returned. She embraced Catherine warmly. "Catherine, I've missed you."

Catherine returned the sentiment. Lord and Lady Chester led the couple into their grand home. After James and Catherine changed out of their traveling clothes in their guestroom, the four of them met in the parlor for tea.

"Oh, Catherine," Constance said, her gray eyes open wide. "I wished to speak with you before the other guests arrive."

Catherine arched a brow at her. "What about?"

Constance leaned closer. "I wanted to tell you that Waltham will be in attendance."

Catherine was taken aback for a brief moment. She recovered and nodded. "I know that you're great friends with Lady Joan. I had wondered why they were not present at your wedding."

"Waltham's estate business kept him away from town," Constance explained. "As you know, his holdings are far to the north of London."

Catherine nodded. "Constance, please don't fret about it. I hold no ill will toward Lady Joan. Or Waltham, for that matter."

Catherine's gaze fell on James where he stood in conversation with Chester. Her smile widened and she turned once more to Constance. "I'm most happy with the way matters resolved themselves."

Constance smiled at her. "Marriage agrees with you, I daresay."

James caught Catherine's eye then. He grinned and winked at her. "Oh, yes." She lowered her lashes. "James is so wonderful to me."

Several of the other guests soon arrived. The ladies' conversation grew livelier as Michelle and Elizabeth joined them in the parlor. Paul strode over to join James and Chester.

"Hello, Chester," he said in greeting. He turned to face James. "Brother." He grinned.

Chester laughed at that. "My, that sounds strange."

"Never mind." James looked over at Catherine where she sat with the women. "I suppose I'm stuck with you, Leed."

Paul cuffed him on the shoulder. "I trust you're keeping my sister happy?" he asked, the serious look in his eyes belying his jovial tone.

James met his gaze steadily. "Yes," he said firmly. "Catherine is very happy."

Paul gave a nod to that. Talk soon turned to the prospect of a marvelous hunt on the morrow.

After a while, James crossed to his wife. "Why don't we go ready ourselves for dinner, love?"

Catherine nodded and excused herself from the others. James led her from the room and back up to the chamber Constance had set aside for their use. James found her seated at her vanity, lost in thought, when he emerged from his dressing room. A frown marred Catherine's delicate features as she sat perfectly still in her chemise and petticoat.

"We're expected downstairs in a few minutes, love," he told her, tying his cravat. "Why aren't you ready?"

She shrugged, her frown clearing.

"Catherine," he said. "What is it?"

She met his gaze in the mirror. "Waltham will be here, James."

"Ah, hell," he muttered. He crossed to his wife and rubbed her shoulders. Catherine visibly relaxed. "Don't let that scoundrel ruin our visit, wife," he said, placing a kiss on her cheek.

Catherine nodded and turned to face him. "I won't."

He cupped her cheek with his hand and gazed down at her. James arched a brow at the confounding play of emotions on her face. She seemed almost . . . wistful.

"Is something wrong?"

She shook her head. "I'll be ready in a moment, James," she said, standing on tiptoe to kiss him lightly.

He watched her go, having the distinct feeling that his wife was keeping something from him. It had better have nothing to do with that bastard Waltham.

Catherine soon stood beside her husband in the parlor, her hand on his arm. Her gown, a beautiful creation of ivory, hugged her curves. James felt Catherine's fingers twitch and turned to see what had caused her discomfort. Lord Waltham stood in the doorway, his wife beside him. The man ran his pale blue eyes over Catherine, his mouth curved in a slight smile. James caught his lustful gaze and bristled.

When Waltham tore his gaze from Catherine, it was only to find James's eyes boring into his. Apparently recovering himself, Waltham crossed the distance between the two couples, dragging his wife along with him.

He wore an insincere smile on his thin, aristocratic face. "Catherine," he said smoothly. "Constance mentioned that you would be here." He turned to James. "Roberts," he said in greeting.

James managed to smile at the miserable man. "Waltham," he said with a nod. He turned toward the man's wife. "Lady Joan."

Waltham turned to Catherine. "I hear best wishes are in order."

"Yes," Catherine allowed.

"I must say I was quite surprised to hear of your nuptials," the man said. "Was the wedding as grand as ours was to be?"

James held his hands in fists at the mention of their aborted wedding. "Waltham," he began. "Don't think to—"

"It was beautiful," Catherine cut in. "Perfect, actually," she added, smiling up at her husband.

James returned the smile, pleased with her show of loyalty.

"I daresay ours was a bit rushed." Waltham sighed dramatically. "But when you're in love, you care not for such matters. Isn't that right, darling?" he asked his wife.

Joan smiled wanly, her face turning nearly white. James was shocked at the girl's appearance. Joan was much thinner than when he last saw her at the Markham's ball. Her eyes appeared nearly sunken, and quite dull.

Catherine must have noticed, as well. "Lady Joan," Catherine said, concern on her face. "Are you feeling all right?"

Joan opened her mouth to speak, but Waltham's hand on her arm stilled her. A shadow of a smile curved her mouth. "Yes," she said finally. "I'm quite well, thank you."

Catherine seemed as doubtful of her answer as James was. She turned to him. "James, look. There are Lord and Lady Kanewood."

James caught her meaning right away. He bowed to Lady Joan and nodded to Waltham. "If you'll excuse us."

Waltham returned the nod, his eyes on Catherine as her husband led her away.

Long after dinner, when the men rejoined the ladies, James stood watching Waltham out of the corner of his eye. Paul obviously caught the scowl on his face.

"Roberts," he asked in a low voice. "What the devil's troubling you?"

James flicked his head in Waltham's direction. "That bastard has been drooling over my wife all evening," he said through clenched teeth. "If he so much as thinks to touch her—"

"Easy, brother," Paul cut in. "He wouldn't dare, not with both you and me in attendance."

James nodded, appeased that Catherine's brother would do anything to protect her. His gaze settled on her where she sat in deep conversation with her friends.

James looked back at her brother. "That doesn't change the fact that every time I look at him, I want to wring his scrawny neck."

Paul gave a small chuckle. "I very nearly did, after the way he treated her last year."

James gazed at his brother-in-law with renewed respect. A

dark thought crossed his mind. He took a few moments to put it into words.

"Leed," he began hesitantly. "Did Waltham ever attempt . . . ?"

Paul's eyebrows shot up in surprise. He laughed heartily at what James was intimating.

"Roberts," he said, clapping his friend on the back. "I barely allowed the scoundrel five minutes alone with her. Never trusted the bastard."

"Your instincts were correct, as always."

Shooting a look of irritation at Waltham, James crossed to his wife's side. He sat beside her and took her hand in his.

She turned to favor him with a smile. "James," she said softly.

"Hello, love," he returned, placing a kiss on her temple.

Paul followed his brother-in-law's lead and joined the ladies, as well. They sat down and played a few games of cards. James didn't take his eyes from Waltham for one second, however. The man didn't even attempt to hide his lust for Catherine.

Catherine's voice called his attention back to the table and the game at hand. He looked at his cards absently, letting the others' conversations go on without his participation. Catherine was *his*. Waltham be damned.

* * *

Later that night, as they readied for bed in their guest chamber, Catherine sat in front of the vanity clad in her nightgown, brushing her hair.

"James, I can't believe how poorly Lady Joan looks," Catherine said.

James shrugged, stripping down to his breeches. "She always was a plain little thing, Catherine."

Catherine put her brush aside and stood, shaking her head. "But she's so pale."

James placed his hands on her shoulders, rubbing the tension from her.

"I had noticed that," he offered. "Perhaps she's expecting."

Catherine nodded and let him lead her over to the bed. "She's frightfully thin, James," she added. "Perhaps Waltham should—"

James placed his fingers over her mouth to quiet her. "You won't speak that man's name, Catherine," he said the command gently with a light kiss. "I want only my name on your lips."

He sounded so possessive. She could almost believe he loved her. She cocked her head to the side for a moment, a smile teasing the corner of her mouth. She reached up and placed her hands behind his neck. "All right," she said as she leaned against him, "James." She kissed his throat. "James," she whispered, kissing his chin. She placed her lips gently on his. "James," she whispered into his mouth.

He grabbed her and kissed her thoroughly, inflamed by her teasing kisses. They fell on the bed, where James proceeded to kiss every inch of her.

Catherine later fell asleep tucked cozily in her husband's arms, his deep, easy breathing telling her that he was as satisfied as she was. He desired her, and demanded that she desire only him. She looked at his dear, handsome face and sighed. It would have to be enough.

* * *

While the men were out hunting the next day, Catherine and the other ladies passed their time in the parlor. They discussed the ball to be held that evening as they sipped their tea.

"Constance," Elizabeth began excitedly, "pray tell me there will be several unattached gentlemen in attendance at the ball?"

Constance assured her that, yes, several were indeed expected. Elizabeth's eyes lit up and Catherine arched a brow at her sister.

"Elizabeth," she teased. "Are you in the market for a husband?"

Elizabeth took no offense whatsoever and nodded enthusiastically. The ladies shared a laugh at that. All but Lady Joan, that was. The thin young woman shook her head sadly.

"Marriage isn't always a desirable state, Elizabeth," she said softly.

The others had no answer to that statement, exchanging glances of confusion. An awkward silence fell over the room, broken when Elizabeth let out a dramatic sigh.

"I suppose I'll just have to wait for my wedding," she said dejectedly.

Catherine squeezed her sister's hand in consolation. "Elizabeth, I've no doubt that you will be betrothed within the year."

"Oh, do you truly believe so, Catherine?" she asked.

Catherine nodded, at which Michelle wholeheartedly agreed. The talk resumed its light tone, though Catherine didn't miss the fact that Joan remained silent.

Readying herself for the ball, Catherine thought to see if Elizabeth possessed some ribbons to match the gown she planned to wear. Her sister did indeed have ribbons to match the violet gown Catherine had chosen, and happily gave them to her. Catherine thanked her and thought to return to her guestroom.

She passed the room being used by Paul and Michelle and noticed the door was slightly ajar. Thinking to say a quick hello, she raised her hand to knock. Paul's voice from within stilled her.

"I wouldn't believe it if I hadn't seen it, love," he said to Michelle.

"They seem incredibly well suited, Paul," Michelle said in answer. "Catherine seems quite happy," she added.

"Yes," Paul allowed. "Roberts as well. Quite remarkable, considering I forced his hand."

Outside in the hallway, Catherine felt a chill go through her. She clutched the ribbons to her chest, her eyes closed tight. Could it be true? Her heart pounded as her stomach churned. Had Paul truly forced James to marry her?

She turned and walked slowly back to her guestroom, numb. As she entered, James turned from where he stood shaving in front of the washstand.

"There you are, love," he said warmly.

She looked up and smiled wanly at him. "Hello," she said in a flat voice.

James arched a brow at her. He grabbed the towel and wiped his face. "Catherine, are you all right?"

"What?" she said absently. "Yes, yes. I'm all right. I suppose the excitement of the ball has me a bit out-of-sorts."

He studied her. "You do seem a bit preoccupied, love."

The endearment tore at Catherine's heart. Not only did James not love her, but he'd been forced to marry her. How could he stand to look at her? To touch her?

With a small smile, James strode into the dressing room to change into his formal attire. She choked back a sob and rang for her maid.

Chapter 12

Catherine turned from the cheval mirror and gasped to find James staring at her.

"My God, Catherine," he said in a low voice. "You look incredible."

The warmth in his gaze told her that he did feel something for her, even if it was only physical attraction. Sad, but it seemed that was all they had.

She held her chin high and smiled at him. "You're most handsome in your formal attire, James."

James shrugged and crossed to her. He placed his hands on her bare shoulders, lightly caressing her. She couldn't ignore the pleasure his touch gave her.

"I believe that I'll have to beat the men away from you, love," he teased. "Remember," he told her as he led her out of the room, "you'll dance with no other man but me."

Catherine nearly tripped, recovering her footing as she nodded. He was possessive, then.

"And will you dance with any other woman?"

He blinked. "I hadn't thought to . . . Do you wish me not to?"

"You're a charming dancer, James." She forced a smile. "Far be it from me to deny any woman your attentions."

He seemed to take her words at face value. God, the thought of any other woman in his arms for anything more than a dance! Again, her stomach churned.

They descended the grand staircase and joined the other guests in the ballroom. James was most solicitous to her as the evening began, keeping her close to his side. They spied Paul and Michelle across the room and he escorted her over to join them. Catherine couldn't look them in the eye, so ashamed of what she'd heard them discussing earlier that evening. Michelle seemed to sense something in her demeanor.

"Catherine," she said, causing her to lift her eyes at last. "Is something wrong?"

"Wh-what?" Catherine stammered, blushing. "No, I . . . No, everything is fine."

Catherine turned and found James regarding her closely, a curious look on his face. She smiled weakly and turned her attention to brushing the nonexistent wrinkles out of her skirt.

Paul asked his wife to dance, and Michelle let him lead her out onto the dance floor. James took the opportunity to ask Catherine to dance. She stared up at him, this handsome, charming man she'd married, and nodded. He held her close to him as they twirled about the room and Catherine fell into rhythm easily, matching him step for step. The familiarity left her feeling more comfortable in his company.

"I so enjoy dancing with you, love," he told her, flashing her a dazzling smile.

"You're a wonderful dancer, James."

By the time the number ended, she'd managed to put the matter of their forced marriage out of her mind. Almost. James led her over to the row of chairs lining the enormous room. She sat down as he held her hand to his lips, seemingly unable to keep from touching her. But how long would his attentions last without any real emotion behind them?

"Would you like a glass of punch, Catherine?"

Catherine nodded her acceptance and watched him go see to the refreshment, admiring the dashing figure he cut. She sighed and turned, surprised to see that someone sat beside her.

"Lady Joan!" She recovered herself. "I'm sorry. I didn't see you there."

Joan nodded as if well used to never standing out in a crowd. Tonight, she appeared agitated. What ailed the girl?

"Catherine," Joan began haltingly, "I . . . I so wish to apologize for what happened between Thomas and myself."

Catherine blinked in surprise. She reached out and placed her hand over Joan's. Her fingers were like ice.

"You've nothing to regret, Joan," she assured her. "If Waltham loves you, then everything worked out for the best."

Joan had paled further and shook her head adamantly. "Catherine, he doesn't—" Joan stopped and leaned closer. "How did you ever manage his fierce temper?"

Catherine was shocked. Temper? Waltham was never anything but calm and solicitous whenever they were together.

"Joan, I don't understand what you're saying. Waltham never showed a hint of—"

"Thomas can be quite cruel, Catherine," Joan sobbed softly. "Why, one time he—"

Joan stopped her diction once more, her thin lips pressed tightly together. Catherine looked up to find James standing in front of them, two crystal glasses in his hands.

He arched a brow at Catherine then looked at Joan and smiled. "Lady Joan, would you like a glass of refreshment?" he asked, holding out his glass.

Joan shook her head and stood, her eyes darting about the room. "No, I . . . No thank you, Lord Roberts."

She said a quick farewell to Catherine and dashed across the dance floor.

Catherine watched her go. "James, did you see how agitated she was?"

"Hmm?" James sat down beside her. "What do you mean?"

"She mentioned Waltham's temper," she whispered. "But he exhibited no such temperament with me."

"She's quite timid, Catherine," he said. "Perhaps she misinterpreted his actions."

Catherine shrugged. "She was just about to tell me about one time in particular—"

"Love," James cut in. "I believe Lady Joan feels badly for running off with that scoundrel. Perhaps she wishes to put a negative face on her marriage for your sake."

"But that's silly, James. I don't wish to be married to Waltham now. Not when I have you."

"You do have me." He leaned over and placed a kiss on her temple. "Forever."

Catherine pondered his words. Why weren't they enough tonight?

Upon Catherine's return to the ballroom, her feelings of unease bubbled anew as she watched the loving exchanges between the other couples of their acquaintance. While James was ever so gallant toward her, his usual charm evident, Catherine longed for the love she saw flowing freely between Chester and Constance, Paul and Michelle. Her gaze settled on Geoffrey and Becca as they twirled about the room, their great affection plain to see. Catherine watched as James danced with Elizabeth, smiling down at her as the girl chattered on. Warm regard was in his gaze. Was that tepid emotion also evident whenever James danced with her? Pitiful.

Suddenly, the room seemed stifling. Before James could return to her side, she took herself out to the terrace. Large lanterns lit and warmed the space. Nevertheless, it was still a bit chilly but she welcomed it, hugging herself as she stared out at the clear November night sky.

"I see you felt the need to escape, as well," Waltham said from behind her.

Catherine started, then recovered her composure and nodded curtly at her ex-fiancé. "Waltham."

Waltham flashed a sly grin, gone in an instant as he stepped closer. "You seem as miserable as I, love," he said softly.

She faced him fully. "What are you talking about?"

"I've made a huge error in judgment, Catherine." He stroked his finger over her bare shoulder. "I never should have married Joan."

Catherine pulled away from him toward one corner of the terrace. "Waltham, you shouldn't speak to me of such matters."

A slow smile spread across the man's coolly handsome face as his pale eyes raked hungrily over her form. "Perhaps we can come to an arrangement."

She gasped at what he was intimating. She shook her head. "I'm married, Waltham. I want no other but my husband. I love him."

It was the first time she'd spoken the words aloud, but she knew them to be true. Waltham shrugged and placed his hands on her waist. She started to pull away, but his next words stilled her.

"Your husband doesn't love you."

"What?" Catherine whispered.

"Roberts is quite a charming rogue, love," he allowed. "But he'll never love any one woman."

Catherine shook her head.

"He charms his way through the young society ladies," Waltham continued, his mouth curved in an ugly sneer. "Leaving naught but broken hearts in his wake."

"You don't know him," she argued. "My husband cares for me." God, the words sounded so weak to her ears.

"Cares for you? Perhaps." Waltham's smile reappeared. "But he doesn't love you. If he did, Catherine, he wouldn't let you out of his sight. If you were my wife, I certainly wouldn't."

He brought his lips to her ear. "If you were my wife, I wouldn't be able to keep from touching you. I would pull up the skirt of this incredible gown and take you right here, all of those people but a few feet away."

She was stunned speechless. A tall figure in the doorway suddenly caught her attention. "James," she whispered.

James stood there, shock on his face. His shock gave way to palpable anger, his hands held in fists at his side.

Waltham pulled back to stare down at her, misunderstanding her meaning. "Roberts doesn't deserve you, Catherine," he said dismissively. "Come with me to my chamber."

"Get your hands off my wife!" James grabbed him and hurled him across the terrace.

Waltham grunted in pain as he landed on the hard stone floor.

James turned back to Catherine. "What the bloody hell did he do to you?"

Catherine found her voice. "N-nothing. He said that . . . that . . ." She couldn't go on.

She turned and fled.

James watched her go, stunned. He turned back to Waltham, his eyes narrowed to slits. He grabbed him up off of the floor and pulled him close. "What did you do to her, you bastard?"

"I assure you, Roberts," he said, sniffing in disdain, "I did nothing to compromise your wife."

James studied him as his mind worked. He believed the man, albeit grudgingly. Physically at least, Catherine had seemed unharmed. But her eyes had welled with tears, her skin turned as pale as moonlight.

"Pray tell me, then. Why is she so upset?"

Waltham shrugged as he brushed off his clothes. "I don't purport to understand the workings of your marriage."

"My marriage?" James repeated. "You son-of-a-bitch." He slammed his fist into Waltham's face.

Waltham slumped against the wall and rubbed his jaw.

James fixed a cold glare on him. "Don't let me catch you alone with my wife again, Waltham."

"Perhaps I'm wrong," Waltham murmured.

"What, you cur?"

Waltham held up his hands. "Nothing."

James turned on his heel and returned to the ballroom in search of Catherine. He had to know she was all right. When he'd seen Waltham with her, an incredible feeling surged through him. She was his! Yes, Catherine had been a virgin when he married her. But had Waltham taken any other liberties with her? What had he been attempting out on the terrace?

He sought out Michelle where she sat in conversation with Elizabeth. "Excuse me, ladies. Have you seen Catherine?"

Michelle blinked up at him. "No. Is something wrong?"

"No, no." He just had to find her. "Excuse me."

James didn't find Catherine in the front parlor, either. Paul was there, however, with Chester. James crossed to Catherine's brother. "Have you seen Catherine?"

Paul shook his head and straightened. "What happened?"

"That bastard proposed an assignation with my wife."

"Son-of-a-bitch. Where is he?"

James placed his hand on Paul's arm. "Don't worry, Leed." James gave him a grim smile. "I took care of him."

Paul nodded and James left him. Running out of places to search, he decided to return to their guestroom. He opened the door, blinking as his eyes tried to adjust to the gloom in the chamber.

"Catherine?" he asked into the dark.

A soft sob was his only answer. He crossed to the bedstand and lit the candle there. He turned then and discovered her, sitting gracefully on the floor. Relief flooded him.

"Catherine."

"James." She breathed, a tear spilling over her long lashes to trail down her cheek.

Catherine stared up at him, her eyes huge. He let his eyes drink her in. Her hair was in loose curls about her shoulders. Her dress pooled around her, her hands clutching the smooth, luxurious fabric of her skirt. She looked like a beautiful, exotic flower.

"What is it, sweetheart?" He crouched down beside her and stroked her cheek with the back of his hand. "Are you hurt?"

She shook her head in answer.

James took her hands in his and studied her once more. "Come," he said finally, standing up.

"No," she said in a small voice.

James ignored her plea and gently pulled her to her feet. She suddenly collapsed against him, fresh tears falling from her eyes to soak the front of his jacket.

"Catherine, what's wrong?"

"Oh, James," she sobbed. "Tell me you care for me, even a tiny bit. Tell me, if only for tonight."

"Of course I care for you," he said, rubbing her back. "Why would you think—?"

"Love me, James," Catherine said, pushing his jacket off his shoulders. "Make love to me. Now."

James sharply drew in a breath, her softly-spoken command making him hard. She untied his cravat and unbuttoned his shirt. She placed hot kisses on his chest.

"Catherine . . ." he murmured, unhooking the back of her gown.

He let her gown drop to the floor, her chemise, stays, petticoat, and stockings soon followed. She stripped him out of his finery and ran her hands over his back, pressing herself tightly to him. James moaned softly and scooped her up in his arms. He laid her on the bed and slowly trailed his lips over her skin. As if unable to withstand his unhurried possession, Catherine pushed at his shoulders. James looked at her in question and rolled onto his back as she came over him.

"I'll be a good wife, James," she said fervently, lightly kissing his shoulder, his chest. "I'll never hurt you."

Those were nearly the same words he'd used when he asked her to marry him. What was she about?

"I'll make you happy, James," she whispered, kissing the flat of his stomach. "Even if I was forced on you."

"Forced on me?" he puzzled aloud. "Catherine, what do you mean? Ah, God—!" he groaned as her lips brushed the tip of his arousal.

All thought left his mind as his sweet wife caressed him. Her delicate tongue stroked the length of him, making him rock-hard. Her lips fairly burned along his shaft, causing him to arch off the bed. When she closed her mouth over the tip and gently suckled it was all he could stand. With a loud groan, he pulled her up to him, crushed his mouth to hers. He kissed her with all the passion she'd aroused, running his hands over her skin.

"God, love," he rasped, nibbling on her ear. "You set me on fire."

Catherine whimpered in response. James moved her legs until she straddled him. He reached between their bodies and stroked her, driving her to the very brink of ecstasy.

Her fingers curled in the hairs on his chest. "James, please . . ."

James couldn't hold his control much longer. He had to be inside of her. He placed his hands on her hips and gently lifted her.

"Lean back, sweetheart," he rasped.

Catherine did as he asked. She gasped as he entered her completely. Over and over again he drove up into her, his eyes closed tight. She soon caught his rhythm. Her body bowed back as she neared her release. James felt her tremors, knew she was close. His thrusts became deeper, touching her very core.

She sobbed as her climax took her and he opened his eyes to watch her in her pleasure. He came in the next moment, letting out a shout as he exploded inside of her.

She collapsed against him, her breath coming fast. He felt her tears on his chest and lifted his head.

"Shh, love," he soothed, stroking her back. "Shh . . ."

"Tell me I pleased you, James." She sniffled and rubbed her cheek against him. "Tell me."

"Pleased me?" James asked, his voice rough. "My God, Catherine. You very nearly killed me."

She smiled shakily at that and rolled off him, turning away to cuddle into her pillow. James puzzled over her actions. She always lay in his arms afterward, her fingers gently caressing his chest as sleep claimed them.

"Catherine?" He reached out to touch her shoulder, but she didn't move.

She was silent for a long while. "Yes?" she finally answered.

"Come here," he gently instructed.

She shook her head. "James, you don't have to—"

He hauled her to his side and cradled her in a tight embrace. "You're my wife." He dropped a kiss on her brow. "You belong here. In my arms."

Catherine sighed and cuddled against him. James echoed her sentiment and placed his hand over hers where it rested on his chest. Her earlier words came back to him.

"Why would you think I don't care for you?" he asked.

She stiffened. "It doesn't signify."

"Doesn't signify?" James repeated. "How can you say that?"

Catherine said nothing, feigning sleep. James sensed her reticence and let the matter drop for the time being. He vowed to get to the bottom of matters in the morning.

She thought he didn't care for her? My God, she was everything to him.

As he drifted off to sleep, a thought teased at the edge of his mind. Did he love her?

Chapter 13

Catherine was the first to awaken the next morning. Her dreams had been strange, her sleep troubled. All of what Waltham had said came back to her. Although Waltham was the last person she'd look to for the truth, he had boldly stated that James didn't love her as though it was the most obvious thing in the world, and if he had noticed then everyone must know the same. How could she face the assembled guests today? Her brother and sister-in-law. Her host and hostess! Her marriage wasn't of the same caliber as theirs.

Thoughts of last evening intruded, when James had found her in their guest chamber. How would she face him when he awoke? She'd thrown herself at him, begged him to take her. To love her! She let out a sob, causing James to shift in the bed beside her.

"Morning, love," he said, stretching his big frame.

"Good morning," she murmured.

James must have sensed something in her tone, for he opened his eyes and regarded her closely. "Catherine, are you still upset with me?"

She shook her head at him. "I was never upset with you, James. I was upset over my own foolishness."

He sat up, causing her to draw away from him. He grabbed her hand and kissed it, holding it close to his chest. "And can you explain this 'foolishness' of yours?"

She ignored the beat of his heart, the heat from his skin, and withdrew her hand. "No I cannot."

James pulled back at her conviction. She watched as his silver eyes began to glitter. "Catherine, last night was—"

"Don't speak of it!" she said, covering her ears.

James pulled her hands away from her ears and stroked her

cheek. "Sweetheart, you pleased me greatly. You're not embarrassed by what we shared, are you?"

Catherine briefly thought to lie, to say that, yes, she was embarrassed. But pleasing him had given her more pleasure than she could have imagined. It seemed to her that her foolishness of the past evening was to accompany her into the new day.

"No, James. I'm not embarrassed. I'm just sorry."

"Sorry?" He arched a dark brow. "Whatever for?"

She buried her face in her hands. "I begged you to make love to me. I shouldn't have done that to you."

He was quiet for a moment then threw his head back and laughed, tears coming to his eyes. "My God, Catherine," he said, getting control of his laughter. "You just look at me and I want to make love to you."

She blinked at him. "Truly?"

"God, yes."

"Then you're not angry?"

"Your boldness pleased me. Surely you could tell?"

Catherine shrugged as he embraced her. He gently stroked her hair, whispering sweet words in her ear, and Catherine fancied she could hear a touch of affection in his voice.

"James, I realize that you care for me."

"You're the most important person in the world to me."

She pulled back to gaze at him.

He cupped her face in his hands and stared deeply into her eyes. "Catherine," he whispered. "What I feel for you . . . That is, I . . ."

Say the words, James. Catherine held her breath. *Say the words!*

But he said nothing more. She lowered her lashes, sighing softly. After several moments of awkward silence, she moved out of his embrace, picked up her nightgown from the end of the bed, and turned her back to him.

Catherine used the brief time away from his gaze to rein in her emotions. He didn't love her. She wouldn't profess her feelings. Not now. Perhaps not ever.

She squared her shoulders and turned to face him, a bright smile fixed on her face. "We don't have to talk of feelings and emotions, James," she said, amazed at the steadiness of her voice.

"Catherine, I—" he began, making a move toward her.

She held up her hand to stop him. "We're fond of each other," she said, flicking her hair over her shoulder in a gesture of nonchalance. "We get along well. Why should we fret over such matters as emotions?"

He watched her, his eyes wide with what, relief?

"I've got to get dressed," she said lightly.

Only after she'd breezed into the dressing room and quietly closed the door did she lean against the wood panel and let out a ragged breath. Her shoulders shook with silent sobs as fat tears rolled down her cheeks.

James sat in the bed for a long moment. He felt immense relief over what she'd said. And disappointment, as well. He hadn't seen any indication that she didn't mean precisely what she'd said. But only last night, as he was falling asleep, he was filled with the certainty of his feelings for her.

He admired her. He was fond of her. He wanted her like no other. He wished to keep her safe from heartless gossip and scoundrels like Waltham. He could love her. But with her dismissal of such feelings in the light of day, he was once more unsure. He knew nothing of love, that was certain.

With a sigh, he rose to ready himself for the day.

When Catherine emerged from the dressing room, she once more wore a smile on her face. She'd chosen a lovely day dress of light blue, the color of the winter sky.

He smiled at the pleasing picture she made and crossed to her. "Catherine, I thought to stay here with you today."

She stiffened, then went to the vanity and settled herself before the mirror. "I thought you were going hunting this morning, James."

He watched her, unsure. If he did join the others for a hunt, he could keep his mind occupied and put aside their halted exchange of the morning. Coward.

He shrugged. "I suppose I can catch up with them."

The relief on her face was clear. She was obviously not as

comfortable as she professed. Pleased to put the matter aside, he kissed her lightly and took himself into the dressing room to don his hunting clothes.

* * *

Catherine went down to the breakfast room. Michelle and Elizabeth were seated there, plates of eggs and ham and sweet rolls in front of them.

"Good morning, Catherine," Michelle said with a smile.

Catherine nodded and crossed to the sideboard to serve herself some of the delicious fare. She sat down as Constance joined them.

"Good morning, all," Constance said. "Catherine, were you ill last evening?"

Michelle and Elizabeth looked at Catherine with concern. Catherine smiled shakily.

"You didn't feel well?" Elizabeth asked her.

Catherine shrugged and concentrated on pouring herself a cup of tea. "I had a bit of a headache, is all."

Constance breathed a sigh of relief. "Thank goodness." She set her plate down and joined them at the table. "I was worried you caught whatever is ailing Joan."

Catherine blinked. "Is Joan ill?"

Constance nodded. "She has terrible pains in her stomach. And last evening, she was frightfully pale."

Catherine had taken note of Joan's pallor, as well. And when she'd spoken of Waltham, Catherine thought she saw fear in the woman's eyes, as well. What was going on?

"Waltham told me she has frequent bouts of stomach problems," Constance said. "But I recall no such thing."

Catherine thought for a moment. Hmm. Maybe she should attempt another conversation with the woman while the men were out.

"Catherine," Michelle began, drawing her attention. "I trust Roberts caught up with you last evening?"

"What?" Catherine asked.

"After his, um, discussion with Waltham, he was most

anxious to find you," Michelle elaborated.

Catherine closed her eyes in shame. What an embarrassment for a man like James to withstand. She opened her eyes and found the other ladies looking at her with open curiosity.

"I . . . Yes, Michelle. James found me," she said. "I went up to our guest room to rest. My head was fairly pounding."

Elizabeth gave a vigorous nod of her head. "I told Michelle that your running off had nothing whatsoever to do with that worm Waltham."

Catherine gasped. This was just too much! She pushed her plate away from herself and stood. "If you'll excuse me. I just remembered that there is a matter that requires my attention."

Upstairs, Catherine walked purposefully toward their guestroom. A tall figure in her path blocked her progress.

"Waltham!" she exclaimed in surprise.

"Shh," Waltham urged. "We don't want anyone to find us together now, do we, love?"

She shook her head. "Waltham, what are you doing?"

He opened the door to her room and urged her inside.

"Waltham!"

He closed the door and faced her. "Catherine, you look incredible." He fixed a look of concern on his face. "I was very worried about you last evening."

"Worried about me? Why?"

"Roberts was quite angry, love." He stepped closer to her. "I was afraid he might do you harm."

"James would never hurt me, Waltham." She reached for the doorknob. "Now if you would please leave . . ."

Waltham raised his hand to his cheek. "Your husband had no qualms about hurting me without cause."

Catherine gasped as she noticed the bruise there. "James did that?" she said, leaning toward him to get a better look.

Waltham grasped her tightly in his arms. "Catherine, how I want you."

Catherine struggled in his embrace. "Let me go, Waltham."

"Call me Thomas, love," he said, nuzzling her ear. "We were very nearly married. You would now be mine if not for that twit I married."

"What a horrid thing to say about your wife." She shook her head and renewed her struggles.

Waltham finally released her, but only after letting his hands roam over her form. "God, love," he said, his eyes on her bosom. "You're absolutely delectable."

"Waltham." Catherine stepped back from him and tried a different tack. "Thomas, you must go."

He gave a deliberate shake of his blond head. "I need you, Catherine," he said, following her across the room. "Joan isn't the woman for me." His lip curled cruelly. "Such a simpering fool. She turns my stomach."

"You shouldn't be speaking to me so." She was disgusted that he could say such cruel things about his own wife let alone behave so toward her. "Leave me, Thomas. Now."

"Not until I show you what we can share," he said, grabbing her once more.

He brought his lips to hers. Catherine turned at the last moment, evading his kiss as she heard the door to the chamber open.

"What the devil . . . Let go of her, you bastard!"

Thank God! She breathed a sigh of relief that her husband walked in.

Waltham immediately stepped back. "Roberts," he said smoothly. "Catherine was upset. I was merely offering her comfort."

James swung his gaze to Catherine then looked back at Waltham, a fierce scowl on his face.

"Get the hell out of our room, Waltham," he said through clenched teeth. "Get out, or so help me I'll throw you out that window."

Waltham bowed graciously to Catherine and beat a hasty retreat, closing the door behind him.

"Son-of-a-bitch," James muttered, his eyes on the door.

Catherine finally found her voice. "What are you doing here, James?"

He turned to look at her, his brow furrowed. "What do you mean? This is our room, wife."

"I thought you'd gone hunting."

James's scowl cleared. "No," he said. "I was unable to catch up with the party, so I rode a bit before returning to the house." He looked at her closely. "Were you sorry for the interruption?"

"No! Why would you think that?"

"I don't know, Catherine," he said, stepping closer. "It seems I'm forever finding you alone with that scoundrel. And in our room, yet."

Catherine gasped at what he was suggesting.

"James, you don't think that I . . ." she sputtered. "That we . . ."

James let out a breath and raked his fingers through his hair. "No, no." He shook his head. "Forgive me for saying that."

She gave him a nod of acceptance.

"Pray tell me, then, Catherine," he began, his voice controlled. "Why was he in here with you?"

"I'm not at all certain," she said. "He told me that he wanted—"

"I know just what the bastard wanted," James growled. "You're my wife, damn it, and I won't have you meeting other men behind my back."

"James, I didn't meet with him. He followed me in here."

"Never mind." He turned away from her in an obvious attempt to rein in his anger. "Ah, hell," he muttered. "I don't know what the devil's wrong with me."

If she didn't know better, she might believe he was jealous. But how could that be? He didn't love her, let alone marry her of his own free will.

She touched his arm. "Don't fret about it, James."

He looked at her in confusion, then drew her into his arms. "Catherine." He kissed her hair, her ear. "Forgive me for my outburst."

She couldn't resist him. He smelled so good and his hands felt so right on her, especially after Waltham's pawing. If only he loved her.

"Why don't we go downstairs, love?" James asked. "Perhaps you would like to play a game of cards?"

Catherine smiled in genuine delight. "That sounds lovely, husband."

He took her hand and led her from the room.

She thought she saw a flash of color in one of the doorways as they passed, maybe an impression of blond hair. Was Waltham hanging about? She wouldn't think about him again. She had her husband to herself today and would focus on that. For as long as it lasted, in any event.

Chapter 14

Two days later, the guests took their leave of Chesterfield. James and Catherine stayed on for another week however, at Lord and Lady Chester's insistence. James and Chester hunted in the mornings while Constance and Catherine passed the time gossiping and working on their needlepoint. Without the others in attendance, the two young women were free to speak of whatever was on their minds. Lady Joan and her mysterious illness were discussed quite a bit between them, leaving Catherine with the distinct impression that Constance was as troubled by it as she.

One afternoon, three days into their extended visit, the four of them sat in the parlor sharing a pot of tea.

"What a pleasant morning's hunt today, eh, Roberts?" Chester said. "I so like it when there's a frost in the air."

"Quite pleasant, Chester." He sat beside Catherine. "And how was your morning, love?" he asked her. "Did you get any work done on that little hanky?"

Catherine slanted a look at him. He and Chester both teased the women mercilessly on the amount of chatter heard whenever the two of them were together, their work all but forgotten in their laps.

"Yes, husband." She laughed.

He draped his arm comfortably over her shoulders and gave a little squeeze.

"Roberts." Chester set down his cup. "I nearly forgot to ask a favor of you."

James straightened and looked at him expectantly. "What can I do for you, friend?"

"I'd like your opinion on some purchases I'm contemplating," Chester said. "Perhaps you could come into the study?"

"Certainly." James stood and looked down at Catherine. "If the ladies will excuse us?"

Constance and Catherine both nodded their assent, and Chester turned to exit the room. James kissed Catherine lightly and followed his host into his study.

Catherine watched him go, a small smile on her face. She turned back to find Constance regarding her closely. "What are you looking at?" she asked, a bit embarrassed.

Constance shrugged, a small smile lifting the corner of her mouth. "You appear quite taken with your husband, is all."

Catherine bristled at the innocent comment. "I . . . I'm, um, fond of James, yes."

Constance laughed. "Fond of him?" she repeated. "You love him. Admit it."

Catherine opened her mouth to protest, but shook her head instead. "You're right," she said in a small voice.

Constance's brow furrowed. "If I didn't know better, Catherine, I'd think you're troubled by that fact."

Catherine looked toward the doorway to make certain the gentlemen were well away from the parlor and leaned toward Constance. "I'm most troubled by that fact, I'm afraid."

"But why?"

Catherine twisted the skirt of her tea dress in her hands. "Because James doesn't love me," she admitted on a whisper.

"Catherine, Roberts loves you. Don't shake your head at me. He loves you."

"You don't understand." Catherine sniffed. "He's fond of me, that is all."

Constance set her teacup aside and faced her. "My own husband has remarked upon the affection between the two of you, Catherine. Don't tell me Roberts isn't in love with you."

But as much as she wished to believe it, Catherine couldn't be swayed by her friend's insistence. He'd had any number of chances to profess such tenderness since the night she'd thrown herself at him.

"No." Catherine wiped at her eyes. "James cares for me. Nothing more."

Constance opened her mouth to make another protest, but

Catherine raised her hand to still her. "Pray, don't speak of it. I've reconciled myself, Constance." She lifted her chin. "Believe me."

To Catherine's relief, Constance bowed to her wishes and turned the conversation to other topics.

* * *

In his study, Chester outlined some of his intended purchases. "I value your opinion, Roberts. I know how well you've managed your father's properties during his illness as well as your own."

"Thank you. I believe you'd do well with that property on the west side, Chester. The water on it would adequately irrigate the fields to the south."

Chester nodded. "That's what I thought. I noticed the stream one morning when I was out riding with Waltham."

James lost his relaxed stance at the mere mention of the man's name. Chester apparently noticed the change in his demeanor at once.

"Roberts," he said with a crooked smile. "What's ailing you?"

"Don't mention his name."

"What happened the night of the ball?" Chester asked. "I heard something of an altercation on the terrace."

"The son-of-a-bitch offered my wife an arrangement."

Chester wore a look of surprise. "You must be jesting," he said. "Surely he'd do no such thing here. Not with you present."

"He would and he did." James stood and paced about the room. "And what's more, I found him alone with her in our room the next day."

"What?"

"The scoundrel said he was comforting her because she was upset," James said, raking his fingers through his hair.

"And was she?" Chester asked. "Upset, I mean?"

"Yes," James admitted.

"Well then, perhaps—"

"The bastard shouldn't have been alone with her. I very nearly threw him out the window."

Chester cleared his throat. “And did, um, anything happen between them?”

“God, no. Catherine would never betray me.”

“I believe you have nothing to fear from Waltham,” he assured James. “He enjoys his wife’s fortune far too much to risk an assignation with another man’s wife.”

“He wanted her at one time, Chester. And from the little I heard on the terrace, he wants her still.”

“He wouldn’t dare to approach her now. Not with you aware of his intentions.”

James shrugged. “This wasn’t the first time.”

“Perhaps if I speak to him, he—”

The butler at the door interrupted Chester. The servant handed a letter to him and bowed, taking his leave. James watched as Chester puzzled over the missive.

“Who sent it?” James asked.

Chester shook his head and broke the seal. As he read the letter, his face went white.

“My God, Chester.” James came to his side. “What is it?”

“It appears our friend Waltham is no longer tied to a wife.” Chester closed his eyes and sighed. “Lady Joan has passed away.”

James froze. “No. That can’t be so.”

Chester handed the missive to him. James quickly read the contents and swore softly.

“Catherine told me she was quite ill,” he said. “And troubled.”

“Troubled?” Chester asked. “In what way?”

“I don’t truly know,” James answered. “I dismissed the lady’s odd behavior as guilt over her marriage to Catherine’s intended.”

A knock came at the door.

“Husband,” Constance called. “I fear Catherine and I are growing quite lonely in the parlor.”

Chester looked worriedly at James.

“You have to tell her, old man,” James said. “I don’t envy you.”

Chester gave a solemn nod. James crossed to the door and pulled it open.

Catherine and Constance smiled up at him.

"I was beginning to believe you gentlemen had forgotten us," Constance chided.

Chester's face was marred with a worried frown. "Constance, I have to speak with you."

Constance lost her smile. She crossed over to him as James gently urged Catherine out the door. As he pulled the door shut behind them, Constance's sudden, heart-rending sob could be heard through the wood panel.

Catherine grabbed tightly onto James's arm. "James, what happened?"

James saw no easy way to word the terrible news. He took her hands in his. "Catherine, Lady Joan died."

She gasped. "But," she stammered, "how can that be? She was so young, I . . . Oh, why didn't I pay more attention to what she was trying to tell me?"

"What was she trying to tell you?"

She shook her head, wiping tears from her eyes. "She mentioned something about Waltham, and—"

"Don't say the man's name, Catherine."

She flinched at the vehemence in his tone.

James caught the motion and hugged her to him. "I'm sorry, love. What were you saying?"

Catherine shrugged as James led her back into the parlor. "Joan mentioned his violent temper. As I told you, he never exhibited such with me."

"But, Catherine, she was quite ill."

She sat. "I know that. I suppose her nerves might have been affected by her illness."

James believed that was precisely what had been troubling Joan. That, and the fact that her husband's former fiancée was in attendance there at Chesterfield.

Catherine sighed as she refreshed her cup of tea. "I suppose we have to attend the funeral."

James nodded. He had little taste for spending time in Waltham's company, but attending the funeral would be the proper course, especially for Constance's sake. Perhaps at his wife's funeral, the bastard would have the sense to keep his hands off Catherine.

It was decided that Chester and Constance would travel to Bradford Hall with James and Catherine, and that they would leave for the funeral at Waltham's estate in Westmorland from there. There was a pall over their gathering that evening, Catherine sitting very close to Constance on the settee in the parlor.

"I can't believe she's gone." Constance sniffed. "She was ill, but I never thought this would happen . . ."

"Shh, love," Chester soothed, coming to stand in front of the ladies.

Catherine stood to permit him to sit beside his wife. She crossed to where James stood by the mantle and he favored her with a small smile. She met it with one of her own and held her hands out to the fire crackling merrily in the fireplace.

"I can't seem to get warm," she said softly.

James took her chilled hands in his and pulled her closer. She leaned against him as he wrapped his arms around her.

"It's all right, love. I didn't know her very well, but she seemed like a sweet person."

"She was, Lord Roberts," Constance added, wiping her tears.

Catherine nodded. "She was too good for Waltham, I can tell you that."

"Why do you say that?" Chester asked, bewildered.

Catherine was startled to find the three of them looking at her closely. "I . . . Waltham made some very unkind statements about Joan to me when . . ."

"You may say it." James smiled ruefully. "When I found him in our room?"

Catherine reddened a bit. "Yes. He was most unkind."

"I daresay the scoundrel would have said anything to sway you toward him, Catherine," Chester offered.

"What's this?" Constance asked. "He was in your room, Catherine?"

Catherine simply nodded. James tamped down the anger the memory gave him.

"It appears Waltham thought to renew his attentions toward my wife," James said.

"No!" Constance gasped. "And with Joan so ill?"

Chester looked sharply at James, his eyes clearly showing his alarm.

"Chester?"

Chester gave an almost imperceptible shake of his head, at which James held his tongue.

He arched a brow at Chester, turning back once more to Catherine. "It's been a long day, sweetheart. Why don't you ready yourself for bed?"

Catherine nodded and left the circle of his arms. He watched as she exited the room. Chester suggested the same to Constance, who was only too happy to retire for the evening.

"Now, what are you thinking, Chester?"

Chester poured them each a brandy and offered a glass to James. "Roberts, could Waltham have had something to do with his wife's death?"

James shook his head. "It can't be possible," he said. "As much as I despise the bastard, I can't believe he'd do such a thing."

Chester breathed a sigh. "I suppose so. But he bears watching, Roberts," he warned. "If only where Catherine is concerned."

James hesitated for the briefest moment, finally downing a large swallow of the brandy.

"Let him attempt to come near my wife again," he said, his eyes narrowed. "It'll be the last thing he ever does."

Chapter 15

The four of them departed for the funeral a few days later. The ride from Bradford Hall to Westmorland was but an hour or so, though it proved most uncomfortable for the traveling party. It was the middle of November, and quite chilly. Catherine and Constance wore gowns of severe black, as was the custom. The gentlemen wore the austere color, as well, with no white to relieve their dress. Not a one of them was looking forward to the visit, least of all James. The funeral notwithstanding, he had no desire to be in Waltham's company for any length of time. He hadn't been jesting when he'd threatened to throw Waltham out the window at Chesterfield.

"The sky looks forbidding," Chester said. "I hope the weather holds."

"Yes," Constance agreed. "We hadn't planned on staying on after the service."

"We won't be staying," James said curtly.

Catherine blinked in surprise at his tone. James saw her reaction and tempered his next words.

"I have no desire to reside under that man's roof for one moment longer than necessary. Grieving widower or no, we won't be staying."

They arrived at Waltham Manor just past noon. The main house was quite large and grand, if in need of a few repairs. Leaving the carriage with the many others lining the stone drive, they alighted and climbed the wide steps to the entrance. A large wreath of black adorned the front door. Chester rapped loudly with the knocker and a liveried servant pulled the door open wide.

The servant bowed low and gave the mourners the requisite black gloves to wear. As Catherine slowly pulled on hers, James didn't miss her shiver. They went into the parlor.

James knew a funeral was an important social event, with every propriety observed. Apparently, Lady Waltham's would prove no exception. After assembling with the other mourners, Catherine and James filed out to follow the hearse to the family graveyard. The service was over quickly, the tolling of the bells for the death knell reverberating through the chilly air.

"I can't get Lady Joan's odd demeanor out of my mind, James," she whispered as they returned to the house.

He nodded and patted her hand at the crook of his elbow.

"She'd seemed ill, but not gravely so. And . . ."

"And what?" James asked softly.

"She looked frightened."

Her words brought Chester's comments to his mind. Did Waltham have a hand in his wife's death?

When they returned to the house, it was required that they pay their respects to Joan's surviving relations. James had heard that Joan lost her parents a year ago, thus coming into the generous fortune that had undoubtedly added to her attractiveness. All that remained of her family was an elderly aunt and three cousins much older than Joan had been. James led Catherine over to them, his ease with such formal matters taking over.

He took the aunt's hand in his and pressed it firmly. "We're terribly sorry for your loss, madam," he said with a bow.

The elderly matron smiled wanly, inclining her head to accept Catherine's condolences, as well. After greeting the cousins likewise, he and Catherine continued down the line. James came to a stop in front of Waltham. The widower caught the motion and gazed at Catherine. Lust was clear in Waltham's eyes. He stared at her as a starving man would contemplate a succulent roast.

"Catherine," Waltham said, pulling her into a tight embrace. "I'm ever so grateful that you came."

James took a deep breath to calm his ire. He stood ramrod stiff, his hands in fists at his side as he waited for what seemed like forever for Waltham to release her.

"I'm so sorry, Thomas," Catherine said softly.

James arched a brow at her use of the man's first name.

"My heart is heavy, Catherine." Waltham held her away from him, keeping his hands on her arms. "But the burden is lighter with you here."

It was all James could do not to grab the man by the neck and throttle him right there. He cleared his throat, demanding Waltham acknowledge his presence.

The grieving widower did at last, nodding his fair head. "Thank you for coming, Roberts."

"I'm sorry for your loss, Waltham," James said, his propriety reasserting itself. "Lady Joan will be sorely missed."

Waltham managed a weak smile and nodded in agreement. With obvious regret, he finally released Catherine and watched as James led her over to the refreshments. James didn't miss the gleam in his eye mere moments before that morose expression once more covered his face.

James fumed as he thought of Waltham placing his hands on Catherine yet again.

Catherine accepted a cup of tea from him, regarding him closely. "Funerals are so difficult, aren't they, James? Is that what is troubling you?"

"What?" he said absently. "No, it isn't that precisely."

"Then what has you in such a state?"

James shrugged and shook his head. He was quite furious with Waltham's familiarity with her but could acknowledge, at least to himself, that something else was troubling him, as well. What the devil was ailing him?

The undertaker had provided "mutes" for the occasion, the silent professional mourners lending dignity to the affair. James balked at their presence. Apparently, Waltham wished to give the appearance of great sorrow. Perhaps the man wasn't as upset at his young wife's passing as he professed.

Before he could make mention of it to Catherine, Constance drew her attention away from him. The woman gestured, bidding her to join her on the settee. Catherine looked at James in question, at which he nodded. He watched as she made her way over to join Constance. He thought once more of her easy use of the widower's first name.

"Just what's troubling you, Roberts?" Chester asked, drawing him from his reverie.

"Hmm?" James answered, turning quickly to his friend. "Nothing. Nothing at all."

Chester eyed him closely. "You looked quite furious just then, friend."

James shook his head. "I'll be pleased when we're well away from here, Chester."

Chester opened his mouth to make a comment about that, but was stilled as James frowned in Catherine's direction. He followed James's line of vision, his brown eyes widening as they watched Waltham settle himself between Constance and Catherine. Two other ladies joined them, sitting themselves across from the threesome.

"Just what is that scoundrel about?" Chester asked.

James snorted in disgust. "He's playing the role of grieving widower to the hilt, damn him to hell," he muttered.

Waltham, a bereaved look fixed on his face, welcomed the attention from the young women surrounding him.

"I can't believe she's gone, Waltham," Constance said, placing her hand on his.

"Nor can I," he said, giving a very convincing sniffle.

"She was so kind," one of the other women, Diane Plymouth, offered.

Catherine nodded her agreement at that. "Joan didn't have an unkind bone in her body."

Waltham turned to face her fully. "Catherine, I'm doubly glad you came today. I desperately wished to speak to you."

"To me?" Catherine asked. "But, Thomas, why would you need to speak to me?"

Waltham bent his head to Catherine's, but James couldn't make out his words. As he watched Catherine inclined her head in agreement, Diane gently patted Waltham's hand before rising to her feet. She and her companion stood and left them, walking in the direction of Joan's elderly aunt. Constance, imparting a look of confusion on Catherine, took her leave, as well.

She joined her husband and James at the refreshment table.

"What the devil was that, Constance?" James asked her pointedly.

Constance gave a small shrug. "I don't know. Waltham said he needed to speak with Catherine."

"What?"

He made a motion to go to them, but Chester's hand on his arm stilled him. "Roberts, you don't believe he'd try anything here with all of these mourners present, do you?"

James's stomach churned, but he had to acknowledge the wisdom of Chester's words. He contented himself to watch the scoundrel, seeking to decipher the blackguard's words from where he stood.

* * *

"Oh, Catherine," Waltham said, taking her hands in his. "I'm so sorry for all that happened at Chesterfield."

Catherine blinked in surprise. "Thomas, what are you—?"

His sudden grin stopped her in mid-sentence. He recovered himself, the dour, grieving look settling upon his features once more. "It pleases me to hear you say my name, Catherine."

She gave a small nod, accepting his words in the manner in which they were spoken. She glanced down at her hands.

"You please me, Catherine," he whispered.

Her head shot up. "What?" she asked, perplexed.

Waltham cocked his head to the side. "Even dressed in mourning, you look delectable."

Catherine's mouth dropped open.

"Forgive me," he said, his tone contrite. "I should never have made such comments to you. Now, or before, at Chesterfield. I suppose I was distraught."

She looked at him closely. He certainly hadn't seemed distraught. No, his pale eyes had glinted with lust then. "But when you—"

"Shh," he said, reaching out to stroke her cheek. "I was upset over Joan's illness and spoke out of turn."

Catherine pulled back at the contact, so Waltham contented himself with placing his hand on her arm.

"I never meant to upset you, Catherine," he said fervently. "I pray Roberts hasn't made it difficult for you."

"He hasn't," she allowed.

"Oh, Catherine," Waltham said, letting out a heavy sigh. "How I wish we could go back in time, love. To last year."

She shook her head. "No, Thomas. I am a happily married woman now. That's in the past, and we can't change that."

James stepped closer, apparently just in time to hear the last bit of their conversation.

"And just what is it you would like to change, Catherine?" he asked.

"James!" she said, startled.

He gently grasped her arm and pulled her to her feet. "We must leave, wife, if we're to beat the foul weather that threatens."

Waltham stood up beside her. "You're not staying?"

James favored him with a dark look that chilled Catherine. It cleared as a grim smile curved his lips. "No," he said. "But we thank you for your generous offer of hospitality."

Before Catherine knew what he was about, Waltham embraced her once more. "Thank you so much for coming, Catherine love."

Catherine was stiff in his embrace. She patted his shoulder and pulled back. "Do take care of yourself, Thomas."

With a curt nod to Waltham, James led her from the room and strode quickly to the foyer.

Catherine took the cloak he unceremoniously thrust into her arms. "James, what—?"

"We're leaving, Catherine," he said, his words clipped. "Now."

He went outside to call for the carriage as Catherine waited for Constance and Chester to join her. Their expressions of bemusement mirrored her own feelings. What ailed James?

The return trip to Bradford Hall was a near-silent one, with James speaking nary a word. Catherine finally ceased trying to draw him into a conversation and stared out the window at the darkening sky.

By the time they arrived at the hall, well toward the dinner hour, an icy rain had begun to fall. Lord and Lady Chester were shown to their room and Catherine watched them ascend the grand staircase with a touch of regret. Without their company at the moment, she'd have to suffer James's very odd behavior on her own. She sighed and turned to face him, startled to find him eyeing her speculatively.

"Go upstairs and change," he tersely instructed. "I'll order you a bath."

"A bath?" she asked. "At this hour?"

James pulled her close, causing her breath to catch in her throat. "I want any trace of that man's hands washed from your body, Catherine," he said, his mouth a breath away from hers.

Catherine lifted her lips to his, stunned when he abruptly set her away from him.

"Go." He raked his fingers through his hair. "Now."

Catherine stared at him as if seeing him for the first time. His back was ramrod straight, his manner brusque. Shaking her head, she turned and climbed the stairs.

Chapter 16

Catherine finished quickly with her bath and stepped out of the tub, covering herself with her wrapper. James's strange behavior was still on her mind, his very odd request for her to bathe still quite baffling to her. She heard the door to their chamber open and turned, surprised to find James there and not her lady's maid. The dark scowl he'd worn for the past few hours was once more evident. She turned toward her dressing room, anxious to bring some normalcy to the evening. Perhaps when they joined their friends downstairs for dinner, James would once more regain his good humor.

"Hello, James," she said with a small smile. "It'll take me a few moments to ready for dinner."

James said nothing as he removed his jacket and waistcoat. Catherine reached the dressing room, but his voice called her back.

"Come here," he said softly.

Catherine blinked and did as he bade her. Her heart pounded as she noted the change in his demeanor. His scowl was a memory, replaced by a look that was blatantly carnal. She stopped in front of him and stared up into his face, her breath catching at the hot glare in his beautiful silver eyes. As if from far away, she watched herself untie his cravat, pulling the black silk from his neck.

He gently grasped her chin and tilted her head up to him. "Catherine," he murmured, brushing her lips with his. "You're mine."

She could smell the brandy on his breath, mingling with the scent that was wholly male and completely James. "Yes, James." She sighed into his mouth.

James crushed her to him, sealing her mouth with his.

Catherine moaned softly and pressed herself against him. He groaned and held her away from him. She opened her eyes in surprise, then smiled as she watched him fumble with the buttons of his shirt. She took over the task and let the garment fall to the floor, running her hands lovingly over his broad chest.

"James." She sighed. "You're mine."

She placed kisses on his chest, his stomach, coming to her knees in front of him. She caressed him through his tight breeches, making him shudder. She unbuttoned his pants and reached inside to stroke him.

"Ah, sweetheart," he said in a near-groan. "Ah, God . . ."

She kissed and stroked him, letting her tongue caress him. When she took him fully into her mouth, he groaned again, loud and low. He quickly grabbed her and pulled her up to him, his hands cupping her bottom and pressing her tightly to him. Catherine gasped as she felt his burning heat through her thin wrapper, the strength of his arousal branding her.

"Can you feel how much I want you, love?" he rasped. "I want you now."

"Take me, James," she said, breathless.

He lowered her onto the carpet in front of the fire and untied the belt of her wrapper. He spread the thin material wide, pausing for a moment to stare down at her. Her breath came fast in response to the desire on his handsome face.

He finally joined her, covering her body with his. He kissed her deeply, his tongue mating with hers. Dragging his mouth from hers, he kissed her throat.

"Ah . . ." he moaned, rubbing his arousal against her. "God, how I want you."

She arched toward him as he moved to nuzzle her breasts. He teased her, circling one hardened nipple with the tip of his tongue.

"Please, James," she whispered. "Please . . ."

He swore softly and closed his mouth over the sensitive nub. Raw pleasure nearly sent her over the edge. He teethed the nipple as his hand stole down to the curls that shielded her womanhood. He found the tiny nub hidden there and gently stroked her.

"Catherine . . ." He trailed kisses down the front of her. "Catherine . . ."

His mouth took over for his hand, his tongue teasing her as it slowly delved inside. She grabbed at his shoulders, his hair, whimpering softly.

The first tremors of her orgasm began. He lifted her hips and entered her with one deep thrust. Catherine cried out and he held himself still.

"Am I hurting you, sweetheart?" he asked, his voice rough.

She gave a quick shake of her head. "God, no," she replied, moving her hips restlessly.

He grinned wickedly and renewed his thrusts. He drove into her roughly and she met him stroke for stroke, whispering his name over and over. She cried out as she came, scoring his back with her nails. He joined her, a shout tearing itself from his throat. He collapsed on top of her.

After a few moments, he held himself above her, staring down at her. "You're mine, Catherine," he said, raining kisses on her face. "Remember that."

She looked at him, her passionate haze slowly clearing. "James," she murmured, "what do you mean?"

He dropped his head to her neck, nuzzling her skin. "I never want to hear another man's name on your lips, wife," he said, nibbling on her ear. "I never want to see another man's hands on your body."

Catherine heard it in his voice, the worry, the conviction. She sighed then, pleased with his possessiveness. Surely if he wished to keep her for his own, he must be making a small place for her in his heart.

She cupped his face in her hands and held it above her. "Yes, James. None but your name. None but your hands."

He grinned at her a bit sheepishly. "It wasn't my intention to take you on the floor."

She shrugged, giving him a grin of her own. He bent his head to capture her lips when her words stilled him.

"We have guests, James," she said.

"Ah, hell," he muttered, sitting up beside her. He stood and pulled her to her feet. "Come, wife," he said. "Let's ready for dinner."

James smiled as he watched Catherine attempt to lend some semblance of order to her dress, her wrapper twisted hopelessly about her legs. She caught his smile and fixed a look of pique at him.

"Go," he said. "Before I tear that garment from you and take you again."

She tilted her head to the side as if considering his blatant offer.

He gave her bottom a light slap. "Lusty wench." He chuckled.

Barely hiding her smile, Catherine took herself into the dressing room.

* * *

Dinner was pleasant, the four of them at last able to put aside the depressing mood of the funeral. James's charm was once more in full force, as he let go of his stilted manner from the afternoon.

That night, in the big four-poster they shared, James cradled Catherine in his arms. She was lightly snoring in slumber, the soft sound bringing a smile to James's lips. He stroked her hair, her back. Letting out a sigh of deep satisfaction, he closed his eyes.

His mind unfettered, he found himself recalling his odd behavior at the funeral. Waltham had no right to touch her. No, Catherine was his. And she had no cause to say that bastard's name with such warmth and ease, either.

By the time they'd returned to Bradford Hall, his anger had seemed excessive even to himself. But, when he joined her in their chamber . . . He smiled as he recalled her boldness, her passion. He had no doubt that his sweet wife was only thinking of him, not that son-of-a-bitch she'd nearly married.

Catherine moved beside him, drawing his attention once more. He looked down at her, this beautiful woman he married, and felt desire stir within him. Amazing, as they had shared their passion just a short time earlier. But she was asleep, undoubtedly exhausted from their long day.

Thinking he was certainly the most gallant of all men, he forcibly closed his eyes once more. They flew open as he felt her delicate hand grasp him.

"Catherine!" He gasped.

She smiled lazily up at him, her hand slowly stroking him. "You want me, James," she said softly.

He laughed shakily at her statement of the obvious. "I always want you, love," he said, rolling her onto her back.

He might not be sure about love, but this unending passion for the woman he'd given his life to? He was surely a lucky man.

* * *

Chester and Constance left after breakfast the next morning, promising to return soon for a long visit. The Earl of Bradford joined James and Catherine in the breakfast room soon after the guests had departed.

"Hello, children," he said, serving himself from the sideboard. "I trust your journey from Westmorland was uneventful."

"Yes, Father." James nodded.

"Catherine," he said, sitting beside his daughter-in-law. "How did you fare at the funeral?"

Catherine sighed and set her napkin aside. "As well as can be expected, I'm afraid."

James's father nodded solemnly. "Funerals are never the most pleasant affairs," he said. "Especially for one so young. Was Lady Joan ill for long?"

James shrugged his shoulders. "Apparently so."

Catherine shook her head. "Constance said that she didn't recall Joan having any such stomach ailment before."

"Perhaps Joan kept her illness a secret," James offered. "It wouldn't be the first time a lady did so."

Catherine sipped from her teacup. "I suppose you may be correct."

"Well," James said, standing. "I must be off."

"James," Catherine said, her eyes flying to the window. "You can't mean to work outdoors today. It's still raining."

He smiled at her concern. “I won’t melt, wife,” he said, kissing her lightly.

Catherine blushed slightly at his display of affection in front of the earl. “I, um . . . Do promise me you won’t stay out overlong.”

“Very well, I promise,” he agreed. “I’ll see you later, then. Goodbye, Father.”

“Don’t get yourself wet through now, son,” the older gentleman teased.

“I won’t, Father.” James laughed as he left.

“Catherine, I wanted to chat with you for a few moments,” the earl said.

“Yes, of course, sir,” she replied as she poured more tea into her cup.

“My dear, you are my daughter now. Please call me Father.” He smiled.

“Of course, Father,” she said with pleasure.

“I can see how happy my son is,” he said warmly, clasping her hand. “And I have you to thank for it”.

Catherine smiled and placed her other hand on top of his.

“James is a wonderful husband,” she replied softly.

“I can see you love him very much.”

She couldn’t keep the truth from someone so closely connected. She took a deep breath and nodded. “Yes, very much, Father.”

“Have you told him of your feelings?”

She sighed and shook her head. “I—I’m not quite sure how to.”

“My son can be very stubborn and set in his ways, my dear. But he is a fine man. Trust in him and trust in your feelings.”

Catherine’s eyes filled with tears as she embraced her father-in-law and kissed him on the cheek.

“Thank you, Father,” she whispered. “Thank you for your kindness.”

“Oh, now. I’m happy to listen any time you need to talk.”

The earl then told Catherine a bit about his late wife and Catherine’s eyes pricked with more tears at the great love he’d had for her. Certainly, having grown up with such warm and loving parents, meant that James could at some point grow to love her. She hoped so with all of her heart.

* * *

Catherine finished her breakfast and accompanied the earl to the library and left him there to read his book. She took herself into the parlor and sat behind the small writing desk. She was startled to find a letter sitting atop, her name penned on it in James's elegant hand. Looking about the room to assure herself that she was alone, she opened the letter and started reading. She blushed hotly at the contents, the paper fairly burning her fingers. James's words set her pulse racing. "Lord, how you pleased me," he wrote. "Just the thought of your lovely mouth on me sets me on fire."

"Oh, my!" Catherine gasped under her breath.

She folded the letter and quickly slipped it into the pocket of her day dress, a small smile curving her lips. She might not have his love, but she certainly had his passion. Sighing, Catherine put the provocative note out of her mind and set about penning a missive to her sister.

James joined her later for tea after changing out of his wet clothes. Catherine was readying to pour when he entered the room. She ran her gaze over him as he joined her and the earl in the parlor. His cheeks were a bit ruddy from the outdoors, his hair a bit damp. He looked strong, virile, and totally male.

Her gaze finally settled on his face, the sparkle in his eyes telling her how much he enjoyed her slow perusal. She blushed hotly and turned to pour tea into their cups.

"Here, James." She held his cup out to him. "Do drink this. You were positively soaked through when you came in."

He gave a small shrug and took the offered cup. "It's nothing some tea and a warm fire won't fix, wife."

"What say you to some brandy in our tea, son?" the earl asked.

"Capital idea, Father," James agreed.

He crossed to the sideboard to retrieve the bottle of brandy. Catherine watched the graceful way in which he moved, their passion of the last evening fresh in her mind. And his letter! What if someone else had happened to read his words?

She soon noticed that James was regarding her with puzzlement.

"Catherine, perhaps you'd like some brandy?" he asked.

"What?" she said quickly. "Oh, no, thank you."

James poured the liquor in his and his father's cups and set the bottle aside. He stepped closer to her. "What has you so skittish, love?" he asked softly.

Catherine shook her head. She couldn't tell him how much his note had affected her. Surely he'd think her a silly chit or, worse, that her feelings ran much deeper than she alluded.

She flashed him a smile. "It must be the weather. I'll be most happy when the rain finally stops."

"Yes," the earl cut in. "In March, I daresay."

James laughed at that. "It does rain quite a bit in the winter. For once I shall be quite content to be housebound, with my lovely wife here to keep me company."

Catherine blushed hotly, throwing a meaningful glance toward her father-in-law. James chuckled at her reaction and quickly turned the topic in an obvious attempt to draw attention away from her.

"I feel the cottages will withstand the winter quite nicely, Father," he said. "I only hope all this rain won't loosen the fence posts."

The earl shrugged and took a healthy sip from his cup. "Easily remedied if need be, James."

Catherine let their voices wash over her, pleased at last to feel her cheeks cooling. Just how dreadful could the weather turn? She hid her own grin at the possibilities.

Chapter 17

The days passed, quickly turning to weeks. Neither Catherine nor James made any further mention of Lady Joan's passing or of Waltham's inappropriate behavior at the funeral. Almost before they were aware of it, the Christmas holiday was nearly upon them. They would spend part of the holiday at Leed Manor, which Catherine was quite looking forward to. She and James were also very happy that James's father seemed to be improving. He seldom fell asleep at teatime and, when he spoke at length, coughs rarely interrupted his speech.

One afternoon, an unseasonably sunny and crisp one for December, James rode the estate to ascertain the fitness of the border fencing. Catherine, unable to resist the lure of a temperate day, walked in the winter-dormant garden, her cloak loosely wrapped around her form. She paused in front of the reflecting pool, once more thinking about her marriage and the love she felt for her husband but couldn't divulge to him. Staring at her reflection, she pondered her father-in-law's advice of simply telling James the truth. What if she did tell him? Would it be so dreadful?

Yes. James would feel guilty over being unable to return the sentiment, forced as he had been to marry her. Sighing in frustration, she took herself back into the house. As she walked through the foyer bound for the grand staircase, she caught sight of a missive set on one of the hall tables. Quite certain that it was another note from James, she snatched it off the table and hurried up the stairs, a smile teasing her lips. Once in their chamber, she swept off her cloak and tore open the letter. She gasped as she read the contents. She sank down into the chair in front of her vanity and read the words once more.

The note was from Waltham, and in it he stated his desire to renew his attentions toward her. He made mention of his great delight in seeing her at Joan's service, and of how her face and figure ignited a fire inside him. He professed a desire to see her.

She dropped the note as if it burned her. How dare he write such things to her! She was a married woman! She stood then, eager to put the letter and its author far from her mind.

Leaving the note on the polished top of the vanity, she went into the dressing room to change for tea.

* * *

James's tasks finished, he returned to the stables, dismounted and handed the reins to one of the grooms. The glorious day left him feeling quite invigorated, the satisfying completion of his duties pleased him. He took quick strides toward the house, eager to see Catherine. Surprised to find her absent from the parlor, he mounted the grand staircase in search of her. Certain she was within, he entered their chamber.

"Catherine?" he called out, shrugging out of his jacket.

He walked through the sitting area. He opened his mouth to call out once more, but a note placed on her vanity caught his attention. He glanced at it absently, his eyes snapping back to it as the name of the sender jumped out at him. He picked up the letter and read the contents.

"Son-of-a . . ." he muttered. "Catherine!"

Catherine hurried out of the dressing room in alarm, clad in only her chemise and petticoat. "James, what are you yelling about?"

"What's the meaning of this?" he demanded, thrusting the offending letter in her face.

"Oh, that," she said dismissively. "You had me worried that something was—"

"How long, Catherine?" he cut in.

She shook her head in confusion. "How long? I don't know what you're—"

"How long has this scoundrel been writing to you?"

She scowled at him. "James, that's the first letter he's ever sent me."

James was confounded. He knew of Waltham's desires where Catherine was concerned, and yet she'd never given him cause to doubt her faithfulness. Then again, just what had they been about those times he'd found them alone?

He narrowed his eyes at her. "Why would Waltham think to renew his attentions toward you, Catherine?"

Her mouth gaped open at what he was intimating. "You can't think that I'd ever encourage such attentions?"

He shrugged. "There must be a reason the bastard believes you'd be open to an arrangement." His anger suddenly flared to full force. "Damn it to hell. You're mine, and no one should even think to approach you."

He brought his fist down on the vanity, hard. The delicate piece of furniture rocked on its slender legs, the drawers sliding open. James took a deep, calming breath and tried to rein in his anger. One look at the neatly tied bundle of letters nestled in the top drawer put any hope of that to an end. Flicking a glance in Catherine's direction, he deftly plucked the stack of papers from their hiding place.

"What the hell . . . ? So, this is the first letter he sent you, is that right?"

"Yes," she answered quickly. "Those others are—"

"I know what they are!" he raged. "I can't believe you'd be so foolish as to save such damning evidence."

Catherine shook her head in mute protest, her eyes filling with tears. James held the letters above his head, his eyes flying to the fire burning in the fireplace. He shot her another scorching glance and took quick strides toward the hearth.

She flew at him. "No, James!" she cried, grabbing hold of his arm with both of her hands. "You can't!"

James froze, stunned by her vehemence. He lowered his arm and tossed the letters on the floor, defeated. They landed in a heap, the violet ribbon fluttering down to rest beside them.

Giving a yelp of dismay, Catherine fell to her knees and began to gather up the letters.

James watched her, a sharp pain settling in his heart. "Are the letters from your lover so important to you?"

"Yes," she answered tearfully.

James combed his fingers through his hair, a ragged sigh escaping him. The proof of her betrayal cut him to the quick.

"You've cuckolded me," he said in a low voice.

She stood at last, the beloved missives clutched tightly to her breast. She blew out a frustrated breath. "You're being completely and utterly foolish," she said, in an exasperated voice.

He fixed a steely glare at her. "I might be foolish, Catherine, but you're a—"

"These are from you!" she cut in, holding the letters out to him.

James blinked in surprise and grabbed the letters from her hands. He thumbed through them, amazed. She was telling the truth. All of the letters were penned in his hand. Why, she'd even saved the note from Leed Manor! He turned to her. The warmth in her violet eyes seemed to confirm what the pile of letters in his hands suggested. Did she love him?

"Catherine," he began, "if you saved all of these letters, then surely you—"

"Shh," Catherine said quickly, placing her fingers over his lips.

He dropped the letters and drew her into the circle of his arms. "I'm so sorry, sweetheart." He stroked her hair. "I never should have doubted you." He held her close, kissing her hair, her cheek. "Catherine," he rasped. "What I feel for you . . ."

He said nothing more. He captured her lips with his, letting his gentle kiss tell her what he couldn't put into words. Catherine melted against him, relishing the tenderness of their embrace as he did.

He quickly removed her underclothes, running his hands lovingly over her. He laid her on the bed and stripped off his own clothes, joining her on the big bed. There he cherished her, kissing every bit of her silken skin. When he entered her, she held tightly to him, her body arching as she reached her peak.

"I love you, James!" she cried out.

He held himself perfectly still for a moment. He finally let go, joining her in fulfillment. He leaned up on his elbows and tunneled his fingers through her hair. "Catherine," he whispered reverently. "Catherine . . ."

She squeezed her eyes shut and turned her face from him, but James wouldn't let her escape him.

"Did you mean what you said, Catherine?" He kissed her brow, her eyelids. "Do you?"

"No," she insisted in a small voice.

James stared down at her. "Tell me the truth, sweetheart," he gently commanded.

She opened her eyes, shiny with tears, to gaze up at him. "Yes, I meant what I said," she sobbed. "I love you, James."

James said nothing, his throat tight. Catherine obviously misinterpreted his silence.

"I'm sorry, James," she said. "I'm so sorry."

"Don't be sorry, darling. I'm pleased that you love me."

She gave a small nod of acceptance and he rolled onto his side, taking her with him.

"I can scarcely believe you saved all of those letters."

"They mean everything to me, James," she admitted shyly.

He turned to her. "Because you love me?" he asked, still unsure.

"I wouldn't have married you if I didn't love you," she admitted.

That night, after Catherine had fallen asleep in his arms, James lay wide-awake in their bed. She loved him! A silly grin split his face. Her simple declaration made him feel as though he were invincible. But did he love her in return? He was still so unsure, so unwilling to return her sentiments. He'd thought himself in love with Becca, and had been quite mistaken. Physical love he knew much about, having bedded many a wench in his time. But his wife's response to him . . .

Why hadn't he realized she loved him? No untried girl could give herself to a man the way she did and not give her heart, as well. He'd have to ascertain his own feelings sometime soon. He dropped a kiss on his wife's tousled head.

But not tonight.

* * *

The day soon arrived to travel to Leed Manor for the long Christmas holiday. Michelle had written to Catherine that the family planned to celebrate together on the night before Christmas. The other guests were to arrive on Christmas Day for the ball to be held that evening. The trip to the manor was not a long one, which was a relief since the weather had turned decidedly colder in the past several weeks. Sharing the carriage with the Earl of Bradford, the couple sat as close together as was proper.

"I daresay this promises to be a most pleasant holiday, James," the earl said with a grin. "'Tis a pity about the dreadful weather."

"I'm well aware you had entertained notions of the hunt, Father," James said. "But given your health, you really shouldn't have given thought to—"

"Bother my health. I feel quite well, thank you very much."

Catherine watched the two men as they conversed. James looked very much like his father, who no doubt had been quite handsome and dashing in his day. His lingering illness had aged him beyond his years, but today's happy grin and easy laughter lent him a more youthful countenance.

She looked forward to spending the holiday with her family, and with her little niece. She'd seen very little of Rose since the wedding and was eager to give the child the presents they'd chosen for her. Catherine glanced over at James once more, her head tilted to one side as she pondered his very handsome visage.

What would their children look like? That question brought her up short. James had yet to tell her of his feelings, despite his easy acceptance of her love. Should she even entertain the notion of having children with a man who didn't love her?

But she loved him, beyond what she'd ever dreamed possible. She'd happily bear his children. And perhaps his love for their offspring would extend to her eventually. How pitiful. Catherine let out a sigh.

"What is it, love?" James asked.

Catherine shook her head and smiled. "I was thinking about

Rose," she told him, a half-truth. "I do hope she likes the doll we brought her."

"She'll adore it, no doubt. Any gift from her favorite aunt would surely please the little mite." After glancing at his father to be certain the man wasn't listening, James leaned closer. "I can only hope she enjoys it half as much as my wife did her present."

Catherine's fingers went to the exquisite amethyst pendant James had gifted her with the previous evening. She could feel the jewel through the thickness of her cloak. Suspended by a thin gold chain, the jewel was pear-shaped, large and flawless. James had told her that the stone was nearly the color of her eyes when they darkened with passion. When he'd fastened it around her neck the previous evening, the pendant resting at the swell of her breast, he'd placed teasing kisses on the back of her neck. She blushed hotly as she recalled the loving that came afterward. He'd insisted she keep the necklace on as he made love to her.

"James," she whispered, scandalized.

He moved closer still. "You quite enjoyed your present, didn't you?" he said, nuzzling her ear.

"Oh, yes." She sighed. She remembered the earl then and straightened, her eyes opened wide. "Stop that, James."

James chuckled and leaned back against the seat, a wicked grin on his face.

She shot him a look of mild irritation, nervously adjusting her cloak. "And what of your present, husband?"

She'd given him a set of monogrammed handkerchiefs, embroidered by her own hand. He reached into his pocket and withdrew one of them, snowy-white with silver threads shaping his initials.

"They're quite handsome, Catherine," he said. "But I much prefer the other gift you gave me."

"Other gift?"

"The words, love."

She couldn't help but smile. Ever since making her declaration the day he found the letters, he insisted she repeat her words each time they made love. And each time she felt more at ease professing her love. He had yet to say the words in his turn, but she put that matter out of her mind. It was enough that he accepted her love and appeared to take pleasure in receiving it.

James wrapped an arm around her shoulders and held her close. He placed a kiss on her temple and settled back with a half-smile.

She leaned back against him once more, staring out the window as they rode on toward Leed Manor.

Chapter 18

The carriage rocked to a stop before the massive stone structure that was Leed Manor. They alighted and James helped his father down. He then took Catherine's hand and escorted her to the entrance. They left their outerwear with the servants and went into the parlor where they found Paul and his wife awaiting their arrival.

"Roberts!" Paul boomed, a big grin on his face. "Come in, come in."

"Hello, Leed," James returned. "Happy Christmas."

Michelle crossed quickly to where they stood and wrapped Catherine in a warm embrace.

"Happy Christmas, Michelle," Catherine said.

"How are you feeling, sir?" Paul asked James's father.

"Just fine, my boy. Has your father arrived as yet?"

Paul shook his head. "We expect him and Elizabeth shortly."

"Catherine, you look well." Michelle tugged on her hand to bring her to one of the settees flanking the fireplace. "And that necklace! It's exquisite."

Paul glanced over at his sister and let out a low whistle. "My God, brother." He grinned at James. "That jewel would rival anything in my wife's collection."

Catherine knew well that Michelle was an heiress who possessed a stunning jewelry collection. James shrugged dismissively and came to stand beside Catherine. He placed his hand beneath the stone, cupping his fingers around it.

"I tried to find a stone the exact color of my wife's beautiful eyes," he said. "I'm afraid this was as close as I could get."

"But Catherine's eyes are blue, Roberts." Michelle laughed.

"Not quite blue." James gazed into Catherine's eyes, his own glinting silver. "Not always. Sometimes they turn violet, like when she—"

"James!" Catherine cut in.

"Now, wife," he said with a crooked grin, "I was merely going to tell them that when you're angry with me, you—"

"And just what is it you do that angers my sister?" Paul asked.

Michelle clicked her tongue at him. "Oh, Paul. Catherine is no longer under your protection. Content yourself with Elizabeth's welfare, at least until Rose is out."

Paul closed his eyes and groaned. "That's a frightening thought. I can't imagine the trials we'll be put through when that little piece of baggage comes out."

"It pleases me to know Michelle and little Rose will keep you on your toes, Paul." Catherine laughed. "You do tend to be . . . overprotective."

Michelle's mother, Lady Helen, was also in attendance for the festive holiday and entered the parlor just then.

"Lord Roberts," Lady Helen began. "Catherine. I'm so pleased to see you both."

James bowed to Lady Helen, flashing her one of his dazzling smiles. "As we are to see you, Lady Helen."

Catherine accepted a warm embrace from the woman and they spoke about the weather and the upcoming Season. Catherine's father and sister arrived shortly thereafter, and they all set about their celebration for the Christmas holiday. Little Rose much adored the doll from her favorite aunt, and carried it clutched in her hands as she toddled about the room. The hour soon grew late for the tot and, after Catherine saw the child up to the nursery, the adults adjourned to the dining room to partake of the splendid holiday repast.

After they finished dinner—a feast of poached pears in port with a selection of cheeses, cream of leek soup, roast lamb with asparagus, and potatoes—they treated themselves to a tempting round of desserts. All assembled around the table raved over the flaky pastries and creamy custard tarts. Pushing aside his glass of sherry, James let out a loud sigh of satisfaction. Paul and the elder gentlemen echoed his sentiments.

"My, I'm quite stuffed," James's father intoned. "Leed, Michelle. Splendid meal."

Catherine and Elizabeth nodded their agreement. Their host and hostess graciously accepted the compliments and came to their feet. The ladies took themselves into the parlor while the gentlemen adjourned to the library for brandy and cigars.

Settling herself near the fireplace with the other ladies, Catherine turned to her sister. "Do you have any news to impart of Society, Elizabeth?"

"Oh, no." Elizabeth sighed. "The winter's been frightfully dull. I'll be most happy when we return to London."

"But what of your friends?" Catherine asked. "Haven't you heard anything from them?"

Elizabeth brightened. "Why, yes." She smiled. "Diane Plymouth wrote me just last week."

"Diane Plymouth," Lady Helen cut in. "Oh, she was with us at Kanewood, wasn't she, Michelle?"

Michelle nodded. Her mother spoke of the ball thrown to celebrate Geoffrey and Becca's nuptials three years prior.

"Pretty girl," the older woman went on. "Though a bit quiet. I believe she was quite taken with your husband, Catherine."

Catherine blinked in surprise at that.

Michelle laughed lightly. "Now, Mother. It's safe to say that most of the ladies in attendance were quite dazzled by Roberts's charm." She turned to Catherine. "That is, before I fell in love with your brother."

"Love is quite different than infatuation, isn't it?" Catherine asked.

"Oh, yes," Michelle said easily. "Love kind of sneaks up on you and hits you over the head."

Catherine agreed whole-heartedly with her sister-in-law on that count. Her love for James had taken her completely by surprise.

"Diane told me that she saw you at Lady Joan's funeral, Catherine," Elizabeth said.

"Yes." Catherine sighed. "What a strange circumstance."

"Strange?" Michelle wondered aloud. "Sad, I would imagine. Why would you say it was strange?"

Catherine shook her head. "I didn't mean strange, precisely. But Waltham was quite out-of-sorts, and—"

Elizabeth snorted.

"Elizabeth, is there something you wished to say?" Catherine asked.

"His wife had just passed away, Catherine," Elizabeth said in obvious irritation. "I would imagine such circumstances would put him out-of-sorts."

The other three ladies looked at Elizabeth, the puzzlement Catherine felt also clear on their faces.

"Elizabeth, I realize that," Catherine began. "What I meant to say was that he made some comments that seemed highly inappropriate."

Michelle arched a brow. "Did he? Paul told me what Waltham did at Chesterfield, but to exhibit such behavior at his wife's service?"

Catherine fought back the urge to shiver at the memory of all that happened at Chesterfield.

"I'm certain you misinterpreted Waltham's actions," Elizabeth said. "Diane told me of his great sorrow. The poor dear was beside himself. He was so distraught over Joan's sudden passing."

Catherine straightened. "I won't discuss what happened at Chesterfield, Elizabeth. Waltham had seemed a bit sad at the funeral, yes, but not distraught. I can't imagine what Diane told you, but I assure you—"

"Waltham has been in contact with Diane, Catherine," Elizabeth said. "She'd know his state of mind far better than you would. He cast you aside, if you recall."

Catherine's mouth fell open in shock.

"Elizabeth!" Michelle cried. "How can you speak so to your sister?"

Catherine took a calming breath and held up her hand. "It's of no consequence, Michelle," she said. "If that's how Elizabeth views matters, then leave her to her own opinion."

With that, Catherine stood and crossed over to the window. She stared out at the night sky and pondered her sister's remarks. Why would Elizabeth take up Waltham's share in any matter? It was passing strange.

* * *

In the library James sat in a large wing chair, holding his glass of brandy and swirling the liquid within it. The older gentlemen passed the time playing cards over at one end of the room. James looked up as Paul folded his big frame and sat down opposite him.

"So, brother," Paul began. "How did you fare at Waltham's wife's funeral?"

James shook his head and took a sip of brandy. "Ah, Leed. It was quite a strange affair."

Paul arched a brow. "How so?"

"For one matter, the man didn't seem very upset over his young wife's passing."

"Well, when he deserted Catherine in favor of Joan, I had the distinct impression that the girl's recent inheritance was a determining factor in his decision."

James nodded. "I suppose so. But that doesn't excuse his behavior toward my own wife."

Paul leaned forward in his chair. "You mean at Chesterfield?" he asked, his voice low.

"No," James grumbled. "At the funeral."

"At the funeral?" Paul repeated. "What did he do?"

"He couldn't seem to keep his hands off her."

Paul smiled crookedly. "I believe you're quite sensitive where Catherine is concerned, brother."

James waved his hand. "Ask Chester, then. He'll surely tell you what the man was about."

Paul's eyes widened. Suddenly, a dark look crossed his face. "Roberts, you don't think Waltham was somehow involved with Joan's death, do you?"

James rubbed his chin. "You know, Chester brought up the same question. I had thought it impossible, but if the two of you are of like minds . . ."

"Perhaps I'm wrong." Paul shrugged. "Perhaps the man seemed strange at the funeral simply because he's unused to such occasions."

James shook his head. "I would agree, Leed, if he hadn't

sent Catherine a letter only last week."

"A letter?"

"Yes." James finished the brandy in his glass. "The bastard wishes to renew his attentions toward her."

"But he was widowed less than a month ago," Paul said. "How could he do that?"

"He certainly had no qualms about approaching Catherine when his wife was still among the living." James shrugged.

"The bastard."

James agreed whole-heartedly with his friend's assessment.

The gentlemen finished their drinks and headed into the parlor to join the ladies. Catherine was staring out the window when the men entered the room.

James crossed over to her and brushed a stray curl away from her eyes. "Hello, love."

"James," Catherine said softly.

He sensed something in her tone. "Catherine, is something troubling you?"

"No, not really," she said. "Elizabeth and I had a bit of a disagreement, is all."

"In all the years I've known the two of you, I've never heard you argue over anything, big or small. You had a disagreement? About what?"

She leaned toward him and lowered her voice. "It seems my sister harbors some misconceptions about a certain widower of our acquaintance."

"Waltham?" James asked, perplexed. "What would your sister know of that scoundrel?"

She shrugged. "Diane Plymouth has apparently been going on about the 'poor man' and his terrible grief."

"Catherine, we were there at the service," James pointed out. "Did you see any evidence of this grief?"

"No, but Elizabeth said . . . Oh, never mind."

He studied her closely. Her brow was furrowed as she wrung her hands. Obviously, this tiny rift between the sisters was gnawing at her.

"I don't like to see you upset, Catherine," he said, a bit bewildered.

She looked up at him in obvious surprise, as if she too was astonished at his statement. She lifted her hand and placed it on his cheek. “Don’t fret, James.”

James turned his face and placed a kiss in her palm, then was seized with the urge to grin. “I was right, love,” he said, staring into her eyes. “Violet.”

She grasped his meaning immediately and blushed. James chuckled as she pulled her hand away.

The midnight chimes rang, heralding Christmas Day. Glasses of festive punch were handed around and glad tidings were shared among those present. Beside him, Catherine stood stiffly as Elizabeth came to stand in front of her.

“Catherine, I . . .” Elizabeth began. She suddenly threw her arms around her. “I’m sorry I spoke so harshly to you!”

Catherine hugged her sister. “It’s all right, Elizabeth.”

The younger girl sniffled as she wiped away her tears. James wished her “Happy Christmas,” and smiled his own pleasure at their reconciliation.

*   *   *

After readying themselves for bed in their guest chamber, James and Catherine climbed into bed.

“I’m quite pleased all was settled between you and Elizabeth, love,” he said, drawing her into his arms.

Catherine nodded and snuggled closer. “I can’t help but wonder what Waltham’s been telling Diane.”

“He’s obviously been playing the grieving widower to perfection.”

She sensed the anger her ex-fiancé never ceased to rouse in him threatening to surface. She leaned up to kiss him quickly on the mouth. “I don’t wish to speak of that man tonight, James.”

His gorgeous gray eyes turned to silver. “And what is it you wish to do then, wife?” he asked, his voice low.

The passion in his voice set a thrill to her toes.

“I wish to give you another present,” she answered huskily, placing teasing kisses at the base of his throat.

When he made a move toward her, she gently rebuffed his

advances. He settled back and she grasped him gently in her hands. Her fingers stroked the deliciously hard length of him.

"Ah, Catherine . . ." he murmured, closing his eyes.

Coming to her knees, she flipped her hair over her shoulder and smiled cheekily at him.

He opened his eyes. "Catherine, what are you about?"

She ran her tongue over her lips as she grasped him once more. His eyes glittered at that provocative action.

"Happy Christmas, James," she purred, lowering her head.

Chapter 19

The next morning, Catherine was slow to awaken. James roused her with teasing kisses.

"Good morning, love," he said, brushing the hair back from her face.

Her eyes fluttered open. "Good morning, James," she said sleepily.

He chuckled softly and stood beside the bed as he pulled on his breeches. Catherine donned her wrapper and stood. The sudden movement made her dizzy and she nearly lost her balance. Her stomach clenched sickeningly.

James must have seen her grimace for he reached out quickly to steady her. "Are you all right?"

Catherine licked her lips and took a deep breath. The nausea was gone as quickly as it had arrived, and her head seemed to ease its pounding.

She nodded slowly and sat down on the edge of the bed. "It must be the excitement of the holiday," she offered with a slight shrug. "I didn't sleep very well last night."

He sat beside her on the bed and took her hands in his. "Sweetheart, was I, um . . . ? Did I hurt you last night?"

"What?" She grasped his meaning and flushed. "No, James. Last night was wonderful."

"Then what's wrong?"

"I suppose I'm a bit hungry."

He studied her for a long moment, then dropped a kiss on her brow, and stood once more. "Then I suggest we ready for breakfast."

She nodded and arose. By the time they joined the others in the breakfast room, she'd all but forgotten her slight discomfort of the morning.

That evening, upstairs in their guestroom, they dressed for the ball. Catherine wore a gown of silver gray, quite daring in cut. The tiniest sleeves draped off her shoulders, the bodice dipping low. Annie had styled her hair simply, sweeping the curls into an artful pile and allowing a few strands to brush her shoulders. Catherine now stood in front of the washstand, trying in vain to check her appearance in the mirror atop. How she missed her cheval mirror back at Bradford Hall.

Giving in to defeat, she turned as James reentered the room. A low whistle coming from his lips.

"My God, wife." He came to stand in front of her. "You look magnificent. Like a dream."

Catherine blushed at his praise. She took in his appearance in her turn. He wore his formal black, his snowy-white cravat in stark contrast. Paired with a waistcoat of charcoal, the effect was devastating.

She placed her hands on his chest and splayed her fingers wide. "You, dear husband, look frightfully handsome."

James simply grinned. He reached out one finger and stroked the skin around her amethyst pendant, making her shiver.

"This does look marvelous on you, love." He took a step back and cocked his head to the side, apparently sizing up her attire. "But something is missing, I fear."

Catherine raised her brows at that. James reached into his pocket and withdrew a small velvet jeweler's box.

"James, what have you done?"

Flashing her a big smile, he opened the box. Inside sat earrings to match her pendant. Stunned, she withdrew the pair and turned to the mirror as she fastened them to her ears. She faced him expectantly.

"They look beautiful on you," he said. "But then again, I was quite certain they would."

He traced his finger over the shell of her ear. "You have such perfect ears, Catherine," he said, bending his head to hers. He gently tugged at her ear with his teeth, causing her to gasp. "Perfectly lovely ears . . ." He breathed, running the tip of his tongue over her lobe.

"James." She sighed as he moved to nuzzle her neck.

"Do you think anyone would notice if we didn't attend the ball?" he asked, rubbing his hands over her bare shoulders.

"I do believe we'd be missed," she answered him, a bit out of breath.

"That," he drawled, bringing his lips to hers, "is a shame."

Catherine closed her eyes and leaned into him as James deepened the kiss, pressing her close to him. Their tongues touched, first lightly, then tangling wildly. James groaned softly. With obvious reluctance, he released her and stepped back.

"If we continue, love," he told her with a crooked grin, "we'll never make it downstairs."

She caught her breath and nodded. He gave her one more quick kiss and, taking her elbow, led her from the room.

They met Paul and Michelle where they stood welcoming their guests as they arrived at the grand entrance. Paul wore his formal black, as well, while his wife wore a dazzling gown of topaz.

Michelle smiled widely at them as they descended the staircase. "Good evening, Catherine. Roberts."

James bowed low to her, turning to nod in Paul's direction. Catherine's brother gave him a hearty slap on his back.

"We were worried, brother," he teased. "Michelle was afraid you'd miss the ball."

"I'm afraid we were, um, delayed," James answered, hiding his grin.

Paul nodded, a glint in his blue eyes. "I daresay we nearly missed our own party, didn't we?" he said to his wife. "Ah, when I saw Michelle in this sinful gown, I simply couldn't resist—"

"Paul!" Michelle cut in, reddening.

James shot Catherine a knowing look and she was certain she turned nearly as red as her sister-in-law.

James turned to Paul. "And what do you think of your sister's perfect ears, Leed?"

"What lovely earrings, Catherine," Michelle said.

Paul shrugged. "I suppose they'll serve to divert attention from her bosom, which even now is in full view of all of our male guests."

"Oh, Paul." Catherine laughed.

"Now, as for my wife's wicked gown," Paul went on, "I fear I'll have to keep very close to her this evening."

The women's eyes met, knowing full well that neither gentleman was apt to leave their respective wives throughout the ball. As if to confirm Catherine's assumptions, James simply nodded and grasped her elbow once more. He led her into the ballroom and to the festive time awaiting them.

The evening proved quite wonderful, full of much merry-making and laughter. Elizabeth seemed her usual cheerful self, much to Catherine's great relief. Even though they'd settled matters the previous evening, Catherine had harbored the disturbing thought that her younger sister would behave oddly again. Instead, Elizabeth spent the evening dancing with several gentlemen in attendance and driving Catherine quite mad with her incessant chatter.

After taking a late supper, James escorted Catherine to the chairs set up around the enormous ballroom. Elizabeth joined them, fairly trembling as she took a chair beside her sister.

"Oh, isn't the ball just lovely, Catherine?" she gushed.

Catherine nodded, smiling at her.

"I'm quite surprised Diane isn't here, however." Elizabeth pouted.

James arched a brow at the girl's innocent statement. "Diane Plymouth isn't in attendance?" he asked, looking at Catherine in puzzlement.

Catherine turned to her sister. "Perhaps the weather kept her away, Elizabeth. It's quite cold outside."

"Yes." The younger girl sighed. "I suppose Lord Henry would worry about such matters. He's positively ancient."

"I daresay he isn't much older than your father, Elizabeth," James said.

"Oh, but Father isn't old," she insisted, looking at her brother-in-law as if he was quite mad. "Tell him, Catherine."

Catherine hid her smile. "No, Elizabeth, he isn't," she agreed. "And neither is Lord Henry, if memory serves."

"I suppose not," Elizabeth allowed. "But I'm miffed at Diane Plymouth, I tell you. I fully expected her to be in attendance."

Catherine opened her mouth to offer some sort of response, but Elizabeth's happy squeal put an end to that.

"Oh, there's Constance!" she exclaimed, Diane's absence obviously forgotten. "I must tell her how much I adore her splendid gown."

With that, she took off toward the other side of the room. Catherine watched her retreating form. James placed his hand on hers and she turned to face him.

"What is it, sweetheart?" he asked.

"Was I ever that utterly disconcerting?" she asked him.

James blinked for a moment. Suddenly, a big grin spread across his features. "That and more."

Catherine tried to look indignant. She failed miserably, laughing lightly at her husband's statement. He stood and tugged on her hands, pulling her to her feet.

"James, what are you about?"

"Dance with me," he said, bringing his lips to her ear. "Puzzle me. Confound me. In short, captivate me, wife."

She felt that familiar warmth course through her. She followed his lead out onto the dance floor, reveling in the fine music and the wonderful way they fit each other.

As he held her a bit closer than was proper, he brought his lips to her ear once more. "Ah, Catherine," he said, his breath tickling her ear. "You truly captivate me. And I must say I love the way you feel in my arms."

Love. He'd said the word and hadn't perished, though it wasn't quite the declaration she so anticipated. She looked at him then and his eyes glittered in response.

He opened his mouth to say what, she could only imagine, but the musical number ended just then.

"You're an excellent dancer, James," she said, unable to step out of his arms.

He dropped a quick kiss on her lips, taking her by surprise. Glancing toward an alcove, he spied the doors leading out to the courtyard beyond. He looked back at her, his eyes offering an invitation.

"The courtyard, love," he whispered, sweeping her off the dance floor.

"But," she whispered back, "it's bitterly cold outside."

They reached the doors and he paused. "I'll keep you warm."

Her eyes widened as she looked about the room. She was relieved to note that no one appeared to notice their departure as James quickly opened one of the doors and slipped outside. Several torches were lit and placed about the courtyard.

"You see, darling?" James nodded in apparent satisfaction and turned to her. "I knew your brother would have such ancient devices. He absolutely relishes all things Gothic."

She smiled and placed her hand in the crook of his elbow as he led her toward the far corner of the space. The air was brisk despite the torches and she shivered.

He took off his jacket and draped it over her shoulders. "Here, sweetheart."

She pulled the jacket close around herself, breathing in deeply. The garment smelled faintly of spice and brandy. And of James. She closed her eyes and sighed.

"Catherine," he said, grabbing the lapels of his jacket and pulling her close.

She gazed up at him and read the desire in his eyes. "James," she whispered, reaching up to place her hands behind his neck. She placed her lips on his and rubbed gently. James sharply drew in a breath and crushed his mouth to hers. His tongue swept inside her mouth, stroking and demanding. He pressed her against the wall and ran his hands over her.

"Ah Catherine, this is what I wanted that night." He breathed, kissing her cheek, her ear. "The night I asked you to marry me."

She nodded and pressed herself to him. "I wanted it, too," she whispered. "Only I didn't know precisely what it was that I wanted."

He smiled and ran his lips over her neck. "And now?" he rasped. "What is it you want now, love?"

He ran the tip of his tongue over the skin above the low-cut bodice. Catherine shivered, hot and cold at the same time. "I want . . . I want . . ."

Grinning, he tugged on her gown. She gasped as a blast of

chilled air hit her flesh. Her nipples hardened before James even touched them.

He trailed one finger over her breast. "Beautiful," he murmured.

He closed his mouth over one tip and she nearly burst into flames. The cold of the air, the wet heat of his mouth, affected her as never before.

"Oh, James," she said in a trembling voice.

He moved to the other breast, gently teething the nipple as he reached under her skirts. Grasping her bottom, he pulled her close. She could feel his arousal through her skirts and rubbed herself wantonly against him. He pulled her hand from his neck and pulled off her glove. He kissed her palm.

"Touch me, darling," he ground out, placing her hand on himself. "Please."

Catherine caressed him through his breeches. Her fingers deftly worked the buttons loose. She reached inside and grasped him gently. His flesh was hot against her cool fingers as he grew even harder.

He moved against her hand, moaning softly. "Ah, what you do to me . . ."

He removed her drawers and thrust his fingers deep inside of her and she cried out.

"Tell me what you want, love," he gently commanded as he slowly drove her mad. "Tell me."

"You, James," she softly sobbed. "I want you. Inside me."

He grinned wickedly. "Never let it be said I don't bow to my wife's wishes."

He placed her arms around his neck once more. He flipped up her skirts and lifted her. Catherine wrapped her legs around his waist as he entered her, hard and deep.

"Oh!" She gasped, the feeling intense.

James pressed her against the wall, his hands wrapping around her to cushion her as he thrust into her again and again.

Catherine sobbed as she neared her release, clinging tightly to him.

"Tell me, Catherine," he rasped. "Tell me you love me."

"Yes, James!" she cried out. "I love you!"

Wave after wave of pleasure washed over her as James drove deeper still. He joined her in fulfillment, shouting out his own intense pleasure.

"My God, love," he said in a hoarse voice. "That was better than I imagined it would be."

"Mmm," she agreed, closing her eyes in bliss.

As their bodies cooled, the chill of the night intruded once more. They quickly rearranged their clothing. As James shrugged into his jacket, Catherine noticed the scratches on his hands.

"James, your hands," she said, holding them to the light of the torch.

James regarded the scratches on his knuckles and shrugged.

"Better my hands than your gown. Or your lovely skin." He grinned. "I am, after all, a gentleman."

"Yes." She tenderly kissed the backs of his hands. "My darling gentleman."

"Come, wife," he said gently, his eyes glittering with an unspoken emotion. "Before we catch our death in this cold."

Catherine nodded as she smoothed her hands over her gown once more. She tugged on her glove and patted her hands over her hair. "How do I look?"

His gaze touched her lips, which were swollen and bee-stung from his passionate kisses.

"You look well-loved," he said with a grin.

He took her hand and led her back toward the manor.

She stopped suddenly and turned to face him emboldened by the incredible passion they just shared. "Am I well-loved, James?"

He stiffened, then seemed to take her question at face value. "You're extremely well-loved, Catherine." He drew her into his arms. "And I plan to keep you that way."

Her shoulders slumped a bit as she realized precisely what he meant. She shook herself and managed to smile brightly at him. They reentered the manor, joining their friends and family once more.

Passion, then. But how long would it be before he tired of a union that offered nothing else save love on her side?

Chapter 20

If anyone had noticed James or Catherine's absence, no mention was made of it. The party was winding down, and most of the older guests had already retired to their guestrooms. James and Catherine strolled over to where Paul and Michelle stood.

Paul regarded them closely. "Brother," he said to James, "what have you been about?"

James saw that Catherine couldn't meet their eyes. He gave her arm a quick squeeze and smiled at her brother. "My wife asked me in a most pleasant tone of voice if I would join her for a stroll in the courtyard."

"But it's quite cold out, Catherine," Michelle said.

"I . . . That is . . ." Catherine stammered.

James took her hand in his, rubbing gently. "I kept her warm," he said. "Besides, Leed, those immense torches warm the space adequately."

"The torches," Michelle scoffed. "I would so prefer lanterns installed, but my husband favors those smoky torches."

"They're quite medieval, love." Paul grinned. "Most fitting when I feel like a good brood."

James laughed at that. Michelle clicked her tongue and asked Catherine if she'd like some refreshment. Catherine nodded and followed her across the room to the refreshments and joined some of the other young ladies present. James watched her go. Lord, she was lovely. And passionate. His friends' voices broke through his musings and he saw that Chester and Geoffrey had joined them.

"Lovely bash, Leed," Geoffrey offered.

Paul nodded and asked a servant to bring some brandy for them. It arrived and Paul offered James a glass.

"This will warm you, brother," he said.

James nodded and took it.

"Roberts, what happened to your hands?" Chester asked.

James glanced at his abraded knuckles. "I, um . . . I suppose I scraped them when I was out in the courtyard."

Paul looked at him strangely, then suddenly threw his head back and laughed. The other two gentlemen exchanged a puzzled look. James bristled nervously as their gazes settled on him.

"You suppose so, brother?" Paul laughed. "Oh, come now. I can't help wondering, however, if you scraped them on the bench or on the wall."

"Never mind." James turned to Chester, his mind returning to the puzzle of Diane Plymouth and her apparent interest in Waltham. "Chester, did Constance mention anything about Diane Plymouth regarding her absence?"

Chester took a sip of his brandy as he nodded his answer. "Yes," he allowed. "Constance was quite surprised to find the lady absent."

"Isn't she here?" Geoffrey said. "My mother told me that Lord Henry was quite looking forward to a visit to the manor."

James frowned. Could Waltham have something to do with her absence?

"What's this about?" Paul asked James.

James let out a breath. "Well, it seems that our dear friend Waltham has been crying on Lady Diane's shoulder."

"How did you hear of that?" Chester asked.

"Elizabeth has been in contact with her. The poor widower has been quite distraught, in the lady's words."

Chester snorted in obvious disgust. "Distraught," he grumbled. "You should have seen him at the funeral, Leed, Kane. The only time he managed to show the least amount of sorrow was when the young ladies were about."

"Really?" Geoffrey asked. "Was that how you saw it, Roberts?"

The memory of Waltham's attentions toward Catherine made his hands fist. "The bastard couldn't keep his hands off my wife, Kane. If Chester hadn't been there, I don't know what I would have done."

Chester barked out a short laugh. "I fear they would have buried two that day."

"I wouldn't miss the worm." James shook his head. "And what of Joan's mysterious illness? I'm still not satisfied he didn't have some hand in his wife's death."

"No," Paul said.

"I'm afraid Roberts may be right, Leed. Constance told me Joan didn't suffer from bouts of stomach problems before, despite Waltham's assertions."

Geoffrey's eyes grew round. "Stomach problems? You don't think . . . No, that can't be."

"What, man?" Paul asked.

Geoffrey leaned toward the others. "There are certain substances that, when taken internally, could cause such problems."

"Hmm," Chester said. "Arsenic perhaps, or—"

"No," Paul cut in. "The man's a bastard, but even Roberts isn't convinced Waltham had a hand in Joan's death."

"There's his continued attention toward Catherine, Leed," James pointed out.

"But what of Lady Diane?" Paul asked. "Did Waltham seem overly attentive to her?"

"Not that I noticed," James said.

"That's not surprising," Geoffrey said with a chuckle.

"And what do you mean by that?" James asked him.

"I simply mean that when your wife is about, Roberts, you can't see anyone but her."

"Don't be obtuse, Kane," he snapped.

Geoffrey raised his brows, but he held his tongue.

James brooded for a few moments as his friends talked, regretting his outburst. He was still a bit perplexed by Catherine's innocent question in the courtyard. Was she asking him if he loved her? Why the devil couldn't he just say the damn words?

Giving his head a shake, he returned his attention to his friends and their conversation. Catherine caught his eye just then. She was currently the recipient of Elizabeth's oration, and appeared to be tiring. As she stifled a yawn behind her hand,

James excused himself from his friends' company. Geoffrey eyed him, an expression of knowledge on his face James didn't wish to consider.

James reached Catherine's side. "Are you growing tired, love?"

Catherine smiled wearily up at him and nodded. "Would you be terribly disappointed with me if I told you I wish to retire?"

"You could never disappoint me, sweetheart."

His words caused her tired smile to brighten. They made their excuses and climbed the grand staircase to their guestroom.

* * *

"What do you suppose is troubling Roberts?" Geoffrey asked.

Paul shrugged his puzzlement. Chester believed that he knew precisely what was disturbing their friend.

"It would appear, gentlemen, that Roberts seems unsure of his regard for his wife."

"That's ridiculous," Geoffrey scoffed. "He's obviously mad for the girl. Leed, surely even you can see that?"

"You're forgetting his charming nature, Kane," Paul pointed out. "He could urge any lady to eat from the palm of his hand."

Chester shook his head. "He cares a great deal for her, Leed," he insisted. "I believe, however, he's uneasy with the possibility of any stronger emotion."

"Ah," Geoffrey said knowingly. "He believed he was in love with Rebecca and, well . . ."

Chester clapped him on the shoulder. "He was mistaken, Kane," he said simply.

"No matter," Paul said. "He obviously makes my sister happy, and that's utmost in my concern."

"But what of Waltham?" Chester asked. "Do you believe that scoundrel will attempt to renew his attentions toward Catherine when we all return to town?"

Paul's eyes narrowed. "Apparently, he wrote a letter to my sister requesting such," he informed them.

"No!" Chester exclaimed.

Paul nodded solemnly. “But I have the utmost faith in Roberts’s ability to keep that bastard away from her.”

* * *

The next morning Catherine was the first to awaken. She donned her wrapper and stood. Immediately, a wave of nausea struck her. Her head fairly pounded as she gripped the bedpost for support. After one long minute, the feeling passed.

She padded over to the washstand. Splashing some water on her face, she rid herself completely of the strange feelings. She dabbed her face with a towel and stared at her reflection. What was ailing her? Suddenly, her eyes widened as recognition dawned on her. My God! Was she expecting?

Catherine glanced quickly at James, certain that he could read her thoughts from where he lay in the bed. He was still asleep, his lashes dark and thick against his finely chiseled cheekbones. What of his feelings on the matter? Would he be pleased? Or would he feel more put-upon than he must already?

Having the marriage forced upon him was one thing, but to bring a child into their union so soon would surely trouble him. She wouldn’t tell him of her suspicions, at least for the time-being. They were to return to London in three short weeks. And if her symptoms persisted, she’d have Dr. Morgan, their family physician, call on her. If she was indeed having a child—James’s child!—she’d tell him then.

James awoke at the moment she reached what she felt was a very reasonable decision. He gave a loud yawn as he stretched his arms above his head.

Placing his arms behind his head, he opened his eyes, immediately settling his gaze on her. “Good morning, love.”

Apparently, her face still wore its look of resignation for James regarded her closely.

“Catherine, why do you look so dour?”

She shook her head firmly and favored her husband with a small smile. “I was thinking of nothing dour or dismal, I assure you,” she said lightly. “Um, I was simply contemplating the aspect of ringing for a bath.”

He nodded and pulled himself to a sitting position. "I'll see to it, sweetheart," he said, swinging his long legs over the side of the bed.

She thanked him and went into the dressing room to see to her morning toilette.

When she emerged, she was quite surprised to see an enormous tub set in the center of the room. Servants were in the process of filling it to the brim with steaming water. Her gaze flew to James where he stood beside the tub, a crooked grin on his face. He wore one of his satin dressing gowns and Catherine thought he looked positively wonderful. Her attention went once more to the tub.

"James, it's so big. Have you ever seen such a tub in your life?"

He chuckled. "Apparently everything in this castle is oversized. Are you displeased?"

She shook her head, her eyes on the huge tub once more. It looked so tempting. She fairly shivered as she imagined sinking into its depths. Surely the water would come up to her chin!

"But, it's so . . . decadent," she finished in a whisper.

The servants left the room then, closing the door behind them. Movement to the side of her caught her eye. James untied the belt of his dressing gown and began to remove it.

"James, what are you about?" she asked, her eyes caressing the hair-roughened skin he was revealing.

"I thought we could bathe together, wife." He stepped into the tub. "Ah." He sighed, resting his back against the rolled edge.

The tub was large enough for him to stretch out his long legs. He held a hand out to her. Catherine stood for a moment, unsure.

"I don't know," she demurred.

"Come and join me, Catherine," he ordered with a grin. "I want you in here with me this instant."

Shyly returning his smile, Catherine untied her wrapper and let it fall to the floor. She grasped her husband's outstretched hand and gingerly stepped into the tub. Turning, she came to rest between his knees, leaning back against his chest. She reveled in the heat of the water, in the feel of his strong arms wrapped around her.

He suddenly stiffened. “What’s that scent?”

Catherine bit her lip to hold back a giggle. “Lavender.”

“Oh, wonderful,” he groaned. “I can hardly wait for your brother to get wind of it.”

Smiling to herself, Catherine thoroughly scrubbed his body with the scented soap, even his thick black locks. James rinsed the soap from his hair and wiped the water from his eyes.

“Equal measure, love,” he said, taking the soap from her.

Catherine turned her back to him once more. James began with her hair, twining the curls through his fingers as he worked the fragrant lather along the strands.

“Mmm,” she murmured, closing her eyes.

James lifted the pitcher of rinsing water and gently poured the water over her head. When all traces of the soap were gone, he picked up the cake of soap and the washcloth. His eyes glittering, he set the cloth aside and worked the soap with his bare hands. Catherine sighed as he ran his hands over her back, past her shoulders and down her arms. She gasped as he cupped a breast in each hand.

“James!” she exclaimed, her eyes flying open.

James nuzzled her neck as he touched and teased her, one hand stealing down to the curls that shielded her womanhood. Catherine turned to face him, thrilling as his hands slid down to her bottom and held her tightly against him. He was unmistakably aroused beneath the soapy water.

“What are you about?” she asked breathlessly.

He grinned and proceeded to show her.

There was more than a little water on the floor by the time they finished their bath. Her head resting against her husband’s chest, Catherine let out a small sigh. James dropped a kiss on her wet locks.

“Ah, the way you love me, Catherine,” he said in a lazy drawl.

She blushed in spite of herself, causing deep laughter to come from her husband. The water had cooled significantly, and they arose from the oversized tub and readied for the day.

James grudgingly informed his wife later that afternoon that his friends did indeed tease him mercilessly about his decidedly feminine scent. The words served to remind her of their time together. She'd never smell lavender and not think of her husband's hands all over her!

How she loved him, she thought. Catherine sighed. But would he ever love her back?

Chapter 21

As the time to travel to London drew near, Catherine was all but positive she was expecting James's child. Stubbornly refusing to tell him of the baby, she was firm in her decision to wait until Dr. Morgan confirmed her suspicions when in town. What would James's reaction be? He continued to be ever attentive, tender and considerate of her in all things. Surely a man as worldly and experienced as he was would be well aware of the consequences of their frequent lovemaking. Why, he'd taken her at nearly every available opportunity since their wedding.

But would he welcome a child from their union? She could only pray he would love the child if not its mother.

They departed for London on a crisp sunny day in late January. James's father stayed on at Bradford, as was expected. The earl had told them he couldn't abide the crowds in town or the dank and dreary London weather, so James and Catherine traveled alone.

Several hours later they arrived at their townhouse. James assisted her down from the carriage and led her to the wide door.

Giles pulled the door open. "My lord! Lady Roberts! How good it is to see you."

Catherine smiled at the butler and placed her cloak in his waiting hands. "Hello, Giles."

"Giles, old man." James clapped him on the back. "I trust you saw to matters in my absence?"

"Yes, my lord." He took his master's overcoat. "I left a bit of correspondence in your study. Nothing of import, I assure you."

"And you're certain of this, I imagine?" James teased. "Nothing from the matrons?"

"No." Giles laughed. "I saw to it that news of your marriage spread quite widely through certain channels."

Catherine looked from one man to the other in confusion.

"Lady Roberts," Giles began, "the cards are all addressed to the two of you. The whirlwind has begun anew, but in a different direction entirely."

She gathered the man's meaning and smiled. She knew of James's enormous popularity among the ton, and was most pleased that he was no longer sought after in the marriage market. He was hers. And because he accepted her love, she was his.

Giles left them and saw to having their belongings settled into the townhouse.

"Do you feel at home yet, love?" James asked her when they were once more alone.

She shook her head. "I find this most strange, James," she allowed with a small smile. "I've been here so many times in the past, but now . . ."

James put his arm around her and led her into the parlor. She went with him to one of the big chairs flanking the fireplace. Recognition dawned on her in an instant, causing her cheeks to flame.

"Ah." He took a seat and pulled her down beside him. "You remember."

She knew then that he too remembered the night of the Markham ball, when she'd come to him in a move that was both foolish and bold.

"Yes." She fingered the pleats of her gown. "Are you sorry I came that night?"

"I was then," he said, softening his words with a crooked smile. "I very nearly ruined your reputation."

She thought back to that night. "You looked so attractive in your dressing gown, James." She placed her hands behind his neck. "I daresay I would have permitted you."

He breathed in sharply at her words, bringing his mouth to hers. His lips took possession as his tongue parted hers, sending a tingle through her.

"Catherine." He rained kisses on her face, her neck. "My

God, I can scarcely believe all that has transpired since that night."

"Mmm," she murmured, her fingers running through his thick waves.

"You're mine," he whispered against her ear. "I could take you right here. Right now."

She pulled back in shock. "You can't!" she whispered.

He gave a slow nod. "We're married now, Catherine. We don't have to contain our passion."

"Oh, I don't wish to contain it, James."

The relief clear on his handsome face caused an odd flutter in her heart.

"The servants . . ." she went on. "That is, we shouldn't . . ."

He grabbed her to him once more. "I'll have you anywhere I wish, love," he said, trailing kisses down to the swell of her breast. "Anywhere and everywhere."

She closed her eyes in surrender.

"My lord," Giles said from the doorway.

Her eyes flew to the door, relief flooding her when she saw that the butler was in the hallway and well out of their view.

Apparently, James wasn't as relieved as she was. He swore softly and turned his head toward the door. "Yes, Giles." He shifted to drape his arm comfortably over her shoulders. "What is it?"

The servant entered the room then, his shrewd gaze quickly taking in the scene. Giles seemed pleased to find his master and mistress seated so close together. Catherine had known Giles since she was a child, and it was gratifying to know that the respected servant approved of James's new wife. But he couldn't possibly know that James was forced into the marriage. Catherine tamped down that thought.

"Giles," James said again, breaking through the man's obvious reverie.

"Yes, um, a letter from your solicitor, my lord," Giles said, handing the missive to James.

James took the letter and waited for Giles to take his leave. "Oh, and Giles?" he said as the butler turned away.

"Yes, my lord?" Giles answered in an even voice.

"Close the door."

The butler did as he was told. James set the missive down on the table and turned back to Catherine, his eyes glinting silver. "I'd imagined our trip to town this morning, love." He came closer to her. "I thought to take you in the carriage."

"James." She couldn't help wondering just how that would have been, though.

"Catherine," he teased. "Yes. Loving you gently and thoroughly as the countryside rolled on past the window."

How lovely!

"You no longer feel ill, do you, sweetheart?" he asked.

Catherine blinked for a moment as she recalled her nausea of that morning. The rocking of the carriage caused more discomfort than she'd imagined it could. Thankfully, any trace of her illness was long gone, as she'd come to expect these last few weeks.

"I feel quite well, James."

"Good." He wrapped his strong arms around her. "I was worried about you."

She couldn't help but smile at that admission, fool that she was. She kissed his chin, his cheek. "You don't have to worry about me."

James moved swiftly to capture her lips, apparently pleased to take up where they left off when Giles interrupted them. He did indeed take her in the big wing chair, catching her cries of pleasure as he brought them both swiftly to orgasm.

After he helped her rearrange herself, Catherine couldn't help but marvel at her attentive husband. Their passion was . . . Well, even in her innocence, she'd never imagined the emotion so linked to the sexual act. She watched him as he read the note from his solicitor. Apparently, he was able to quickly shift his mind from their incredible release to his business matters. Well, it wasn't as if his heart was engaged.

"I have quite a few papers to review with my solicitor, Catherine." He folded the note and smiled in her direction. "I'll see to this tomorrow, however. I don't wish to leave you alone on our first day back in town."

She nodded. That was something. Resignation struck her

then. “And no doubt I’ll find many invitations to keep us busy in the coming weeks.”

That afternoon she sat in the parlor at a small writing desk placed in front of a beautiful bay window overlooking the courtyard in back of the house. James, planning on that visit to his solicitor on the morrow, was in his study reviewing his ledgers in preparation. She opened the cards, amazed at her husband’s popularity and hers by association. She penned answers to the notes congratulating them on their nuptials, setting aside the invitations to dinners and the like until she could discuss the dates and times with her husband.

She neared the bottom of the pile when one particular note caught her eye. It was written in a lady’s delicate hand and addressed solely to James. From whom could this be? Catherine set the note aside, quite surprised by the prick of jealousy that flared through her. She shook her head as she chided herself. No doubt this was brought on by her condition.

That put her in mind to dash off a note to Dr. Morgan, which she handed to Giles, instructing him to see to it right away. With James sure to be busy with his solicitor, tomorrow afternoon would be ideal for a visit from the doctor.

Returning to her task, Catherine once more perused the letters, pausing every so often to glance at the mysterious note at her elbow. Teatime soon arrived. Giles set a tray laden with tea and biscuits on the table before the hearth, then bowed to her and left the room.

“A bit bogged down with the correspondence, love?” James asked from the doorway a short while later.

She started in surprise, then smiled. “Not too terribly, James.” She came to her feet. “And what of your ledgers?”

He shrugged dismissively. “Just the usual tangles, wife,” he answered easily. “It’ll take a bit to straighten them with the solicitor, however.” He crossed to her and gave her a sweet kiss.

“Are you going in the morning?” she asked him.

“I suppose I must.” His gaze touched on the amount of paper littering the top of the small desk. “My God.” He picked up some of the letters in his hand. “We don’t have to attend all of these functions, do we?”

She laughed at the look of dismay on his face. His dark brows were arched sharply over wide-open gray eyes.

"I daresay you're quite popular in town, James. We've been invited to an inordinate number of functions in the coming weeks. I'll leave the decision of which to attend and which to forego to you, however."

He set the papers back down and hugged her, resting his chin on the top of her head. "I would prefer to forego all of them, love, if I believed for a moment we could stay quietly tucked in here at home."

She closed her eyes and leaned against him. As for her, she much preferred keeping his company to herself rather than sharing him with the society matrons. She straightened, suddenly remembering the missive addressed solely to him.

"James, a letter came for you." She plucked the letter off the desktop and handed it to him.

"A letter for me?" He looked at it, curiosity stamped on his face. "I don't recognize the handwriting."

She nodded as he released her and opened the letter. She watched him as he scanned the contents, puzzled as a dark scowl darkened his handsome features.

"Of all the . . ." He visibly collected himself and managed a small smile. "This is nothing of consequence, Catherine. I'll take care of this."

She watched as he crumpled the letter and thrust it into his pocket. *Of no consequence?* Catherine wouldn't press him for an explanation, not now. They set about sharing their tea and discussing the upcoming evening, neither saying any more about the letter.

She couldn't put it out of her mind, though. Who had written it? And why had it made James so angry?

* * *

Alone in his study after tea, James withdrew the offending missive from his pocket. It was from Priscilla Brooks, Lady Brookdale. The widow wished to have an assignation with him? Apparently, his earlier decline of such an offer was of no consequence to the grasping witch. The lady intimated in her letter that, since he was now a married man, no one need learn if they met for a tryst. Nearly all of the married men of her acquaintance indulged themselves, she informed him in the note. And with a young and inexperienced wife like Catherine Talbot, she had added with a large dose of venom, he must be sorely ready for such an arrangement.

He threw the note into the trash. "That little bitch."

He withdrew paper and pen and swiftly wrote a reply to her offer. He managed to remain cordial while at the same time allowing no chance that the widow would think him open to such an arrangement. His social aptitude and innate charm gave him the words and nuances to keep from calling her every derogatory name he could think of. As if he would dally with such a woman. As if he would ever betray his wife.

"Not bloody likely," he growled, pressing his seal into the wax.

He left the letter with Giles to see it delivered and dismissed all thoughts of Priscilla and her distasteful offer from his mind.

That night in their chamber, in a bed nearly as large as the one they shared at Bradford Hall, Catherine cuddled against her husband's side. James cradled her gently, stroking her hair as she breathed slowly and evenly in slumber. He recalled the amazing passion they'd shared just a scant half-hour earlier. God, she was incredible. She could drive him wild with just a glance, let alone a kiss. And what she did to him with that perfect mouth of hers . . . He'd never felt such passion for another woman as he did for his sweet wife.

That thought brought the distasteful subject of Lady Brookdale's letter to his mind. How could Priscilla think he'd have anything to do with her? Catherine was everything he could ever want, both in bed and out. She was sweet and kind, caring and passionate. And she loved him.

She shifted beside him and let out a tiny sigh. He brushed the hair from her brow and kissed her there, gently. Perhaps he should rethink this love business. He could easily love Catherine. So easily that it sometimes scared him senseless.

Letting out a sigh of his own, he put the matter out of his mind and concentrated on just how wonderful she felt in his arms. He soon fell asleep, a small smile curving his lips.

Chapter 22

The next morning, soon after taking breakfast with Catherine, James took his leave. He was off to his solicitor's office, a thick stack of papers tucked under his arm. Catherine watched him go and thought to begin work on a new project to occupy her time, one meant solely for their residence in town. She'd work on a new fire screen, this one for their chamber upstairs.

The bedchamber of the townhouse was decorated much like the one at Bradford, but with a lighter touch. The huge four-poster dominating the space was of dark wood, and draperies of burgundy and ivory hung at the windows. An Oriental rug in nearly the same colors covered the floor. The mantle of the fireplace was gilded, and Catherine thought it quite a regal touch. Flanked by two ivory wing chairs, the fireplace would benefit nicely from the addition of a fire screen covered with flowers. Catherine thought to place several vases of flowers in the space as well, further softening the masculine room.

As she sat in the parlor that morning tracing a pattern upon the screen, she noted with pleasure that flowers were now placed about that space, as well. Obviously, Giles's work, and most certainly for her benefit. She recalled seeing no such feminine touches that night she'd called on James after the Markham ball. She smiled as she recalled his surprise at her arrival. Oh, how she'd melted when he kissed her so passionately! Humming to herself, she took pains to carefully sketch the floral design on the screen, mentally selecting the colors to be painted in afterward.

After dining alone for dinner, she sat once more in the parlor, anxiously awaiting Dr. Morgan's visit. The doctor had sent a note after breakfast, informing her that he would be most pleased to come for a visit that afternoon. He'd been their family physician for years, having seen to her health as a child as well as delivering her little niece. While Catherine trusted the man implicitly, she was more than a bit nervous about what she would do if he confirmed her suspicions about a baby. Suspicions? She was all but certain. What would she tell James?

Would he take a mistress when she grew large? She knew that some men acted in such a manner, although she suspected that her brother and Lord Kanewood had remained ever faithful during their wives' times of confinement.

But they loved their wives. James certainly desired her at present, but would he cast her aside when she grew too large and uncomfortable for their vigorous lovemaking?

Dr. Morgan arrived shortly thereafter, to her great relief. Giles led the doctor to the parlor, a curious look stamped on his face.

Catherine quickly dismissed the butler and turned to face the doctor. "Hello, Dr. Morgan."

"Lady Catherine," the man said with warmth, his blue eyes sparkling. "Or should I say 'Lady Roberts?'"

Catherine smiled. "I'm pleased you were available to see me this afternoon."

She sat down on one of the chairs by the fireplace and waved to the man to follow her lead. The doctor nodded as he sat across from her.

"Catherine," he said with a familiarity borne of long-acquaintance, "I daresay this is more than a social call, yes?"

She glanced nervously at the parlor door, noting with relief that the door was closed tight, then folded her hands in her lap and managed a smile. "I believe you're too astute by half, Dr. Morgan."

She quickly explained her symptoms to Dr. Morgan, who nodded thoughtfully as he listened.

"The nausea, the dizziness, are quite indicative, my dear," he said at last. "And when was your last monthly?"

Catherine blushed as she mentally calculated the time. "October," she said softly. "Shortly after we were married."

"Hmm," the man said to himself. His blue eyes ran over her with a thoughtful glint. "I would like to examine you, if I may."

She nodded and hurried upstairs to the bedchamber, changed into a dressing gown and lay under the covers, trembling ever so slightly. Would he confirm her suspicions? What then? Dr. Morgan followed a short while later, putting an end to her mind's wanderings. Managing somehow to set aside her embarrassment, she allowed the doctor to perform a rudimentary examination. He gently probed her belly through the bedclothes as she lay still beneath the sheets.

He straightened and smiled widely at her. "I'm happy to say, Lady Roberts," he said brightly, "that you're nearly three months along."

Catherine blinked in surprise. Goodness. Three months! The doctor chuckled at her obvious surprise, causing a blush to color her cheeks.

"And what of the viscount?" the doctor smiled, taking a seat. "Will he be suitably surprised to learn precisely how far along you've progressed?"

"Oh!" she exclaimed. "James doesn't . . . That is, I don't believe James suspects . . ."

"I understand, Catherine," the man said. "You wish to choose the proper time to present him with your news."

"Yes."

The doctor nodded and stood to take his leave.

"What of the sickness?" Catherine had to know. "How much longer should it last?"

Dr. Morgan patted her hand reassuringly. "You should feel right as rain in a few weeks, my dear."

Catherine smiled at the man's words. After advising her on the proper foods to eat and to take frequent walks for exercise, the doctor let himself out of the chamber. She changed into her tea gown and left the chamber, bound for the parlor once more. Surely James was due to arrive shortly. She must weigh her words carefully. Such unexpected news had to be given in just the right manner.

As if summoning him with her thoughts, the sound of James's voice reached her from the entryway belowstairs. She froze for a moment, quickly retreating into their chamber. Oh, no. She listened intently to the exchange between her husband and Dr. Morgan.

"Morgan!" James said in obvious surprise. "What on earth are you doing here?"

"I was merely paying a call, Roberts," she heard the doctor say smoothly. "I was disappointed to find you absent."

"Then you must take tea with Catherine and myself," James invited. "I take it she's in the parlor?

"Your wife is abovestairs," the man said.

Catherine squeezed her eyes shut, groaning softly. Her heart pounded as she waited for her secret to be revealed in a most embarrassing manner.

"Abovestairs?" James wondered aloud. "Why would she—?"

"I believe she's changing for tea," the doctor cut in. "I was just seeing myself out."

Catherine breathed out a sigh of acute relief. Thank you, Dr. Morgan! The doctor took his leave then, having deftly avoided any mention of Catherine's condition. She shook out her skirts and left her seclusion, taking herself down the stairs. James stood gazing at the front door, a thoughtful look on his face.

"Hello, James," she said.

James turned to her. He wrapped his arms loosely around her and gave her a gentle kiss.

"Good afternoon, love," he said. "What did Morgan have to say?"

"Dr. M-Morgan?" she stammered.

"Yes." James eyed her with open curiosity. "I saw him as he was taking his leave."

"Oh," Catherine replied with forced lightness, turning away from him to walk toward the parlor. "He wished to pay a call, husband."

If James thought there was something amiss, he said nothing. He strode into his study and set his papers on his desk and soon joined her in the parlor for some tea and relaxation.

* * *

That night Catherine stood in the dressing room, nervous about her coming conversation with James. There was no putting it off now. When he took himself into his study after dinner, she'd been quite relieved. But now, with him waiting for her on the other side of the door, her stomach was tied in knots. How would she tell him her news? How would he take such surprising tidings?

Steeling herself, she tied the belt of her wrapper and opened the door. She was surprised to find him seated in the chair. His head rested on the back of the chair, his eyes closed as he slowly swirled the brandy in his glass.

"James?" she called softly.

He lifted his head and smiled crookedly at her. "Hello, love," he said, straightening in the chair. He placed the glass on the table beside the chair and rubbed his hands over his face.

Catherine crossed to him, drinking in his appearance. He wore no jacket or waistcoat and his white shirt was open at the collar. His glossy black hair was tousled, obviously from endlessly raking his fingers through the thick mass. A dark stubble covered his well-chiseled cheeks, lending him a decidedly rakish appearance.

"Are you tired, husband?"

"A bit, yes. The ledgers are not my ideal companions, believe me. Once I catch up with the winter's ledgers, I should be able to keep up with the ongoing task of seeing to the estate's business."

She stepped behind the chair and began to massage his shoulders and neck. "I have every faith in your skill."

"Mmm, that feels good," he said in a low voice.

Catherine gently and thoroughly kneaded his muscles. "You're quite tense, James."

"Ah, love," he said, closing his eyes. "Pray, give me a fence to mend or a cottage roof to repair any day."

She smiled absently as she ran her fingers through his silky hair. She'd tell him of the baby later. After they made love and were cozily tucked in bed. Surely he'd be in a far better frame of mind than he was at present.

James interrupted her train of thought when he grabbed one of her hands and brought it to his lips. "You're so good to me, Catherine," he murmured.

At his insistent tugging, she came around the chair to face him. They shared a sweet kiss, one that she ended just as he began to deepen it.

"Sweetheart, what—?" he asked in surprise.

She shook her head to silence him and bent to remove his boots. Running her hands over his long, strong legs, she reached the waistband of his breeches. She stopped to glance at her husband's face. His eyes glittered in response as she slowly smiled at him. She caressed him through the thin fabric, making him hard beneath her fingers. With a flick of her hand, she unfastened the top button of his breeches. James placed his hand on hers to still it. She arched a brow at him.

"Not yet, love," he said, pulling her to her feet.

Laughing softly, Catherine unbuttoned his shirt and pulled it from the waistband. She removed the garment and ran her hands over his chest, his skin warm and firm beneath her palms as she teased him.

James reached for the belt of her wrapper. "I need to touch you."

She stood still as he pushed the garment off her shoulders, baring herself to him.

His breath caught, sending a thrill through her. "It may be a trick of the firelight love, but your breasts are so . . ." He gently cupped her breasts, one in each hand. "And your nipples. They look darker." His thumbs caressed her and she felt herself shiver at his touch. "Sweeter."

His words flooded her with heat. Just the thought of his beautiful mouth closing over her flesh!

"My God." He breathed. "You grow more beautiful each day."

She gasped as he placed his hands on her waist to draw her closer to him. He flicked his tongue over first one nipple then the other, the teasing motion driving her mad. She strained toward him. "James, please."

He gave her what she craved, closing his mouth over one hardened nub and drawing it into his mouth. The wet heat, the gentle tugging suction . . . Her breasts were no doubt extra-sensitive due to her condition. When he fondled her other nipple with his strong fingers, she nearly climaxed.

She trembled before him, whimpers of pleasure coming from her parted lips as he kept up the most exquisite torture. His mouth left her flesh and she groaned softly.

James let her wrapper fall to the floor as he lifted her onto his lap.

"Catherine," he said, his mouth close to hers. "Kiss me."

She did as he asked, running the tip of her tongue along the curve of his lower lip. He shoved his hands into her hair as he crushed his mouth to hers. Their tongues tangled as he pressed her tightly to him. She shifted to straddle him, feeling his arousal so strong and firm against her.

He brought his lips to the crook of her neck, licking and kissing her most sensitive places.

"Oh, James." She sighed, letting her head fall back as he kissed the hollow of her throat.

His lips found her breast once more. He gently teethed one nipple as she writhed against him. Reaching between their bodies, he found her. She knew she was wet and ready for him, but she wasn't embarrassed. He thrust his fingers inside of her. She moaned low in her throat.

"God, love," he rasped.

As she wriggled in his lap, he somehow managed to unbutton his own breeches. She was sobbing now, so close to her release. She felt as though the fire behind them burned her very skin.

"Please, James," she whispered. "Please . . ."

"Yes, sweetheart," he ground out. "Yes."

He grabbed her hips and thrust up into her. She cried out as she came, wave after wave of pleasure washing over her. He wouldn't be still, driving up into her even as she tightened around him once more. He gave in to his release as she found hers again, letting out a shout as he drove higher still.

She collapsed against him, her arms wrapped around him as she rained kisses on his neck, his shoulder. She couldn't stop the tears when they came, hot and stinging on her cheeks.

"What is it, love?" he asked after a while, kissing her hair, her cheek.

She couldn't find the words. It was incredible. He was still deep inside of her, his child was nestled beneath her heart, and she loved him more than her own life. She cuddled closer, trying to rein in her emotions.

"James," she managed to say, still crying. "I love you."

"Thank you, Catherine." He buried his face in her hair and ran his hands over her skin. "Oh, the feel of you." He breathed in deeply. "The smell of you."

She'd tell him now. He'd know that she carried his child. She lifted her head to face him.

"James," she began, "I've something to—Oh!"

James grinned wickedly as he moved beneath her. He was hard again within her, smooth and hot and ready to take her again.

"But how is this possible?" she couldn't help but ask.

He shrugged his shoulders, his eyes glittering. "It's all you, love." He kissed her. "I can't seem to get enough of you."

She closed her eyes and moved her hips slightly. The burst of pleasure took her by surprise. He grabbed her hips to still her. With an extreme exercise of control, he lifted her off himself and stood, cradling her in his arms. She gazed wide-eyed up at him and a strangled laugh came from him.

"The bed, sweetheart," he ground out.

He carried her swiftly to the bed and laid her in the middle of it. He stripped off his breeches and came down on top of her. He held her hands above her head as he entered her with one powerful thrust. They rocked together, Catherine's legs wrapped tightly around his waist as he drove her to a stunning climax. He shouted out her name as he joined her, driving even deeper.

A few moments later he rolled off her. She cuddled up beside him in the big bed, running her hand over his chest. "You're a wonderful lover, James," she said softly.

He managed a smile. "Only with you, love," he said, thrilling her. "I've never felt passion for another woman like I do for you."

She turned to stare up at the ceiling. Now. She'd tell him now. "James, I have something to tell you."

He nodded, his eyes still closed. "What is it, sweetheart?" he asked with a yawn.

"Well, this afternoon while you were out . . ."

"Does this have something to do with Morgan's visit?" he asked absently.

"Yes," she answered. "You may recall how I've been ill of late. Well, Dr. Morgan told me that—"

He sat up in bed. "Tell me you're all right, Catherine. It's not serious, is it?"

She smiled at the wording of his question. "Yes, James. Quite serious," she answered. "I'm having your baby."

She might have found the look of surprise on his face comical if she wasn't so worried about his reaction. His beautiful gray eyes stared at her blankly, his well-formed mouth hung open. She waited for what felt like a hundred heartbeats. Oh, surely he was displeased. Suddenly, a smile brighter than she'd ever seen spread across his handsome face.

"A baby?" he asked softly. "Are you certain? Of course you're certain. Morgan was here, after all," he said quickly. "Ah, love!" he exclaimed. "A baby!"

He grabbed her to him in a great hug, letting out a loud whoop of joy. She laughed as she allowed his joy to envelop her.

He pulled back to gaze at her, a frown suddenly wrinkling his brow. "Are you all right?" He cupped her cheek in his hand. "What did Morgan say?"

"I'm fine, James. And nearly three months along."

"Well." He smiled once more. "That didn't take us very long now, did it?"

Catherine's laughter joined his as he hugged her once more. Finally, he lay back down on the bed, taking her with him. He leaned up on one elbow, his eyes running over her from head to toe. He trailed his fingers over her, his hand coming to rest just below her navel.

"Our baby is in here," he said reverently, kissing her belly.

She nearly wept at the tenderness in his voice. He loved the baby. And one day he'd love her, she was certain. She ran her fingers through his hair as his head rested on her stomach.

"Ah, hell," he muttered suddenly.

"What is it?"

He lifted his head, anger and worry both clear on his face.

"Before, love. When I took you. I was far too rough."

"No, James," she said, shaking her head.

"Yes," he insisted. "I'm a bloody selfish bastard."

"You're no such thing," she assured him. "You're a magnificent lover, James. And no doubt you will make a magnificent father."

He blinked. "A father," he said in wonder.

He drew her into his arms and kissed her gently. "I can scarcely believe it, sweetheart," he mused, yawning once more. "We're having a baby."

Catherine sighed in answer, pleased to her toes over his joyful acceptance of her incredible news. She drifted off to sleep, content to bask in her husband's love for their unborn child. Its reflection was bright and warm.

And enough for now.

Chapter 23

The next morning, James reached for Catherine and kissed her awake. "Good morning, love."

Catherine groaned as she rolled over in bed, clutching her belly.

James saw her grimace and sat up. "Are you all right?"

She closed her eyes and took a deep breath in what he guessed was an attempt to regain herself.

"I shall be, James," she murmured. "Just as soon as you cease rocking the bed."

"So sorry." He held himself still as she slowly sat up. After a long moment, she opened her eyes and smiled at him. She looked a bit pale but otherwise she was her usual gorgeous self. "Well?"

"It only persists for the briefest time in the mornings," she explained to him. "Dr. Morgan said that soon I shall feel fine all the time."

"That's a relief." James ran his eyes over her, still amazed that she carried his child. "And soon you'll be round and plump with our baby."

A strange look crossed Catherine's face at his innocently spoken comment, something akin to fear or worry.

"What is it, sweetheart?" James placed his hands on her shoulders. "Are you feeling ill again?"

She shook her head, averted her gaze to her lap, twisting the bedclothes in her hands. "James, will you take a mistress when I'm big with child?"

He was stunned by her question. A mistress? "What? Why the devil would you think that?"

Catherine shrugged her shoulders and looked up at him. He saw the tears in her eyes then and forced himself to lower his voice.

"Why would you believe such a notion?" he asked, gently this time.

She brushed a hand against her cheek. "I know that some men do."

"Well, not this man. Never. You're all I want."

To prove his point, he gently eased her back down on the bed. He kissed her gently and cupped her face in his hands. "I'll never want another woman, Catherine."

That doubt was still evident in her eyes, damn it. "But what if you no longer desire me?"

He threw his head back and laughed.

"This isn't funny." She sniffled.

"No. It's ludicrous." When she blinked in response, he dropped a kiss on her brow and grinned. "That will never happen, love. Even when we're old and gray, I daresay you'll still be able to set me on fire."

She smiled up at him finally, a bright expression that caused his heart to do a little flip.

"Truly?" she asked.

"God, yes," he answered. "You, darling, are stuck with me. For the rest of your life."

"I love you, James," she said, pulling his face down to hers.

James kissed her, hoping to convey his passion and high regard for her. Take a mistress? Odd that his wife would suspect his future unfaithfulness the day after Priscilla had sent him that note with her offer. Both women were wrong. He'd been completely truthful in his refusal yesterday.

And he'd never meant a promise more than the one he made Catherine today.

* * *

Nearly two weeks later, they prepared to go out for the evening. Although Parliament was open, signaling the start of the Season, most of the ton remained in the country through the end of the winter. Catherine was pleased and James apparently was as well, since they'd discussed how delightful it was that they could attend the theater and the opera without a maddening crush of people in attendance. After Easter, the true Season would begin, with its whirlwind of bashes and forced frivolity, which James told her he'd been so pleased to miss the previous year.

Paul and Michelle also returned to town early, as they had many speeches to prepare for their clients. That night, James and Catherine were to join them at the theater. Catherine couldn't wait to share their wonderful news with them.

James emerged from the dressing room, clad in gray breeches topped with a silver waistcoat. "Sweetheart," he said, hugging her from behind, "you look absolutely delicious."

Catherine smiled at his choice of words. Her hair was piled atop her head, long curls falling to brush her shoulders. He pushed the tendrils aside and ran his lips over her skin, making her shiver.

She turned in his arms and favored him with a smile, placing her hands behind his neck. "Hello, husband."

James kissed her, gently at first. He pulled her close and ravaged her mouth, causing her to gasp. His hands were all over her, touching and teasing her through her blush satin gown. When he lifted his head, he was grinning broadly.

"I'm so glad you're no longer treating me like a piece of porcelain, James," she said.

"After that first night, love, you gave me no choice."

Her cheeks flamed. He'd nearly driven her mad with his gentle possession until she'd grabbed him and forced him deep inside her. He hadn't wanted to hurt her, he'd said. But now having gotten used to her condition, he held nothing back from her, much to the delight of both of them. Catherine clicked her tongue at him as she readjusted her gown, which he'd nearly worked down off her shoulders.

He walked over to the mantelpiece. "I've got something for you, love."

He picked up a jeweler's box of gold velvet and Catherine eyed him closely.

"James, what is this?"

"For you," he said again, opening the box with a flourish.

She gasped as she saw the long strand of pearls, large and round and perfect. There were matching earrings within the box, as well. James withdrew the necklace and draped it over her. The pearls reached the swell of her breast and felt cool against her skin.

"James." She gazed in the mirror. "These are breathtaking."

"They look beautiful against your skin, Catherine," he said, trailing his fingers over the round beauties.

He hesitated for a moment then slipped his hand into the bodice of her gown, cupping one breast. She gasped as he brushed his thumb over her nipple.

"James, we can't," she said without any real conviction. "We'll be late."

He lowered his head. "Do you want me to stop, sweetheart?" He ran his lips over her flesh. "Do you?" He pushed her bodice down and closed his mouth over her hardened nipple.

She closed her eyes in bliss. "No." She breathed. "Don't stop."

James gently teethed her nipple as one hand worked its way under her skirts.

"James." She sighed as his fingers caressed her through her drawers.

She placed her hand on him and felt him grow hard. He groaned as she gently stroked him. He was soon tangled in her skirts.

"Ah, hell," he muttered.

With obvious reluctance, he released her. Catherine let out a whimper of protest and he let out a choking laugh.

"I want you, love," he said, his voice deep. "But not this way."

"Take me, James," she said, throwing her arms around his neck.

He grabbed her hands and kissed them. "We have to pick up Leed and Michelle at their home," he said. "If we're late, your brother is certain to guess what kept us."

"Yes, you're right." She sighed. "We must go, then."

Catherine fixed her gown and pulled on her long satin gloves. Taking her elbow, James led her downstairs. He assisted her with her cloak, a thick wrap of deep rose with a large and graceful hood. He adjusted the front of his breeches and pulled on his greatcoat. “Thank God it’s cold out.” She smiled as they went out to the waiting carriage.

As soon as Paul and Michelle joined them in their carriage, they shared their news about the baby.

“Catherine!” Michelle squealed happily, hugging her tight. “How wonderful!”

Paul flashed a bright smile as he congratulated his friend and brother-in-law with a hearty slap on the back. “Quite expedient, brother,” he teased James. “I daresay you didn’t waste much time.”

“Never mind.” James shook his head, hiding the grin Catherine didn’t miss.

Talk in the carriage became quite animated as they made their way toward the theater.

They found the play quite enjoyable, one of Shakespeare’s comedies. After the performance, most of the theater crowd adjourned to the large and beautifully appointed lobby. Refreshments were set up at one end of the space and, after asking Catherine if she’d care for a cup of punch, James strode to that side of the room. She watched him as he went, a faint smile on her lips. Her sister-in-law’s voice soon drew her attention.

“Oh, Catherine,” Michelle began. “I’m so happy for you and Roberts.”

“Thank you,” Catherine said. “I can scarcely believe it myself.”

“And how did he take the news?” Paul teased.

She thought back to the comical shock on his handsome face, the love she’d seen shining in his eyes as he spoke of the coming babe.

“James was quite pleased,” Catherine answered with a genuine smile.

Over on the other side of the room, James waited patiently for the refreshments. The punch was ladled out by one of the elderly matrons who enjoyed being involved in the theater organization. James felt a small hand grasp his arm and turned with a smile, fully expecting Catherine to be at his elbow. He promptly lost that smile.

“Priscilla.”

"Hello, Roberts," Lady Brookdale purred, her eyes running over him. "My, you look ever so handsome this evening."

James extracted his arm from her clutching hand and took a step back from her. The widow, not to be deterred, stepped closer.

"I received your missive." She pursed her lips in a practiced pout. "I must say I was quite disappointed with your response."

James shrugged. "You should expect disappointment when you approach a happily married man," he said in a low voice.

Priscilla visibly bristled at his harsh tone. She threw a glance over to where Catherine stood with Michelle, then looked back at James and sighed dramatically.

"I'll say that Catherine Talbot is a pretty little thing, but—"

"Catherine Bradford," James corrected in a firm voice. "Viscountess Roberts."

"Um, yes," Priscilla allowed with a cool nod. She grabbed his arm once more and leaned toward him. "She was innocent when you wed, Roberts," she whispered. "Surely she can't please you in the manner to which I'm capable."

"I thought I made my meaning clear, Lady Brookdale." James held his hands in fists at his side, anger coursing through him. "Don't proposition me again."

Once more pulling out of her grasp, he picked up two glasses of punch and returned to his wife.

Priscilla followed him with hungry eyes. A voice at her side broke through her reverie.

"Hello, love," Waltham said.

Priscilla turned and flashed a smile at her friend and frequent bed partner. She sidled up close to him and placed her hand on his arm. "Thomas." She sighed. "Whatever are you doing in society so soon after your wife's unfortunate demise?"

Waltham laughed softly at her statement. "I couldn't bear to stay in the country another moment," he told her. "There were some pressing matters needing my attention."

Priscilla cocked her head to the side as she flashed him a grin. "Were there no country girls willing to indulge your particular tastes, Thomas?"

Waltham's pale eyes narrowed slightly. His tastes were quite vigorous, as she well knew.

He recovered his usual coolly handsome façade and smiled at her. "Not in the manner to which you indulge me, Priscilla," he said in a low voice. "I saw you with him." He flicked his head in James's direction. "What did the ever-charming scoundrel have to say?"

Priscilla couldn't keep her disappointment from her countenance. "I offered him a bit of sport." She snorted. "The gentleman refused me without ceremony."

"He's married now, love." Waltham chuckled. "Ah, but how could he resist charms such as yours?"

She clicked her tongue. "He seems content with that child." She sneered. "Although I don't know how she can possibly . . ."

Her voice trailed off as she caught Waltham's eye roaming freely over Catherine's form. The lust in his pale gaze angered her.

"Thomas," she hissed. "What captivates you so?"

"God, she looks absolutely delectable," he murmured.

Another swain fallen under that chit's spell? No. She might not have Roberts in her bed yet, but she knew Thomas's particular tastes. She wouldn't let him think to practice them on the prim Catherine Talbot.

Priscilla straightened her shoulders and tugged firmly on Waltham's arm. "Thomas, take me from here."

Waltham turned back to her with a contemplative look on his face. "Take you?" he teased. "Just where is it you wish me to, um, take you?"

Priscilla felt her pulse race. Waltham was the most inventive lover she'd ever known. And if his methods sometimes left marks on her flesh the next day, she didn't mind. Just the thought of his lean body poised above her. Behind her. Ooh.

She leaned toward him. "My place, dear boy," she answered in a whisper.

Waltham's lips curved in a slight smile as he gave her a nod. They departed the throng of theatergoers and went out into the chilly night.

* * *

Catherine sipped delicately from her glass of punch as the four of them discussed the more humorous aspects of the play. James's rich laughter washed over her and she smiled in reaction.

"Paul," Michelle said, drawing Catherine's attention. "Isn't that Waltham?"

Paul and James both turned to the wide glass doors leading out to the street. The thin man accompanying Lady Brookdale did indeed resemble Waltham, but from their particular vantage point, they couldn't be certain.

"It can't be," Catherine said. "He shouldn't be out in society so soon, should he, James?"

James shrugged, a dark look crossing his face. "If Waltham is indeed with Lady Brookdale, I couldn't think of two people more deserving of each other."

"But, if he—"

"There's no telling what that bastard is capable of, Catherine," he growled.

Catherine sensed his anger rising and placed her hand on his arm. He lost his scowl and smiled down at her. James's jealousy where that man was concerned was something they seldom discussed after Lady Joan's funeral. In silent agreement, they spoke no more of Waltham that evening, either.

Once upstairs in their chamber following their return from the theater, James quickly removed his boots and was in the process of taking off his waistcoat and shirt.

"Catherine," he admonished. "Do hurry."

She laughed as she struggled with the hooks on the back of her gown. "You're quite impatient tonight," she teased.

James divested himself of all save his breeches and came up behind her. "Here," he said, working the tiny hooks free. "Let me play lady's maid if just for tonight." He quickly stripped her gown from her as she unpinned her hair.

She turned to face him, wearing nothing but her pearls.

His eyes glittered as they ran over her. "Magnificent," he said, pulling her close.

Catherine reached behind her neck to remove her jewelry, but he halted her movement.

"Leave them on," he gently ordered.

She dropped her hands to her sides, her pulse beating frantically. He traced his fingers over the pearls as he did earlier that evening, this time cupping a breast in each hand. His hands were gentle and insistent, and she reveled in his touch.

"Love me, James." She breathed.

He did.

Chapter 24

When James awoke the next morning, he wasn't surprised to find Catherine still fast asleep. He'd taken her twice before letting her sleep, loving her with his hands and mouth until she'd been as wild for him as he was for her. His eyes fell on the strand of pearls where they lay coiled on the bedstand. In his mind he pictured Catherine as she was last night, her skin as lustrous in the firelight as the pearls. He knew full well that if he continued his train of thought, his delicate, and pregnant, wife would be denied her much-needed rest.

He had quite a few errands to run that day, errands that would more than likely keep him busy well into the afternoon. He quickly penned a note for his wife, leaving the paper on her vanity. He dropped a kiss on her tousled head and strode from the chamber.

When Catherine awoke and read his note, she gasped with bashful delight. As was his custom now, James alluded to the incredible passion they'd shared the previous night. She was touched that he reminded her to take care of herself that day, and to rest when she tired. With a loud, unladylike yawn, she rose and set about her morning toilette.

"Good morning, Giles," she said brightly as she entered the breakfast room.

"Good morning, my lady," the servant answered with a bow. "I trust you slept well?"

Catherine nodded as she helped herself from the sideboard. "Very well, thank you."

After setting down a silver tray carrying a steaming pot of tea, Giles took himself off to see to the running of his master's house.

As Catherine nibbled at the eggs and bacon on her plate, she thought of the few errands she needed to accomplish. It was only a matter of time before she'd need new dresses. She looked down at her still-flat stomach and happily imagined it round with their baby. Having been around Michelle during her time, she knew it was altogether possible for a woman to still look quite pretty while expecting, although she doubted she'd look as radiant as her sister-in-law had. She decided, however, to pick out some lovely fabrics and speak to the seamstress regarding fittings and such.

She also wished to pay a visit to Elizabeth. Her younger sister had not sent as much as a note since she and their father returned to town, and Catherine could scarcely wait to tell the two of them about the baby. James had encouraged her to share their news in his absence, as he didn't wish her to wait until they could visit them together.

She finished her tea and dabbed her mouth with her napkin. She pushed her empty plate aside and sighed contentedly. Her bouts of morning sickness had all but disappeared, much to her relief, and she was able to eat a substantial amount at the morning meal. After asking Giles to have the carriage brought around, she went upstairs and donned her cloak and gloves. It was quite damp and chilly out, and she stepped from one foot to the other as she awaited the carriage. Accepting the driver's hand up into the carriage, she gave the man his instructions and settled back against the cushioned seat.

* * *

Priscilla Brooks alighted her carriage that afternoon, parked farther down the street from Lord Waltham's townhouse in an attempt at discretion. She walked briskly toward his residence. She tugged alternately at her gloves, making certain that the leather cuffs covered the faint red marks on her wrists. Waltham had been demanding the previous evening, much to her delight. He'd been quite insatiable. Shivering from the memory of all they'd shared, she stepped down to cross the street.

She came to an abrupt halt as the front door of Waltham's townhouse opened. Pulling back to stand behind one of the trees that lined the thoroughfare, she watched as a young lady emerged. Her head was all but hidden in the voluminous hood of her cloak and Priscilla narrowed her eyes as she sought to ascertain the girl's identity. The wind suddenly picked up, sweeping back the girl's hood. Dark glossy curls billowed in the breeze as the girl hurriedly recovered her hood. She ducked around the corner, but she wasn't fast enough to prevent Priscilla from seeing her profile.

Catherine Talbot! How dare she go to Waltham when she was the reason Roberts wouldn't come to her! Squaring her shoulders, she hurried to Waltham's door and rapped sharply upon it. The butler, with his customary blank expression, escorted her to his master's study and left her there to cool her heels. Catherine Talbot, that little bitch. She thought to have Waltham *and* Roberts? Not bloody likely.

Waltham soon entered the parlor, wearing his smooth smile. "Priscilla, what a surprise," he said glibly. "I would think that after our night together, you would need your rest."

"Never mind that!" she snapped.

He arched a fair brow at her.

Priscilla pulled off her gloves and wrap and turned back to him, her hands on her hips. "What was that silly chit doing here?" she demanded to know.

"Silly chit?" he repeated. "I don't know to whom you're referring, my dear." He brushed his long fingers over the sleeve of his brown jacket. His clothes looked a tad rumpled, his cheeks a bit ruddy. Had he engaged in love sport with that girl?

Priscilla glared at him. "You know damn well whom I mean, you cur," she spat. "That Talbot girl!"

Waltham laughed low. "Ah, that silly chit."

"You won't dally with her, Thomas," Priscilla warned. "I forbid it."

He lost his smile, the dangerous glint in his eye putting her on her guard. "My dear Lady Brookdale," he began, his tone harsh. "Don't attempt to tell me my business."

Priscilla saw the flash of anger in his pale eyes and chose to ignore its implications. She stepped closer to him. "You won't have her."

His brows arched. "Oh, I haven't had her. Not yet." He licked his lips. "But her skin was delicious." His smile was devilish. "Her release was . . . surprising."

"You . . . you won't have her," she stated again. "Not before Roberts warms my bed."

Waltham let out a grunt of frustration, losing any appearance of control now. "What is it about that scoundrel that so captivates you?" he asked, his voice shaking.

"He's most charming," Priscilla answered. "And a more handsome man I've yet to meet."

Waltham's anger flared to full force. "Roberts, that bastard," he growled. "I'm sick and tired of that man's many attributes falling from the lips of every woman in England!"

"What?" Priscilla asked. "Does another woman have designs on him?"

Waltham shook his head as if to clear it and managed to smile once more at her. He grabbed her roughly by her arms, bringing his lips to her ear. Priscilla gasped as she felt his body pressed so intimately to hers. She could smell the scent of arousal on him, could feel his hardness against her belly.

"Priscilla," he said, his voice as smooth as velvet and as hard as his cock. "You have no claim upon the charming Lord Roberts. Nor any upon my own manly self, for that matter."

Her mouth gaped open at that. She struggled to release herself from his hold on her. "How dare you?" she sputtered, incensed. "If you believe that you can simply use me and—"

Waltham pushed her away from him, letting his eyes run over her. Priscilla's blood raced at the carnal glint in his pale eyes.

"You need to remember your place, my dear," he said, his eyes boring into hers.

Her breath caught as she ran her own eyes over him, his aroused state obvious through his thin tan breeches. She licked her lips in nervous anticipation. "And," she began in a whisper, "precisely where is my place, Thomas?"

Waltham grinned savagely as he began to unbutton his breeches. "Why, on your knees, of course."

* * *

When Catherine returned to the townhouse, she was quite done in. Her errands were not without success, as she'd managed to choose quite a few fabrics and designs during her visit with the seamstress. However when she stopped at her father's home, she'd curiously found her sister absent. Despite the fact that she'd wished for her father and Elizabeth to be together when she told them about the baby, she'd given her happy news to the earl alone. Lord Talbot was so pleased that his blue eyes had fairly shone with it, his strong arms grabbing her up in a great bear hug. She'd laughed and laughed as he'd twirled her about the room.

After stopping to pay a few overdue calls on several friends of hers, Catherine was quite relieved to step back up into the carriage and head for home. When she arrived back at the townhouse, she was famished, as well. Why, she'd eaten a hearty meal with her father only a few hours ago! Perhaps she'd have need of those new dresses sooner rather than later.

She quickly changed into her tea gown and went downstairs to the parlor. She settled herself upon the oversized chair, brushing her hands over her skirt as Giles entered the room with a heavily-laden silver tray. She took note of the fact that Giles had thoughtfully included a pot of honey to accompany her tea and biscuits and smiled cheekily at him.

"Giles," she playfully chided, "you'll spoil me terribly."

"Never, my lady," he returned with a bow. "The viscount would have my head if I didn't anticipate your every whim."

Catherine laughed at that ridiculous and endearing statement and poured herself a cup of tea. Giles bowed once more and left her to her repast.

Still smiling, she chose a biscuit from the tray and reached for the honey pot. The fluffy cookies were delicious on their own, but with the honey drizzled over them, she found them absolutely scrumptious. She happily proceeded to consume her fill of the sweet tea and the delectable biscuits.

"Mmm." She sighed as she finally sat back, one hand pressed to her stomach.

She lifted her other hand to her lips and daintily licked at her fingertips.

"That good, is it?" James said from the doorway, startling her.

"James!" she exclaimed, her eyes flying open.

He walked into the room, a wide smile on his face. "You resemble a cat who's just finished off a bowl of cream, love."

She sat up and grinned at him. "Not quite," she answered. "But I did eat a fair amount of these biscuits. They're heavenly, James. You must try them with the honey."

James joined her on the chair and reached for a biscuit. Her hand stilled his.

"Let me," she said, breaking off a piece of the sweet cookie.

She drizzled honey on the cookie and held it before him. James let her feed him. After a few bites, he gently grasped her wrist and licked the honey from her fingers, his eyes staring into hers. He pressed her hand against his chest.

"Catherine," he said. "I've missed you."

"I've missed you too, James," she said in a whisper.

He brought his lips to hers, letting his tongue slowly explore her mouth. "You taste incredible."

"It's the honey."

"Mmm. Honey." He kissed her again. "And Catherine." He pulled back and smiled, gently patting her stomach. "How do you feel today, love?"

"Fine," she returned, placing her hand over his.

"And you, little mite?" he directed toward her belly.

Catherine smiled. "I'm certain the babe is fine, as well," she said. "And as happily stuffed on biscuits as its mother."

His laughter joined hers as he hugged her gently. They finished their tea and discussed the coming evening's activities.

"I ran into Chester this morning," he told her. "He and Constance returned to town early, as well."

"Oh, we simply must call on them," Catherine said with a smile. "How are they?"

"Constance wasn't with him," he answered. "Apparently, she's been feeling a bit under the weather."

"Oh," she said, "I do hope it's nothing serious."

"Chester didn't appear overly worried. They'd like us to visit them this evening. For cards and other amusements."

"That would be most pleasant, James."

"Eager to make the rounds?" he teased.

"I confess that with Michelle busy helping Paul with their speeches, I've been quite starved of female companionship of late."

James chuckled and held her close. "Then we shall remedy the situation directly. Perhaps then, love," he added with a grin, "you can show your poor husband some much needed companionship."

"Oh, James." She laughed, throwing her arms around his neck.

* * *

That evening at the Earl of Chester's townhouse, the four of them sat in the parlor and played a game of Whist. As play went around the table, they chatted amiably about the coming round of parties as Easter was but two weeks away.

"Constance," Catherine said, looking absently at the cards in her hands. "You've been ill?"

Constance nodded, a small smile on her face. Chester nodded to his wife, an obvious sign of encouragement.

She set her cards down on the table and widened her smile. "Catherine," she began, "Roberts. We're expecting."

Catherine gave an excited squeal and stood, embracing her friend. James shook Chester's hand, pulling the man up out of his chair.

"Oh, Constance!" Catherine gushed. "I'm so happy for you both." She pulled back. "Have you seen Dr. Morgan?"

"Yes," Constance returned. "Our children will be born scarcely a month apart, Catherine."

Catherine blinked and looked at James.

"You know, then?" James asked them. "Morgan told you?"

"No," Chester answered, hiding his grin.

"Then how did you learn of it?" James asked.

Chester barked out a laugh. "You don't believe your brother-in-law is capable of keeping such news a secret, do you?"

"Hardly," James allowed with a chuckle.

Chester crossed the room to retrieve a bottle of brandy. "To celebrate, friend?"

"Indeed. But only the smallest amount for the little hens, please," James added with a grin.

Catherine clicked her tongue at him and sat once more. As the ladies compared symptoms, the gentlemen fairly beamed with pride. Catherine wouldn't think about the love match Constance had made. They were both blessed with attentive husbands and would soon be doubly blessed with their babies.

They called an early end to the evening in deference to the ladies' conditions. After making plans to attend the opera together the next week, James took Catherine home. They readied for bed shortly thereafter.

"James," she said as she sat in front of her vanity, "I'm so happy for Chester and Constance."

"As am I, love," he returned, stepping from the dressing room.

"I'm afraid that Constance still has a few weeks of sickness ahead of her."

She rose and walked over to where he stood beside the bed, magnificent in his satin dressing gown. She had fond memories of this dressing gown. That first night, when she'd gone to him.

He placed his hands upon her shoulders, lightly caressing her through her nightgown and wrapper. "And what of you, sweetheart?" he asked, rubbing her shoulders. "Are you truly fine now?"

She smiled up at him. "Yes, James," she said, untying the belt of her wrapper. "Quite fine."

His eyes glittered as he ran his gaze over her. He placed his hands on her waist, easily spanning the space with his hands.

"You're still so small," he said, his brow slightly furrowed. "Are you certain all is well?"

"I daresay I'll soon swell, husband," she said, moving his hand down to the spot just below her navel. "Do you not feel that?"

James's hand cupped the tiny bulge she showed him. He

looked up at her, a big grin on his face. "Our baby grows," he said in awe.

Catherine simply nodded. He placed a kiss on her belly and she drew in a breath. He came up quickly and captured her lips. She opened for him as she wound her arms around his neck. Holding her beneath her bottom, James turned and fell with her upon the bed. Their nightclothes were soon in a heap on the floor as he placed teasing kisses over every inch of her body. He lavished attention on her sensitive nipples, nipping and licking them thoroughly. She whimpered as he brushed his lips over the sensitive skin on the inside of her thighs. She could feel his hot breath near her very center.

"James, please," she urged, wild for his possession.

"Hmm?" he murmured. "What is it, darling?" he asked between kisses.

She cried out in frustration and pulled his hair. "James . . . !"

He laughed then, a slightly-strangled sound. With a soft groan, he lowered his head and touched his mouth to her.

Catherine nearly screamed as his tongue flicked over her hot flesh, driving her toward ecstasy. Her body arched wildly. When his fingers moved inside of her, she did scream, her climax running through her like a bolt of lightning.

James lifted his head and stroked her as her passion eased. "I love the way you respond to me, Catherine," he rasped.

Before she could ponder that statement, he was inside of her, his thrusts deep. She clung to him as he drove into her, bringing her closer to her second release.

"Please—" she whimpered, her nails raking his back.

James whispered her name in answer, his control rapidly falling away. When she pulled him down to her for a kiss, he lost that control, giving a great shout as he exploded inside of her. Before he could ease his thrusts, she joined him in fulfillment, arching off the bed and taking all of him deep inside of her.

When their breathing eased, he lifted his head. "There's no other woman in the world for me, Catherine."

Sweet words, if a little strange. She opened her eyes, gazing up at him.

"I love you, James," she whispered, stroking his face.

"Catherine," was all he could say. "I . . . Ah, Catherine."

Catherine fancied she could see the love in his beautiful eyes. If he never said the words, it wouldn't matter.

Chapter 25

The week after they learned of Chester and Constance's happy news, Catherine and James prepared for an evening at the opera. She realized with regret that the opera house would no doubt be much more crowded than the theater had been scant weeks earlier. It was nearly Easter, and all and sundry would be returning to town with a vengeance.

Catherine donned a beautiful gown of emerald green, quite sophisticated in design. The low-cut bodice hugged her figure and, while her waist was still small, her breasts were larger than they'd been when she was measured for the dress prior to her wedding. As she had for weeks now, she left off her stays.

She patted the curls piled on top of her head and stood in front of the cheval mirror, worrying over the expanse of flesh fairly threatening to spill over the top of her gown. Taking one of the thick curls, she draped it over her bosom, chagrined that it did nothing to hide her bosom from view. She turned her head as James strode out of the dressing room.

"Oh, James," she said in mild irritation. "What am I going to do?"

"About what, love?" he asked absently, his attention focused on the precise tying of his cravat.

He wore black breeches with a waistcoat of deep blue. After shrugging into his charcoal gray jacket, he crossed to her. As his gaze swept over her, his eyes widened in obvious masculine appreciation.

"My God," he whispered, his eyes on her creamy flesh. "You look . . . You don't think to wear that dress to the opera, do you?"

"Yes." Catherine placed her hands on her hips and cocked her head to the side. "What am I going to do about these?"

He chuckled. "I believe I may have a notion or two."

"James, I'm serious."

"Don't fret about it, love," he said, placing his hands on her waist. "We're sharing a box with Chester, and he's hopelessly devoted to his wife."

"Thankfully, yes," she said with a sigh.

"But know this, wife," James added. "Don't think to step one foot out of that box without me on your arm."

"I wouldn't dream of it," she returned with a cheeky grin. She glanced once more in the mirror. "Perhaps I'll keep on my wrap," she muttered.

Still chuckling, James led her from the room and down to the waiting carriage.

There was quite a crowd of patrons at the opera when they arrived and they hastened to join Chester and Constance in their box. Catherine was thrilled with their position, as it was well above the main floor and she could watch the people milling about below. Their friends were already there and she and Constance immediately began to remark upon all that were in attendance, spying several acquaintances whom they hadn't seen since the conclusion of the previous Season last August.

As the ladies ogled the crowd below, James and Chester spoke of some business matters. It was soon time for the performance to begin. They settled back in their velvet and gilded chairs and watched the stage intently as the musicians tuned their instruments.

The voices of the performers on stage were quite overpowering, and soon Catherine yearned for intermission to arrive. She fidgeted in her seat and let out a soft sigh.

James took her hand in his and leaned over, placing his lips near her ear. "Are you growing tired, sweetheart?"

"What? Oh, no," she answered with a sheepish grin. "Although I do admit that I find the performance quite tiresome."

He laughed out loud at that, causing several heads to turn in their direction. Schooling his expression, he simply nodded.

"There will be a break soon, love," he promised. He flicked his head toward the stage, indicating a very large woman with a very large mouth. "Surely her voice is driving the horses out front quite mad," he added in a whisper.

Catherine bit her lip to keep her own laughter from bubbling out. She shook her head at him and held more tightly to his hand.

Intermission soon arrived, much to Catherine's relief. She stood and stretched with a soft groan. As she looked over at Constance, she found her friend looking a bit pale.

"Constance, are you feeling quite all right?"

Chester's head turned sharply toward his wife. "What is it, love?" he asked worriedly.

Constance managed a weak smile. "I assure you all that I'm just fine, if a little tired," she said easily. "I could do with some refreshment, however."

"Allow me," James said, coming to his feet.

He dropped a kiss on Catherine's cheek and left the box, bound for the refreshment table. Constance turned to find her husband still wearing his worried frown.

"Perhaps we could take a turn about the lobby, husband?" she asked him.

Chester, relief clear on his face, nodded and took his wife's arm. "Catherine, do you care to join us?"

"No thank you, Lord Chester," Catherine answered. "I believe I'll wait here for James's return."

Chester nodded and led his wife from the box. Catherine sat herself down once more and peered over the railing at the crowd below, her eyes searching for James's dark head, his fine figure. Unable to spot him in the throng, she sighed and settled back in her chair.

"Are you having a pleasant evening, Catherine?" a feminine voice asked from beside her.

Catherine turned with a start. "Lady Brookdale!" She recovered herself and managed a small smile. "You startled me."

"So sorry," Priscilla said smoothly. She sat herself in the chair James had recently vacated and brushed her fingers over the sleeve of her brocade gown. "The performance leaves something to be desired, does it not?"

"A bit, yes," Catherine allowed.

Priscilla ran her eyes over Catherine, apparently searching

for some flaw. She gave a false smile. "I believe we share the same taste in a great many endeavors, wouldn't you agree?"

"Hmm?" Catherine murmured. "I'm afraid I don't understand your meaning."

"Oh," Priscilla began with a sly grin, "we both recognize what a simply remarkable man your husband is."

Catherine puzzled over the lady's confounding words. "What does James—?"

"He's so very charming, Catherine," Priscilla cut in. "Ever solicitous." She paused and leaned toward her captive audience. "He knows how to give pleasure, that's certain."

Catherine gasped at what she was intimating. "You can't . . ." she sputtered. "He's never . . ."

Priscilla simply smiled. She turned from her to gaze down at the crowd. Catherine blinked rapidly as she studied the very pretty widow beside her.

"He's quite the gentleman, however," Priscilla went on. "When we were last in contact, he told me that—"

"What?" Catherine cut in, her hands in fists in her lap, her cheeks hot. "You've had no contact with my husband."

Priscilla smiled wickedly. "Oh, haven't I?" she countered. "Why, I sent him a missive just two weeks ago."

Catherine felt ice settle in the pit of her stomach. The note. The one James had stuffed into his pocket, saying he'd take care of it. Could it have been from Lady Brookdale?

"I admit I wanted to renew our, um, relationship," Priscilla went on. "I believe he feels some sort of loyalty to you, however."

Catherine paid scant attention to the irritation in the widow's voice. She felt as if her heart was breaking. James lied about the note from this woman. What else had he lied about? She vaguely noticed when the woman stood, brushing her hands over her skirts.

"I wouldn't count on that loyalty lasting much longer, my dear," she said in parting. "Remember how easily Waltham cast you aside."

With that she swept out of the box, the velvet curtains softly rustling in her wake. When Chester and Constance returned a few moments later, Catherine smiled wanly at them. They obviously noticed something amiss in Catherine's demeanor but said nothing of it, much to her relief. No doubt they thought her fatigued. But when James returned with their drinks soon after, Catherine couldn't meet his gaze.

"Catherine," he said, holding her glass out to her.

She looked up at last, blinking back tears. James saw them and visibly blanched.

"Are you all right?" he asked, setting down the glass to take her hands in his.

She looked up at him, this charming man she loved, this handsome man whose child she carried. The possibility of his betrayal cut her to the bone. Favoring him with the smallest of smiles, she nodded.

"I'm fine, James," she said in a small voice.

James took his seat beside her just as the curtain rose on the second half of the performance.

When the curtain fell for the last time, Constance looked quite done in. Bidding farewell to their friends, Chester gently grasped his wife's elbow and helped her to her feet. They went downstairs to have their carriage brought around.

James had watched Catherine closely throughout the performance and even now his brow was furrowed as he stood and escorted her downstairs to the exit.

An icy rain had begun to fall, causing much delay in bringing the carriages around to the waiting patrons. James retrieved their wraps and led Catherine away from the milling crowd.

"Why don't you wait here, love," he said. "It's frightful out. I'll see to our carriage."

Catherine nodded absently, barely noticing when he thoughtfully draped the cloak over her shoulders. But she couldn't keep her eyes from following his form as he worked his way through the crowd toward the glass doors at the front of the opera house.

James instructed the attendants at the front of the house and turned, intent on swiftly returning to Catherine's side. She looked tired and upset, a combination he found troubling. When he was barely halfway across the room, a slight figure suddenly stepped into his path. His eyes widened in surprise for a moment, quickly narrowing in disgust.

"Lady Brookdale," he said coolly, giving a curt nod.

He made a motion to step around her, but her hand on his arm stilled him.

"I wish to speak to you, Roberts," she said with a sly smile.

"I have nothing to say to you, Priscilla," he replied through clenched teeth. "I have to get back to my wife. Excuse me."

Priscilla's lip curled. "Your loyalty is to be commended, Roberts," she said as he began to step away from her. "I do wonder, however, if your wife holds the same loyalty toward you."

He stopped and turned. "Catherine is ever faithful to me, Priscilla," he said in a low voice. "As you recall, she is a lady of virtue and honor."

Priscilla apparently chose to ignore that thinly-veiled insult. "Then why, dear boy, did she pay a call upon Waltham just last week?"

He grabbed her by her arms. "What?"

She smiled. "She was at Waltham's, Roberts. I saw her there with my own eyes."

He blinked as he tried to absorb what the woman was telling him. "When?" he couldn't help asking. "When did you see her?"

She shrugged her shoulders and tilted her head to the side. "So now you wish to speak to me?" she goaded.

He gave her a quick shake, his eyes flashing. "Tell me, Priscilla," he ground out.

Priscilla closed her eyes for a moment, as if she enjoyed his rough handling. He dropped his hands from her. She opened her eyes and stared up at him, triumphant. "Last Monday," she said with a sneer. "I saw her leaving his townhouse in a most furtive manner. I would know her anywhere, Roberts, with those mousy brown curls of hers, tendrils loose and in a tangle—"

He lowered his face to hers, effectively stopping her tirade. "You won't spread your lies, Priscilla."

She pulled away from him, sniffing in disdain. "I'm not

lying. Waltham admitted she was there, although he wouldn't admit that he dallied with her."

James's stomach clenched. Saying nothing more to the woman, he turned on his heel, bound for his wife.

From her vantage point on the other side of the room, Catherine watched James coming toward her. She'd seen him speak with Priscilla Brookdale and had felt a raw pain tear through her heart. When he'd held her arms, his head bent to hers, she couldn't help but imagine the two of them together, pressed intimately to each other. Had he touched Lady Brookdale the same way he touches her? Suddenly feeling quite ill, she closed her eyes and leaned against the wall for support. James reached her side, causing her eyes to flutter open.

"James," she whispered wearily.

James managed a small smile and led her outside to their carriage.

On the ride back home, Catherine noticed James's discomfiture but didn't remark on it. Surely he was busy thinking about his mistress and her offer to renew their relationship. She closed her eyes once more and leaned her head back against the cushioned seat.

When they arrived home, James helped her down from the carriage, albeit grudgingly. He obviously wanted to put some distance between them so he could ponder Lady Brookdale's offer.

"Go on upstairs, Catherine," he said stiffly. "I'll be up shortly."

She stared at him for a long moment, sensing anger in his tone. She was too tired to ask about it, too hurt by what she'd learned this evening. Nodding slowly in acceptance, she climbed the stairs to their chamber. She changed out of her beautiful gown and set it aside for Annie's attention. The lady's maid would certainly click her tongue at her when she saw the water stains on the hem. She donned her nightgown and sat at her vanity, happy for the cheery fire blazing in the hearth. She was chilled to the bone, but only part of that condition was due to the icy rain pouring down in sheets against the windowpane. She unpinned her hair and pulled her brush through the curls, letting the simple act soothe her.

How easily James could fall back under the pretty widow's charms. Surely it was only a matter of time.

James entered the room, his mood fouler than even thirty minutes earlier. He scowled in her direction, but she had no desire to guess the cause.

"You'll tell me the truth," he said roughly.

She jumped, dropping her brush to clatter on the smooth surface of the vanity. She turned with a jerk. "What are you talking about?"

He slammed the door and crossed to her. "Where did you go last Monday, Catherine?"

She thought for a moment. "Last Monday?" she repeated, confused. "I went out, but I don't see what—"

"Tell me," he cut in, glaring down at her.

She stood and stepped away from him. "I don't know what you wish to know, James," she said, her brow furrowed. "I went to the seamstress and then to my father's."

"Where else?" he asked, grabbing her by the arms.

She lost her confusion in a heartbeat. She narrowed her eyes at him in anger. "Don't think to manhandle me, husband," she said sharply. "Your mistress may prefer that sort of treatment, but I don't!"

"My what?"

She pulled out of his grasp. "Your mistress!" she shouted back. "I know all about you and Lady Brookdale."

He shook his head. "You believe that Priscilla and I—?"

"I know you were together before," she went on. "But you promised you'd honor our marriage vows."

He shook his head as if to clear it. "I've honored our vows, Catherine," he stated. "You can't believe I would play you false." His eyes narrowed. "And what of you, wife? Just what were you doing at Waltham's townhouse last week?"

Her mouth fell open in shock. "I didn't go to Waltham's," she insisted. "Not last week, not ever."

"Priscilla saw you there," he countered, his eyes dark.

"Oh, and you would take the word of your mistress over mine, is that it?"

He grunted in obvious frustration. “She’s not my mistress. How dare you go to another man, with my child inside you.” His eyes flashed silver fire at her. “If it is my child.”

She cracked her palm across his cheek. “I won’t dignify that with a reply,” she said, tears threatening. She turned and pulled on her wrapper. Curling her fingers in toward her stinging palm, she hurried toward the door.

He caught her arm to still her. “And where do you think you’re going?”

She jerked out of his grasp. “I won’t spend the night with a man who thinks so ill of me. You can sleep alone, with thoughts of your mistress to keep you warm.”

With that, she exited the chamber and took herself off to one of the guestrooms and proceeded to sob herself to sleep. Tears, of pain and anger, clung to her lashes as her sobs quieted. How could James think so little of her? And what of all Lady Brookdale had told her? He’d been with the widow, no matter his denial. Would he return to her when Catherine was large with child?

How dare he think she’d involve herself with Waltham! She was too tired to puzzle it through any further tonight. She placed her hand on her stomach, cradling the child within. At least she’d have her child’s love. That would have to be enough.

Sighing in defeat, she let sleep claim her.

* * *

James collapsed into the chair beside the fire and closed his eyes, letting his mind work as he rubbed his cheek. His dainty wife certainly packed a wallop.

His anger cooled quickly, turning to shame as he recalled the pain evident in Catherine’s beautiful eyes. She believed he was involved with Priscilla? That was utterly absurd. He wanted none other than Catherine. He’d never want any other woman. Couldn’t she see that? And what of Waltham? Surely his sweet wife would never betray him. He’d been a bloody fool to give any credence to Priscilla’s ranting.

He suddenly came to his feet and left the chamber, bound

for the guestroom. Finding her in the pretty little room did little to soothe his guilty conscience. Tracks of tears showed silver on Catherine's smooth cheeks, causing guilt to slump his shoulders. Bending over her still sleeping form, he brushed a damp curl away from her brow.

"I was wrong, Catherine," he said softly so as not to wake her. "Forgive me."

He suddenly shivered. He turned toward the hearth and quickly noted that the fire was banked within. He took a few moments to stir it into flames and returned to stand over her. Lord, she was lovely. And he'd never known a sweeter, gentler woman. He smiled when he touched his sore cheek this time. Dropping a kiss on her brow, he took himself back to their chamber.

He stripped off his remaining clothes and settled into the big bed. He buried his face in Catherine's pillow, breathing in her scent. Tomorrow. He'd make amends for his hurtful words tomorrow. And he'd happily accept her forgiveness, and kiss her tears away.

He fell asleep with that final thought, a smile teasing the corner of his mouth.

Chapter 26

James came awake with a start. Catherine stood before the bed, obviously on her way to her dressing room.

"Catherine," he said as he sat up quickly, the sheets falling down to his waist.

Catherine ran her eyes over him and he felt her gaze like a caress.

"Good morning, James," she returned.

"You . . ." He swallowed and tried to ignore the way her dressing gown hugged her beautiful curves. "You slept well?"

"I slept deeply." She met his gaze. "I must commend your attentive staff."

"My staff?"

"Yes. I saw the remnants of that fire. What they must think to find me sleeping in the guest chamber . . ."

"I lit that fire."

He read the relief in her eyes. "Oh. Then I thank you."

James came to his feet, clutching the linens at his waist. "Catherine, we need to talk."

"No." She turned from him. "We have nothing to discuss."

He could only watch as she walked into the dressing room and shut the door with a quiet click.

"Ah, hell."

He saw to his own morning toilette and pulled on his breeches. When Catherine emerged after what seemed like an eternity to him, she was fully clothed, wearing a lovely day dress of soft violet. She stood still when she saw him, her eyes huge. His breath caught. She looked exquisite. But he couldn't ignore the hurt visible in those incredible eyes.

"Catherine," he began.

She held up one slender hand to quiet him. "We have

nothing to discuss, James," she said again. "What was done can't be undone."

She looked so brave to him, standing there completely composed. He swiftly saw through that composure, for she couldn't keep one fat tear from spilling over her lashes to slide slowly down her cheek. Wiping at it in frustration, she ran back into the dressing room.

James closed his eyes and sighed, loud and long. He'd get through to her. She had to listen to him, damn it to hell! Determined, he hurriedly dressed himself and sent her lady's maid in to her.

He waited for her in the breakfast room. She soon sat across from him barely picking at the plate of eggs in front of her. Giles set down a fresh pot of tea and shot a dark look at him, the accusation clear on his face. No doubt Giles knew that he was the cause of her distress. Returning the man's scowl, he silently ordered him to keep his opinions to himself.

Giles sniffed and turned to Catherine. "I brought you more honey, my lady."

James blinked at the pleased expression on Catherine's face. She managed a smiled for Giles today.

"Thank you, Giles," she answered. "I believe this baby has developed quite a fondness for it."

Returning her smile, Giles left the room. James sighed audibly. Catherine kept her eyes downcast as she sipped at her tea. He watched her closely as he started on his meal, chewing mechanically. They ate in silence for long minutes. He took a long drink of tea and set his cup down. Suddenly, he slammed his fist down on the table, causing her to flinch.

Her head snapped up, her eyes round. "James!"

"We need to talk, Catherine," he said again. "This isn't finished."

Catherine dabbed her mouth with her napkin. Her hands shook but whether from hurt or anger, James couldn't guess.

"I've said all I will on the subject," she said evenly. "If you persist in your ill opinion of me, there's nothing I can say to dissuade you."

James grunted in frustration. "Catherine, I don't believe that you—"

"Excuse me, my lord," Giles said from the doorway.

James spat out a curse. "What is it, Giles?" he ground out.

"A missive has just arrived, my lord," he returned, holding the letter out to his master.

James took the note and gave a curt nod. Giles remained in the doorway. James saw it then, the protectiveness in the man's demeanor, and was more than irritated. As if he would ever harm a hair on Catherine's head!

"That will be all, Giles."

After a brief hesitation, the butler took himself off. James tore open the letter and quickly scanned the contents. It was a note reminding him of a meeting he had need to attend, one with his solicitor and that of a neighboring property in Yorkshire. The meeting was unavoidable and would probably take up much of the day. He swore softly, causing Catherine to raise her brow in question.

"I have a meeting today. Some estate business." He folded the note and set it on the table. "Now, where were we? Ah yes, Waltham—"

"That's enough, James!" she snapped. "I don't have to defend myself to you."

James was pleased at the anger in her eyes. At least the hurt was cast aside for a moment. "Catherine, I know you didn't betray me with that bastard."

Her lips pursed. "I wish I could be as certain of your loyalty."

His mouth gaped. "You doubt me? How can you believe I would ever betray you?"

"You've forgotten one very important fact, James. A large difference in our circumstances, if you will."

"Catherine, our marriage vows are sacred."

"You don't love me," she stated.

"What?"

Catherine stood then, her tears running unchecked down her face. "You don't love me."

She held herself ramrod stiff as she quit the room. He heard her footsteps quicken as she hurried away from him. James watched her go, speechless. He didn't love her? My God, he loved her more than his own life!

He'd never told her of his feelings. Coward that he was he'd been afraid of being wrong, afraid of opening himself up for hurt. Cursing himself for every type of fool, he stood and thought to go to her.

No. Catherine would never believe the words now, not given after such an altercation. She'd think them an apology or worse, given out of guilt or pity.

He snapped his fingers as a thought came to him. He'd tell her in a letter. She so loved to get his letters. She still kept all of them, tied in that neat little bundle in her vanity. Thinking himself the cleverest of men, he went into the parlor and penned her a note. In it he told her of his love for her, of his loyalty. He apologized for thinking ill of her for even the briefest moment. He even went so far as to apologize to the babe she carried, professing his love for the little mite. After signing the note, he sealed it with wax and a kiss.

Smiling to himself, James left the note for her on the small writing desk, certain she'd find it as she spent much time in the room doing her needlework and seeing to her correspondence.

He glanced at the clock on the desk and saw it was nearly time for his meeting. He slipped on his greatcoat and called for the carriage.

* * *

Catherine dried her tears as she sat at her vanity, James's many letters held in her hands. She read over them, searching for any indication of his returning the love she felt for him. His passion was evident, that was certain. But apparently a man's heart didn't work at all like a woman's. She thought to discard the letters, to stir up the embers in the fireplace and burn them there. In the last moment, she couldn't. Calling herself every kind of fool, she retied the violet ribbon and set the pile of letters back in their place of honor in the vanity drawer.

After taking her midday meal, Catherine went to the parlor.

The note on the writing desk caught her eye immediately. Slowly, she walked over to where the desk stood. She tentatively reached for the letter, stopping when her fingers were scant inches from it. No. She wouldn't allow James's very charming, very passionate, words to cloud her thinking.

Nodding to herself, she walked away from the desk and grabbed up her needlework, sitting herself down on the settee near the fireplace. She lightly fingered the stitches, her mind working. If she didn't have his love, she didn't want his passion. Ha! Even she couldn't believe that bit of nonsense for a moment. No matter. She loved his child and she loved him. She wouldn't think about the rest. About whether or not he was involved with Lady Brookdale.

Catherine sat there for a long while, her needlework forgotten, her hand on her belly. She lightly caressed the tiny bulge as she slowly cleared her mind of the beautiful widow and the very hateful words she'd said.

Perhaps she should pay a call on her father and sister. She hadn't visited Elizabeth in some time, and now that they had returned to town seeing her family would go a long way toward forgetting her troubles this afternoon.

"My lady," Giles said from the doorway. "You have a visitor."

Catherine turned, her brows arched. "A visitor, Giles?"

"Yes, my lady." Giles stepped farther into the room, his lip curled in disdain. "Lord Waltham would like to speak to you."

"Lord Waltham?" she repeated in surprise. "Surely you're mistaken."

"No, my lady," he insisted. "If you wish me to send him away, I will."

What on earth did Waltham want with her? "Yes, Giles if . . ." Perhaps he could tell her why Lady Brookdale believed that she visited him last week. "No, no." She set her work aside and brushed her hands over her skirts. "You may send him in, Giles."

Giles bowed and left, returning shortly with Waltham on his heels. "Catherine, love," Waltham said, rushing over to where she sat. "Hello, Thomas," she returned politely.

Waltham smiled and sat down beside her, closer than was proper. His pale eyes were bright, intent in their gaze. “Catherine, I need to speak to you,” he said fervently.

Catherine blinked at his vehemence.

“I wanted to . . .” He stopped, flicking a disgruntled look in the butler’s direction.

Giles frowned at him and looked at Catherine. “My lady, is there anything I can get for you and your guest?”

“No thank you, Giles,” she said with a smile. “I’ll call you if we have need of anything.” She thought of something then. “Oh, Giles! Do have the carriage brought around. I would like to visit my father’s townhouse this afternoon.”

“Very well, my lady.” After another long look at Waltham, Giles nodded and took his leave.

“Quite forward.” Waltham sniffed. “Apparently, Roberts doesn’t possess the skills to train his staff properly.”

Catherine clicked her tongue. “Giles has been in the service of the Bradford family since he was a young man, Thomas,” she pointed out. “He’s quite proper. And loyal, as well.”

Waltham shrugged, obviously dismissing the man from his thoughts. “No matter.” He took her hands in his. “Oh, Catherine, how I’ve missed you.”

“Thomas, you shouldn’t speak so.” She pulled away from him, no longer even caring why Lady Brookdale would make up such a story. “Please state your business and go.”

Waltham suddenly hung his head, sobs coming from deep in his throat.

“What is it?” she asked, placing her hand on his arm.

He looked at her, his mouth turned down in misery. “I’m so alone, Catherine,” he said. “I have no one.”

Her brow furrowed at that. He didn’t expect her to think him distraught over poor Joan’s death, did he? She’d seen no indication of his grief at the poor young woman’s funeral.

“Thomas,” she began firmly. “You have many friends here in town. I don’t know what you’re thinking, but I assure you—”

“I need someone special in my life, Catherine,” he told her. “I recognize now that I wasn’t a good husband to Joan,” he went on. “We were never a good match, that’s certain.”

"Joan was a lovely person."

A dark look crossed his face for a split-second. He quickly schooled his expression. "Yes," he allowed. "Everyone has been so wonderful to me since her passing. Why, even Diane Plymouth has been most kind."

"You've seen Diane? No one has heard from her in weeks."

Waltham let his mouth curve in a small smile. The expression seemed almost sly to her, if not for the anguish in his eyes. "Diane was most sympathetic to me, I daresay," he said. "I had hoped to see her in town, but she and her father remain in the country, I imagine."

Catherine stared into the fireplace, her thoughts on Diane. Where was the girl? And when had Waltham seen her last? She barely noticed when Waltham moved even closer to her. He ran his gaze over her, his tongue darting out to wet his lips. She caught the motion and jerked her head to face him.

He grabbed her to him and nuzzled her cheek, her ear. "Oh, Catherine, it's you I need!"

"Thomas, please!" she cried, pushing him away.

Loosening his hold on her, he relented. Waltham cast a furtive glance toward the door. Was he checking for Giles?

"I'm sorry, love," he said, sincerity clear on his face. "I'm beside myself, is all. I so need to speak to a friend." He leaned closer to her. "We were almost married, my dear. I always did care about you. We are friends, aren't we?"

"I suppose so."

His face suddenly brightened. "Come for a ride with me, Catherine," he beseeched. "Around the park, perhaps?"

"Thomas, I am a married woman. That would not be proper."

"Please?" he cajoled. "I need to talk to someone, someone who is kind and compassionate. Someone with a sympathetic ear. You're the only person I can trust."

She chewed her lower lip, contemplating the wisdom in joining him for a ride. Waltham did look quite put out, upset nearly to the breaking point. She'd never seen him look so distraught. And she wasn't exactly feeling warmth toward her husband at the moment. She loved James with all of her heart but knowing that he didn't return her love hurt her unbearably. She looked closely at Waltham. He wore a look of abject misery . . . No. She was still wary of Waltham's past actions. She wouldn't give possible gossip-mongers any credence to Lady Brookdale's lies by spending undue time with him now. Besides, his particular company would do nothing to soothe her state of mind. Only her family could do that.

She came to her feet. "I am off to visit my family, Thomas. I'm afraid I must bid you good day."

He scowled, then gave her a rueful smile. "As you wish, Catherine."

Giles brought Catherine her cloak, all the while eyeing Waltham with open suspicion. "My lady?"

"Lord Waltham was just leaving, Giles," she told him. "Is the carriage ready?"

"Yes," he answered. He stared at Waltham until the man bristled.

Waltham sketched her a quick bow and left the parlor.

Giles then turned to Catherine. "When will you return, my lady?" he asked.

"I shan't be gone long, Giles," she answered. "Please tell Lord Roberts . . ." She remembered that she wasn't even speaking to her husband at present. She wouldn't let Giles speak in her place. "I shan't be gone long," she said once more.

She went out the front door and into the chilly February afternoon. She was shocked to find Waltham waiting for her on the walk, steely intent in his pale eyes.

"We will have our ride, Catherine," he said.

Irritated, she shook her head. "I am going to visit my family, Thomas."

He stepped closer, grasping her elbow tightly. "I shall drive you."

She began to refuse, then she felt the prick of something sharp in her side. She didn't dare breathe lest the blade cut her.

"Thomas." She gasped in alarm.

"Get in my carriage, Catherine."

With no other recourse left to her, she let him escort her into his carriage.

* * *

James returned from his meeting by teatime. He shrugged off his greatcoat in the entryway, a smile on his face. Surely Catherine had read his love note and was ready to welcome him with open arms.

"Catherine!" he called, striding into the parlor. He glanced about the empty room and turned, bound for the stairs. "Catherine?" he called once more, taking the steps two at a time. No doubt he'd find her in their chamber, sitting at her vanity readying for tea. And looking so soft and lovely and . . .

"She isn't here, my lord," Giles said, bringing him up short.

"What?" He descended to the entry and faced Giles. He could read the worry on the man's face. "My God, Giles. What happened?"

"Lady Roberts went to the Earl of Talbot's, my lord." Giles shook his head. "I thought she'd be back by now."

"When was this?"

"Approximately two o'clock, my lord." Giles frowned. "And after Lord Waltham's visit."

"That— Lord Waltham was here?"

"Yes. I called for the carriage as she requested, but she did not take it."

"What do you mean?"

"Lord Waltham was here and they talked for a time, but I believed he left before she did. She must have let him drop her there."

James's mind worked. Catherine went with Waltham? He could scarcely fathom it. What could she be thinking, being alone with that man? Unless she still believed he didn't love her. Would she throw in with him in retaliation?

"No." Catherine loved him. She'd never betray him. "Had my letter meant nothing?"

"My lord?"

"Doesn't she know I love her?" He paced the entry. "I should have made certain she knew, damn it. From the very beginning."

"As you say," Giles offered in a soft voice.

"Ah, God." James stopped his pacing and sat down on the stairs. "How could I be so dense?"

"No, my lord," Giles said. "If she did go in his carriage, it couldn't have been willingly."

"What are you saying?" James asked sharply.

"Lord Waltham was cajoling her, my lord. I had to give him my fiercest stare to get him to vacate the house."

James came to his feet. "Son-of-a-bitch!"

"Indeed."

"Where did he want to take her?"

Giles widened his eyes and fixed an innocent look on his face. "My lord, you don't think I eavesdropped, do you?"

James slanted him a look. "I'm counting on it, Giles."

Giles managed a small smile. "He wanted to take her to the park. To talk," he said. "He said he needed a sympathetic ear."

"That bastard wants something from Catherine," James growled. "And I would wager it has nothing whatsoever to do with her ear."

James grabbed his coat and dashed back out. He'd find her. He'd bloody Waltham's fine straight nose and bring his wife home.

Chapter 27

Catherine grew more nervous by the passing moment. Waltham was nearly silent on their ride, a dark brooding look on his thin aristocratic face. There was no appearance of the knife again, thank goodness. Had she imagined it? There was no imagining the change in his demeanor since leaving her parlor. Gone was the grieving widower. She now saw no sign of the lonely man desperate for a sympathetic ear. The sun was setting, the hour growing late. She was hungry and tired.

Squaring her shoulders, she faced him. "Thomas, take me home."

Waltham turned slowly toward her, a wicked smile on his face. Catherine's breath caught in her throat at the mad glint in his pale blue eyes.

"Oh, no, my love," he said, his eyes sparkling. "You'll be staying with me."

Catherine shook her head in disbelief. She opened her mouth to protest when his actions stilled her. He opened the window and signaled to the driver with two sharp whistles. He closed the window slowly, deliberately, and turned back to her once more.

The carriage gave a lurch in the next moment, quickly changing direction. She glanced out the window. Even in the fading light, she could see they were riding away from the park, away from the main thoroughfares. Away from James.

"No." She hugged herself. "God, no."

Waltham flashed his knife and an ugly smile, an expression she'd never before seen on his face.

"Oh, yes, Catherine," he countered, reaching for her. "Oh, yes."

*   *   *

Where the devil was she? Yes, the man would drive her to her family's townhouse. But surely only after pouring his wounded heart out to her in the park. Taking his fastest horse, James had raced to Hyde Park. He'd ridden nearly every trail, even the ones too narrow for a carriage to pass. There was no sign of them. He stopped at the Earl of Talbot's townhouse but was shocked to learn that neither Catherine's father nor Elizabeth had seen her that afternoon. He'd somehow managed to contain his worry at that discovery and left them. Now he rode on to Waltham's townhouse, his anger and concern mounting. If that bastard dared to touch her . . . He couldn't finish the thought, a sharp pain twisting through his gut.

He reined in his horse and bounded up the steps to the front door. Pounding on the door, he demanded entry.

"Where's your master?" he barked at the servant who had the misfortune of answering the summons.

"My lord!" the slight man said, his eyes wide. "Lord Waltham isn't home at present."

James closed his eyes and took a deep breath, reining in his anger. "When do you anticipate his return?" he asked in a strained voice.

The butler blinked at that. "Why we don't, my lord," he told him. "We understand he'll be gone for nearly a fortnight."

The truth settled on James in an instant. Waltham had Catherine and didn't plan on bringing her back. "Bastard," James growled, taking his leave.

He mounted his horse once more and rode home to question Giles more closely. Perhaps the man had heard something else. Something that would give James a clue as to where Waltham had taken her. Forcing himself as well as his horse to a slower pace, he made his way back home.

He questioned Giles again, learning no more than what he had already. He waved the worried man out of the parlor and paced, frustrated and angrier than he could have imagined. Damn Waltham to hell for taking advantage of Catherine's kind heart! No doubt he'd played the poor widower to the hilt.

He noticed the letter then, still resting on the writing desk.

He grabbed it up and saw immediately that it was still sealed. She hadn't even opened it. He sank down into the chair behind the desk. She hadn't read his heartfelt words so carefully penned upon the paper.

"Ah, hell. She doesn't know." He covered his face with his hands. "She doesn't know."

A strangled cry tore from his throat.

* * *

Inside his carriage, Waltham clutched at Catherine, tearing her cloak from her. She struggled in his arms until he forced her against the interior wall of the carriage.

"You should have been mine, Catherine." He ran his lips over her cheek. "You will be mine," he added, bringing his mouth to hers.

Catherine gagged as his tongue probed her mouth, her stomach churning. Waltham slipped his hand into the bodice of her dress, squeezing painfully at her breast.

He sheathed the knife and rubbed himself against her. "Ah, Catherine," he moaned. "You're incredible."

His caresses became rougher. Catherine struggled with renewed vigor. "Thomas, stop." She gasped. "You're hurting me!"

Waltham didn't stop, didn't loosen his hold on her. He reached behind her and unhooked her dress. He tugged sharply, ripping the dress at the shoulder.

"Stop it!" she cried, flailing at him with her fists. "Stop it, Thomas!"

He laughed and grabbed her wrists, pinning them to her sides. She was gasping for breath, her chest heaving. Waltham stared at her breasts, nearly visible through her thin chemise. "No stays. Naughty girl." He bent his head and bit her, right above her nipple, nearly drawing blood. Catherine cried out in pain, twisting away from him.

"That's it, love." His breath came fast. "Struggle. Cry out. God, yes . . ."

Waltham ran his hand over the front of her, reaching up

under her skirts. He froze as his hand brushed her slightly-swollen abdomen.

"What the devil—?" he muttered. He shot her a look of shock. "You're carrying a brat?"

Catherine was too frightened to answer. Would he leave her alone if he knew she was expecting? Or would it enrage him further? He'd loosened his hold in his surprise and she managed to pull away from him.

"Yes," she said proudly. "I'm carrying my husband's child."

She watched as Waltham's shock turned swiftly to anger.

"You bitch!" He raised his hand and struck her across the face, hard. Her head snapped back, striking the side of the carriage. Blinking away stars, she sought to collect her wits. She licked her lip and tasted her blood there. She furtively cast a glance at him. He muttered to himself, obviously torn.

"That damn Roberts," Waltham ground out. "The rogue has everything." He suddenly looked at her once more, an evil smile twisting his features. "But he'll no longer have you," he promised. "Not you or that brat you carry."

Catherine felt her blood run cold as he ran his eyes over her, staring at her midsection. Her hands quickly covered her stomach, protecting the tiny being within.

Snorting in disgust, he picked up her cloak and threw it at her. "Cover yourself," he growled. "I won't take you now."

Her relief was visible and only angered him further.

"Oh, don't fret about it, love," he taunted. "I'll take you. But not until I have enough whiskey in me to forget you carry Roberts's brat in your belly."

Shivering in fear, Catherine pulled the cloak tightly around her.

* * *

James sat in the big chair near the fire, his brow furrowed. His clothes were rumpled, his cravat twisted. He sighed aloud and raked his fingers through his hair in frustration. It had been hours since she'd left. The darkness pressing against the windows showed him that. Where the devil was she? She hadn't read the letter. She still believed he didn't love her. What if he never saw her again? She'd never know how much she meant to him. So sweetly she'd asked him for his love and he couldn't open his heart fully to her. "Fool."

Suddenly, a vision came to him. His muddled mind could barely make it out, but there she was, the girl from his long-ago dreams. The sweet angel asking for his love. My God. It was Catherine all along! He closed his eyes and leaned his head back.

"My lord," Giles's voice reached him.

James looked up, forcing his eyes open. "What is it, Giles?"

The butler started at his master's strange appearance, shaking his head in compassion.

"Lords Leed and Chester to see you, my lord."

James sighed once more. "Send them in."

Paul strode into the room, Chester close behind.

"What on earth is troubling Giles?" Paul asked. "He looks as though he swallowed a lemon." His gaze settled on James then. "My God, man. What the devil happened to you?"

"He's got her, Leed," James answered. "He's got Catherine."

Chester and Paul exchanged a look.

"Roberts," Chester began, "what are you talking about?"

"Waltham." James rubbed his hands over his face and looked closely at his friends. "The bastard has Catherine."

"No," Chester whispered.

James nodded and slowly came to his feet. "He came here and cajoled her into going for a ride," he explained, his anger resurfacing. "He tricked her and took her from me and I don't know where the devil she is!"

"Easy, brother," Paul soothed, placing his hand on James's shoulder.

"When was this, Roberts?" Chester asked.

"I wager it was around two o'clock." James shrugged off Paul's hand and began to pace the room. "Waltham made like he was leaving, but he must have waited for her on the walk."

"That's nearly five hours ago," Paul mused aloud.

"Don't you think I know that?" James cut in angrily. "They

could be anywhere by now. Damn him to hell!"

"Do you think he'd harm her, Roberts?" Chester asked.

James thought for a moment, thought about Joan's mysterious death, and shuddered. He gave a small shake of his head in denial. "No, I . . . I don't know."

"I do hope Catherine keeps her head about her," Paul said. "She can be quite silly at times."

"No, Leed," James said. "You're wrong about Catherine. She's no longer a young girl. She's an intelligent woman. And sweet and kind and . . . Ah, God. What would I do without her?" he finished in a groan.

Paul looked at James closely then. "You love her."

"Yes, I love her! Only, bloody fool that I am, I never told her that."

Paul placed his hand on his shoulder once more. "We will find her," he said in a firm voice.

The conviction in Catherine's brother's voice reached through to James. He looked up then, hope blossoming in his chest.

* * *

Catherine shivered in the cold room, only one candle lighting the space. The room was damp and dark and smelled of mold and whiskey and some other odors she didn't wish to identify. From the sounds filtering up from the street below, she ascertained that Waltham had taken her to the waterfront. She'd smelled the brackish water when they'd alighted the carriage, and now she could hear the raucous laughter of drunken sailors as they sang a ditty about women and how they were as fickle as the sea. A crash came, surely a bottle breaking on the cobblestone street. Angry shouts could be heard as a fight erupted. Catherine was almost glad to be tucked into the filthy room, safe at least from the hooligans downstairs.

Waltham had all but thrown her into the room, leaving immediately on some unknown errand. He'd locked the door behind him, dashing any hope she had of escape. She now huddled deep within her cloak, perched on the edge of the moldy mattress in the corner of the room. Her mind raced as she imagined the horrible deeds Waltham might do to her when he returned. He hadn't touched her again, not since learning she was with child. But she knew that would only give her a temporary reprieve from his sadistic appetites. The injury to her breast still pained her. She hadn't forgotten about that wicked-looking knife of his, either. Lord, could she have been more wrong in her judgment?

She thought of Joan then, of the fear in the girl's eyes when last they spoke. Surely Waltham had abused her. Catherine felt guilt wash over her. But what could she have done about it? A woman was her husband's property to do with as he wished. Thank God all men were not like Waltham.

She thought of James then, of his gentleness and his passion, and felt a pain settle in her heart. Would she ever see him again? Would he care enough about her to come looking for her? And what of their baby?

Her hand went to her belly, to the child sleeping within. Waltham could do whatever evil deeds he wished to her, as long as no harm came to her baby. If he so much as threatened harm to the child, she'd fight him to the death.

Catherine cringed as the door opened and slammed against the thin wall with a bang. She turned her eyes toward the doorway. Waltham entered the room, a bit unsteady in his gait. He ran his eyes over her, licking his lips.

"Hello, Catherine my love," he slurred. He slammed the door shut. "Did you miss me?"

She wisely held her tongue. He clutched a whiskey bottle in his hand, and it was obvious to her that it wasn't his first of the evening. His hair was tousled, his clothes disheveled. His color was high. Was he completely sotted? Or just drunk enough to forget that she carried a child? She shivered as she imagined what he'd do to her if the latter were true.

He came closer. "Ah, you look lovely there in the candlelight."

She shrank back from him. He blinked at her reaction, then threw his head back and laughed. She shivered at the ugly sound.

"You're afraid of me, aren't you, love?" he taunted. "Good.

That tells me you're not as silly as I thought you were."

"Let me go, Thomas," she asked in a soft but firm voice.

"No!" he shouted. "You're mine now, and mine you will stay."

Waltham took a long drink from the bottle, wiping his mouth with his sleeve when he finished. He walked to the window, apparently dismissing Catherine from his thoughts. She watched him warily as he consumed more of the whiskey.

"How could you leave me?" he asked, still staring out the window. He turned back to her, a haunted look in his eyes. "How could you leave me, Beatrice?"

Catherine blinked in surprise. He stared at her for a long moment, his eyes finally clearing. Rubbing a hand over his face, he groaned.

"Who's Beatrice?" Catherine couldn't help asking.

"Don't speak her name!" Waltham yelled, slamming his fist down on the scarred table beside the window.

Catherine flinched as if he struck her. He drank more of the whiskey, his eyes never leaving her face.

"You're quite like her in looks," he said absently. "I never noticed that before. More fool me."

She kept silent, her eyes huge as she watched him pace about the small room. He stopped in front of the table, setting the bottle down deliberately so as not to spill it. It took a great deal of effort on his part, as his hands were fairly shaking. He turned back to Catherine, that haunted look once more in his eyes.

"Beatrice," he said in a raw whisper that sent chills down Catherine's spine. "Ah, Beatrice . . ."

He suddenly lunged at her, pushing her flat on her back upon the dirty mattress. She struggled as he ripped the cloak from her, her torn dress leaving her exposed and vulnerable.

"Thomas, please," she begged. "Don't do this!"

"Beatrice, my love," he murmured, running his hands over her.

Waltham stretched out on top of her, settling himself between her legs. Groaning, he rubbed himself against her.

Catherine pushed at his shoulders, tears coursing down her

cheeks. "Thomas, no," she sobbed as his hands found her breasts, pawing and squeezing.

He unbuttoned his breeches, flipping her skirts up out of his way. She brought her knee to his groin but only just grazed him. He growled and slapped her, hard.

"Bitch!" he spat. "You'll have me, Beatrice. Even if I have to force you as before!"

Catherine realized that he still saw her as Beatrice, whomever that poor girl was. He released his manhood, closing his eyes as he held himself.

Catherine increased her struggles, almost sick with fear. "No, no, no. I'm not Beatrice!"

Waltham held himself above her, his eyes clearing. "Catherine," he said to himself. He shook his head. "God, you're my Catherine."

In the next moment, he crushed his mouth to hers. She arched up off the bed, trying in vain to throw him off of her.

"Let me go, Thomas!" She gasped as he moved his lips to her throat. "I'm not yours. I'm carrying another man's baby!"

That stopped him. He pulled back, a dark look on his face. "Roberts, that bastard!" he growled, pushing away from her. "What the devil is the appeal of that scoundrel?"

Waltham sat at the edge of the bed, his head in his hands. Catherine used those moments to fix her dress as best she could, managing to fasten a few of the hooks in the back. She watched him as he stood awkwardly and buttoned his breeches with shaking fingers.

He picked up the bottle once more. "She was in love with him, too."

Catherine said nothing as he resumed his pacing.

Chapter 28

James, accompanied by Paul and Chester, arrived at the Earl of Talbot's townhouse, once more. James knew Catherine's father had the right to know what was going on. And, certain that he had dealings with Waltham before Catherine's betrothal to the man, James fervently hoped he could advise them of any other properties Waltham had in his possession. Surely the scoundrel spirited her away to a location far from town. The four gentlemen now stood in the Earl of Talbot's parlor, the air thick with tension.

"He took her?" the earl asked, incredulous. "The devil, you say!"

James nodded. "Sir, we need to know what other properties, if any, Waltham keeps in town."

"Properties?" the older man mused aloud. "I don't believe the blackguard has any others here in town."

James's shoulders slumped. "Ah, hell," he muttered. "He took her to Westmorland."

James referred to the location of Waltham's country home, quite far from London. He turned to exit, stilled by Chester's hand on his arm. He looked at the blond man in question.

"I don't believe he'd take her to Waltham Manor," Chester pointed out as Paul nodded in agreement. "You could track him there too easily."

"Yes, yes. But where then, Chester?" he asked in irritation. "Where the devil has he taken her?"

Paul opened his mouth to make a suggestion just as Elizabeth entered the parlor. The men exchanged a look, silently agreeing not to tell the girl of her sister's disappearance.

"Where can she be?" Elizabeth wailed.

James looked at her closely, his heart pounding. “Who, Elizabeth?”

“Why Diane Plymouth,” she answered quickly. “I still haven’t heard from her.”

The earl rolled his eyes. “Elizabeth, dear. You’ve been going on about that girl for weeks now. I’m quite certain that she’ll return to town shortly.”

“No one has heard from her?” Chester asked.

James looked at him sharply, a dark thought flitting through his mind. “Elizabeth,” he said, coming to stand in front of the girl. “When did you hear from her last?”

“Lord Roberts, I haven’t heard from Diane since before Christmas,” she answered. “Not since soon after she returned from Lady Joan’s funeral. Waltham said—” She snapped her mouth shut.

“Waltham?” James asked, his eyes narrowed.

“Yes,” she said guiltily.

“What?” James asked, confused. “What about Waltham, Elizabeth?”

Catherine’s sister pulled back, apparently startled by the intensity in his gaze.

Paul stepped over to her, placing his hand on her arm. “Elizabeth,” he began in a low voice, “what of Waltham?”

Elizabeth clutched her hands in front of her, her brows drawn together. “I went to Lord Waltham’s townhouse,” she admitted in a small voice.

“You what!?” Paul shouted.

“He was the last one to see her,” she rushed out. “I thought he could tell me where she was. If something had happened to her.”

James swore an oath, causing the others to turn to him. “It was you,” he said to Elizabeth. “Ah, I’m a fool.”

“What are you talking about, Roberts?” Chester asked.

James shook his head at his own folly. “Lady Brookdale told me she saw Catherine leaving Waltham’s townhouse last Monday.” He turned back to Elizabeth. “But it was you, wasn’t it, Elizabeth?”

“Yes,” she answered in a small voice. “I had to know about Diane,” she said tearfully. “I had to know!”

James stepped in front of her, protecting her from the dark scowl on her brother's face. He placed his hands on her shoulders. "It's all right, Elizabeth," he soothed. "Why don't you go upstairs and ready for dinner?"

Elizabeth nodded vigorously and ran from the room.

"How could she be so foolish?" Paul grumbled.

"No more foolish than I've been," James put in. "Priscilla told me she saw Catherine leaving Waltham's and I believed her."

"And what, precisely, was Priscilla doing at Waltham's?" Chester asked.

"I don't know," James countered. "Perhaps she and Waltham—"

The earl's butler came to the doorway at that moment. After a quick bow to his master, he turned swiftly to the man's son-in-law. "Lord Kanewood for you, Lord Roberts," he said.

"What the devil is Kane doing here?" James asked Paul.

Paul's face mirrored his surprise. He shrugged his shoulders in answer.

"Roberts, thank God I've found you," Geoffrey said as he strode into the room.

James regarded Geoffrey closely. His hair was tousled, his cravat askew.

"What is it, Kane?" Paul asked him. "I thought you would remain in the country for at least a fortnight."

Geoffrey shook his head. "I returned to town as fast as I could, Leed." He turned again to James. "I went to your house, Roberts, and your butler told me you came here."

"Thank the Lord for Giles's big ears," James said.

"What is it, man?" Chester asked. "You look as if you have the devil chasing you."

"A devil, indeed," Geoffrey said ominously. "Diane Plymouth has been found."

"Found?" Paul repeated. "What do you mean, 'found?' When?"

"Weeks ago, I'm afraid," he answered. "Apparently, Lord Henry was too upset to let anyone see her."

"Upset?" James's stomach clenched. "Why was he upset?"

Geoffrey's lip curled in distaste. "His daughter had been raped, Roberts," he said. "Raped and beaten."

"My God!" James said. "Is she all right?"

Geoffrey shrugged. "As well as can be expected," he said. "Rebecca and my mother are looking after her. The girl was uncommunicative. Nearly catatonic. She wouldn't say who hurt her. She would only say it was a gentleman."

James shook his head in denial, backing away from his friends. Please, God. Don't let it have been Waltham.

"Rebecca was finally able to get the truth out of her, bless her kind heart," Geoffrey went on. "Diane named her attacker just this morning."

"Who was it?" James asked haltingly.

Geoffrey took a deep breath and expelled it. "Waltham."

"No," James murmured. "No. God, no!" He sank into a chair, burying his face in his hands.

"What is it?" Geoffrey asked.

Paul quickly told him about Catherine's disappearance, of Waltham's abduction.

"And there's no sign of them?" Geoffrey asked.

Chester shook his head.

James recovered himself and stood, his hands in fists. "If that bastard harms so much as one hair on Catherine's head, I'll kill him with my bare hands," he ground out.

"Roberts," Chester said suddenly. "You started to say something earlier. Something about Lady Brookdale?"

"What?" James asked, blinking rapidly. "Yes. Priscilla informed me that she saw Catherine at Waltham's house. Perhaps she herself is involved with that reprobate."

Paul straightened. "Well, gentlemen," he said. "Perhaps we should pay a call on the bitch."

The gentlemen filed out of the room.

The Earl of Talbot halted James's progress with a hand on his shoulder, an anguished look in his eyes. "You'll find her, son. I know you will."

James nodded, his throat tight. Saying nothing in return, he joined his friends, bound for Lady Brookdale's home.

* * *

Waltham paced the small waterfront room, the nearly empty whiskey bottle clutched in his hand. Catherine followed him with her eyes. Long minutes had passed since his attack there in the room, and she was ever wary of another one. He'd had a tray brought up from downstairs for her dinner, but the only food palatable upon it was a few crusts of bread. Catherine chewed the stale bread slowly as she kept her eyes on her captor.

"She was mine," Waltham grumbled. "It was all set."

Catherine knew he spoke of Beatrice, once more. She shrank back against the bed rail and tried to keep still. It didn't matter really, for Waltham's mind wasn't in the little room. She guessed he was firmly in the past. In the time when Beatrice had been his.

"We were cousins, she and I," he went on. "Second cousins. Our families approved of the match, a feat in and of itself, considering her fortune far exceeded my own. She was so beautiful, was my Beatrice." He turned to Catherine then. "And she loved me, Catherine. Me!"

He took another pull on the bottle, then slammed it back on the scarred table. Raking his long fingers through his hair, he tried to collect his thoughts.

"We went to London, a mistake to be sure," he went on. "But she wanted a Season, and I could refuse her nothing. More fool me, for she took to society and it to her. Men began to call upon her. Men with more than matrimony on their minds, I was certain. I will say my little dove wasn't enamored of any of her gentlemen callers. Oh, no. She'd set her cap on a different gentleman altogether." He cast a baleful glance in Catherine's direction. "Can you wager a guess as to who it was that stole my Beatrice's heart?"

Catherine shook her head, mute.

"No?" He sneered. "Why, Beatrice found herself enamored of the ever-charming, ever-dashing Viscount Roberts! He was so handsome, she'd tell me. And he danced divinely, she'd gush. How I wanted to strangle him for dallying with her feelings."

"No, Thomas," Catherine cut in. "You're wrong. James would never—"

"Keep silent!" Waltham shouted. "I'm telling this story. You will sit there and hold your tongue!"

Catherine froze and did as he ordered.

He gave a satisfied nod and resumed his tale. "This was four years ago, you see, and I wasn't the established gentleman you see before you. I didn't have Joan's money as yet and, while the ladies found me pleasing, I didn't have much to recommend myself. Nevertheless," he sighed, warming once more to his tale, "our betrothal was to be announced before the Season was concluded. Beatrice, however, had other intentions, which would be made known to me very soon after. She intended to wed Roberts, she told me. He was the only man she wanted. The only man she'd have as a husband or a lover."

Waltham's coolly handsome face wore an ugly sneer as the memory rankled. "Thinking to change her mind, I took her for a ride in my father's carriage. Much like our pleasant ride of this afternoon, Catherine," he interjected.

Catherine's stomach clenched as she imagined the horrid story to follow. "Thomas, you don't have to tell me anymore," she said shakily, knowing she'd barely be able to withstand the tale.

"Oh, you will hear all of it, my love," he jeered. "You will see what your husband's charm had wrought."

Waltham returned to the window, staring out into the darkness as the ugly truth spilled from his lips. "I asked her to marry me," he said in a low voice. "I begged her to put aside any ideas she had of marrying that rogue. She laughed at me, Catherine. She told me that she'd never be mine." He turned back to Catherine, a glint in his eye. "So I took her. I took her there in the carriage. Oh, she fought me at first, for she was a young lady of virtue. But once my fists convinced her of what my words couldn't, she was mine." He closed his eyes, lost in the memory. "God, she was so sweet."

Catherine ran to the chamber pot, barely making it before bringing up the bit of bread she'd only just consumed.

Waltham laughed softly at her distress. "Did I offend your delicate nature, my love?" he taunted. "No matter. You'll hear the rest of it."

She wiped her mouth and stood on shaking legs. Sinking back down onto the lumpy mattress, she closed her eyes and sighed. "Thomas, I don't know what any of this has to do with James."

"It has everything to do with that bastard!" Waltham raged. "If he hadn't stolen her heart, I wouldn't have had to force myself on my delicate angel."

She couldn't argue with such perverse logic. She held her tongue once more as he finished his dark tale.

"It was too much for her," he said at last, his voice a low croak. "She fell into a stupor, showing no reaction to anything or anyone except for myself. Whenever I entered her chamber, she screamed and screamed. She got hold of a knife somehow . . . The servants were all questioned afterward as to how one made its way into her chamber." He looked at Catherine, once more. "She took her own life, Catherine. She's gone from me and it's all the fault of that charming rogue you married!"

Catherine sobbed quietly, her heart clenching for what the poor girl must have endured.

"He'll learn. Damn him to hell," he muttered, once more brandishing his own knife. "Roberts will learn what it feels like to lose someone he loves!"

She shook her head then, the shadow of a smile curving her lips as she stared up at him. "You're wrong, Thomas," she said softly. "James doesn't love me—you said so yourself, remember?" She wanted to keep him talking.

Waltham snorted. "*Foolish girl.* I lied! He loves you, Catherine," he spat. "I've seen him with you. You can't tell me he doesn't love you. He worships the ground you walk on, for God's sake!"

Saying no more, he set his knife beside his bottle and drank what little was left inside.

Catherine sat there, stunned as the truth settled on her. How could she not have seen it before? She *had* been a foolish girl allowing herself to be easily swayed by the spiteful words of others. She should have had more faith. In herself and in her husband. Her dear, wonderful James. Suddenly a vision came to her, an image from a long-ago dream. It was him. James was her dream lover, the wonderful man promising to protect her and cherish her forever. *Oh, please find me, James!*

Chapter 29

They arrived at Lady Brookdale's townhouse and James raced up the steps to the front door. The woman's butler showed them into the parlor, where they were left waiting. After ten minutes had passed, minutes that felt like hours to James, Priscilla breezed into the room. She blinked to see the four gentlemen standing there in her parlor.

Turning to her favorite, she smiled coyly. "Lord Roberts. To what do I owe this unexpected visit?"

"Where is he, Priscilla?" James asked without preamble.

Priscilla lost her smile as his eyes bore into hers. She looked from one gentleman to another. She swallowed with an audible gulp. "I don't know who you're—"

"Waltham, Lady Brookdale," Paul cut in. "Where is Waltham?"

She looked down and brushed her hands over her skirts. "Why, I haven't spoken to Thomas since last evening," she insisted, still not meeting his gaze.

James grabbed her by her arms. "Don't lie to me, Priscilla!" he ground out. "You will tell me where that son-of-a-bitch took her!"

"He's with her, isn't he?" Her lovely mouth twisted into a very ugly smirk. "He's with that Talbot trollop!"

James gave her a hard shake. "You won't speak of Catherine that way!"

With more than a little bit of force, Chester pulled him away from Priscilla. "Easy, man."

James raked his fingers through his hair in acute frustration.

Chester turned back to the widow, his brown eyes intent. "Lady Brookdale, we know you're involved with Lord Waltham. We need you to tell us if he keeps another property here in town."

Priscilla glared at James and turned back to the Earl of Chester. “He has no other property, save in Westmorland.”

James took a deep breath to calm his ire. “Priscilla, we know he has Catherine. We need to know if there’s any place he would take her.”

“I told him not to dally with her,” she said. “But he was adamant, the fool!”

The gentlemen exchanged puzzled glances.

Geoffrey cleared his throat. They all knew he could barely stand to be in her company after her involvement with his late brother. “Lady Brookdale,” he said sharply, drawing her attention. “You’re not aware of the foul deeds of which the man is capable.”

Priscilla scoffed at that. “You’re wrong in your assumptions, Lord Kanewood,” she said smugly. “Lord Waltham and I . . .” She suddenly smiled slyly. “Well, a lady doesn’t speak of such matters. But capable of foul deeds? No. You’re quite mistaken.”

James rolled his eyes, his patience stretched to the breaking point. “He’s a despicable bastard, Priscilla,” he growled. “A blackguard, a despoiler of young women, a—”

“No!” Priscilla cut in. “Thomas would never—”

“He raped Diane Plymouth,” Geoffrey said. “My God, he beat her and left her for dead!”

Priscilla gasped, her eyes wide. She shook her head in shock.

Paul stepped in front of her and regarded her closely. “You seem quite astounded.”

“Of . . . of course.” She gasped.

“We need to find him, Lady Brookdale,” Paul said firmly. “He has my sister. She’s with child, and we’re frantic with worry about her.”

Priscilla raised a shaking hand to her face and told them of the place Waltham liked to keep available to him, a disreputable room down by the waterfront.

“The waterfront?” James questioned her.

“H-he . . .” she explained unsteadily, “he told me he enjoys mixing with that rabble.”

James nodded. “Thank you, Priscilla.”

The four of them left her home, bound for the inn at the waterfront.

* * *

Catherine watched Waltham closely, her fear having increased tenfold over what it was when he'd first brought her to this place. He muttered to himself as he stalked about the small room, the now empty whiskey bottle clutched in his hand.

"He'll learn," he said, more to himself than to her. "The bastard will learn. And then he'll be all alone, with nothing but his charm to warm his bed."

Catherine took a deep breath, thinking to try a new tactic. "Thomas," she began in a soothing voice. "Please let me go. I know you're not a bad man. You've been hurt."

"Don't give me your pity, Catherine," he said sharply. "You were to be mine! Instead, you gave yourself to that scoundrel. I'll never understand you women and your constant fawning over that man. Even Diane Plymouth sang his praises to me, the foolish chit."

"Diane?" Catherine murmured.

His lip curled, showing his teeth in a snarl. "She couldn't stop talking about him, Catherine. Even when we were together after Joan's funeral, she went on and on about your dashing husband and how you were the luckiest woman to find someone like him to love. It sickened me. But I silenced her for a while. Now the poor girl is soiled. No longer desirable. And I lay the blame precisely at Roberts's feet!"

Catherine could make no sense of his ranting. What had he done to Diane? And how could he blame James for it all? Biting back the denial she longed to scream at him, she watched him closely.

"Your sister came to me, you know," he went on. "On the pretense of looking for Diane." That slick smile was on his face once more. "She's more than passable, your sister. Quite a fine piece."

Catherine's heart stilled. "You didn't, Thomas. Please tell me you didn't."

He blinked. "What? No. She's not quite . . . ripe enough for me."

She nearly swooned with relief. "It . . . it must have been Elizabeth Lady Brookdale saw, then."

"Indeed? I'd thought dear Priscilla's jealousy quite misplaced." He waved a hand. "I never should have married Joan." His lips curled. "Joan, that stupid cow. Her inheritance was little reward for my suffering her company for over a year." He looked at Catherine, his brows arched. "It was quite simple to rid myself of her, I must say. Just a bit of something in the tea she drank each and every afternoon and she soon fell ill."

"No." Catherine breathed. "You didn't. You couldn't!"

Waltham laughed, the sound echoing in the small space. "Oh, yes," he returned. "Pity she didn't succumb earlier, my love. For you would be married to me instead of Roberts."

Catherine squared her shoulders, her hands in fists in her lap. "You're wrong, Thomas. I love James, not you. I never would have married you."

Waltham lost his smile, his expression chilling her to her toes. "You won't speak to me in such a manner," he said through clenched teeth. "You will hold your tongue or I'll make our mating most difficult."

Her bravado soon fled and she sought to calm him. "I'm truly sorry, Thomas." She shrank back against the bed rail.

He tipped the bottle to his lips once more, finding naught but a drop of the liquor inside. "Damn it to hell!" He threw the bottle against the wall. The bottle shattered with a resounding crash. Catherine shivered, pulling her cloak around her once more. She watched as he stalked her, lust burning brightly in his pale eyes.

"I'll take you now, Catherine," he said in a low voice. "I'll take you despite that brat in your belly." He came down on her, tossing her cloak aside and grabbing her roughly.

She began to sob, pushing against him with all her strength. "No!"

"Yes," he said, grabbing her hands and pulling them over her head. His fingers dug into her flesh. He ran his lips over her cheek, her neck. "You'll scream with the pleasure I give you, Catherine," he rasped. "I admit that my taking of your fair person will be unlike any you've known before." He pulled back and smiled at her. "I daresay by this time tomorrow, that brat in your belly will be but a memory."

Catherine reached her breaking point in that moment. She fought him, thrashing about to throw him off of her. She kicked furiously with her legs, letting loose with a bloodcurdling scream.

He smacked her across the face. "Shut your mouth!"

Her cut lip split once more, her blood flowing anew. "No, no, no, no!" She screamed again.

Waltham balled his hand into a fist and struck her again, his blow landing squarely below her left eye. Sparks lit behind her eyelids as her head fell back on the mattress. She couldn't make her limbs move, could only cringe as she felt his hands roam freely over her.

"That's it, love," he said, ripping her drawers off her now-still legs. He began to unbutton his breeches. "Yes . . ."

"Get off her, you bastard!" James roared as he rushed into the room.

He pulled Waltham from her, sending his fist into the man's face, his gut.

He plowed his fists into Waltham again and again. "You miserable blackguard!"

Blood pounded in his head as he soundly beat Waltham. The bastard soon ceased his struggles, all but limp in his hands.

"Roberts!" Chester yelled, holding James's arm.

Geoffrey grabbed James around the waist. "You'll kill him!"

James threw another blow before letting go of Waltham. The man crumpled into a heap at his feet. James turned quickly to the bed, shocked at the sight he found there. Paul cradled Catherine in his arms, brushing the hair away from her bloodied face.

"Catherine!" James cried, coming to her side. His eyes flew to Paul's.

"She's coming around," Paul said, his voice thick.

Catherine moaned as she opened her eyes. She started as her eyes fell on James, obviously still in the throes of her distress. "No, no, no," she sobbed, twisting away from him.

"Shh, love," James soothed, placing his hand on her cheek. "It's me, Catherine. James. Shh, sweetheart. Everything's all right now."

Catherine ceased her struggles as his voice reached through to her. She held herself still, staring at him for the longest moment. Finally, recognition broke through her haze of horror. "Oh, James!" she sobbed, closing her eyes once more. "Thank God you've come. Oh, thank God."

James held her close as Paul spread her cloak to cover her body. He ran his eyes carefully over her. Her clothes were in rags, her face covered with blood.

Tamping his anger down, James kissed her brow. "Ah, Catherine. I love you."

Catherine opened her eyes and smiled at him, wincing slightly at the discomfort caused by her sore lip.

James bent his head and placed a tender kiss on her injury. He gazed at her. "I love you, Catherine," he said once more. "I've loved you for so very long."

Her eyes, darkened to violet, stared into his. "For how long, James?" she asked softly.

He suddenly grinned, recalling he'd asked her nearly the same thing weeks ago. "I believe I fell in love with you at Chester's wedding," he said. "When I held you in my arms."

Catherine nodded and hugged him, letting out a breath.

Paul crossed to where Waltham lay on the floor, his body bruised and bloodied from James's sound beating. "Is he dead?" he asked Chester.

"No, more's the pity," Chester replied.

Catherine struggled to a sitting position, her eyes wide. She grabbed tightly onto her husband's arms. "He killed her, James," she cried. "He killed Joan."

James swore softly and looked over at his friends. "Summon a constable," he said. "There should be someone from the Watch down in the street." Geoffrey and Chester left together to find the constable. James turned back to Catherine, taking in all of her injuries and the condition of her dress. "Sweetheart, did he . . . ? God, love, did he hurt you?"

"No, James," she answered quickly. "He didn't hurt me in

that . . . manner." She shuddered. "He tried to . . ." she sobbed, biting her lip. "He said I'd lose our baby."

"Shh," James soothed once more, stroking her hair.

Catherine then gazed up at James. "James, do you remember a young lady from several years ago? One named Beatrice?"

James thought for a moment, shaking his head slowly. "No, love," he answered. "I don't."

"She was Waltham's cousin and he was to marry her, or so he told me," Catherine went on, her brow wrinkled. "He said you charmed her, James. That you stole her heart from him."

James took her hand in his, kissing the frown from her brow. "I remember no such lady, love," he assured her. "Before I saw you at Chester's wedding, I had no desire to win any young lady's heart."

Catherine considered him for a moment. "You do have my heart, James," she said, hugging him once more.

"Wait, I recall a Lady Beatrice Thornton," Paul mused. "She died some years back—something about consumption—or so that's what her family put about."

"Waltham said she killed herself," Catherine said sadly. "She stabbed herself with a knife."

"My God!" James exclaimed hugging her close to him. "That bastard probably drove her to it."

"I'm not surprised, given what he did to poor Lady Diane," Paul added.

"What did he do to Diane?" Catherine said shocked.

"He attacked her," Paul said grimly.

Catherine choked back a cry and leaned into her husband's strong embrace.

A constable arrived shortly thereafter, duly shocked at Waltham's condition. The stout man's shock soon gave way to anger as he learned of the man's evil deeds. Holding tightly to James's hand for strength, Catherine told the constable of Joan, of what Waltham had admitted. With obvious regret over Catherine's presence in the room, Geoffrey recounted the horrible crimes the man had committed against Diane Plymouth in Westmorland.

After assuring the gentlemen that he'd keep them apprised

of the man's punishment, the constable gave them permission to leave the dirty little room.

"Take me home, James," Catherine pleaded, her hand cupping his cheek.

James nodded, kissing her palm. Cradling his wife in his arms, he carried her downstairs to Paul's carriage. He didn't release her until they arrived at their townhouse.

"My lord!" Giles exclaimed as he opened the door for his master and mistress. "My lady, are you all right?"

"I'm fine, Giles," she answered wearily.

The man breathed an audible sigh of relief. "I knew that the viscount would find you, my lady," he said with a small smile. "He's a man who loves his wife."

Catherine nodded and looked at James once more, her eyes a dark violet.

James shook his head at the butler, unable to hide his own grin. "Never mind, Giles," he chuckled. "Please see to a bath for Lady Roberts."

The man bowed and turned, leaving them alone in the foyer. James bent his head to Catherine's, his forehead touching hers.

"I do love you, Catherine," he said huskily.

She threw her arms around his neck. "I love you too, James."

He carried her up the stairs to their chamber. Assisting her out of her torn clothing, he waved Annie away and saw to her bath himself. The lady's maid, after expressing her sincere happiness for her mistress's well being, left them. James washed Catherine gently, hiding his anger over the bruises that darkened her face and limbs. She winced as he washed the blood from the corner of her mouth.

"I'm so sorry, Catherine," he said, his throat tight.

"It's all right James," she said with a smile. "It just stings a bit, that's all."

He nodded and continued his gentle ministrations.

After her bath, after he patted her dry and ran his fingers through her damp hair, he pulled her nightgown over her head and laid her on the bed. Peeling off his clothes, he settled himself beside her in the big four-poster.

"We'll send for Morgan in the morning, Catherine," he said, embracing her once more.

"I'm fine, James," she insisted.

He gave her a squeeze and closed his eyes. She drifted off to sleep but he knew he wouldn't find slumber tonight. When he'd heard her scream, when he'd found her in that room with Waltham hurting her so, his heart had nearly stopped. He gave an involuntary shudder at his mind's wanderings.

"My God. I nearly lost you," he whispered against her hair. He held her closer, silent prayers of thanks ringing a litany in his mind.

He didn't know how much time had passed, but sometime later Catherine started to struggle in his arms. Her eyes snapped open and she cried out. The sound was sharp and full of terror.

"Shh, Catherine," he soothed. "I'm here."

She thrashed about, crying, until his soothing voice and touch began to calm her. She came out of her daze. Her eyes focused on his face and a sweet smile of relief curved her lips. "It's you."

He stroked her cheek. "Always."

"I need you, James," she said, staring up at him.

"Catherine . . ."

"I need you to love me, James," she said. "Please. I want to feel you holding me. Loving me."

Desire flared in him at her request. He tamped it down and shook his head at her. "No, love," he said. "I fear I'll hurt you."

She smiled brightly, taking him completely by surprise. "You can't hurt me, James," she said simply. "You can't."

He remembered the words, spoken on their wedding night, and grinned. "God, how I love you," he said, pulling her into his arms. He brought his lips to hers and kissed her gently. Running his hands lovingly over her, he removed the nightgown he'd so carefully put on her. His eyes narrowed as he noted the bite mark on her breast. He kissed the injury, soothing her. His lips moved to her nipple.

"James . . ." she murmured as his mouth closed over the tender bud.

He reached down to the curls that shielded her womanhood,

gently spreading her legs. She moaned as his finger delved inside.

"Ah, Catherine," he rasped, thrilled by her response.

Catherine arched as he found the hidden nub in the folds of her, arousing her further. "Love me, James," she urged, her eyes closed tight. "Love me."

He kissed her once more, laying his body atop hers. He entered her slowly, clenching his teeth as he struggled to hold on to his control. Passion soon took that control from him as Catherine's hands clutched at him. His thrusts became deeper, taking her closer and closer to her release. She sobbed his name as her climax took her, her nails digging into his back. With a shout, he joined her in fulfillment.

"I love you, Catherine," he said when his breathing slowed.

She let out a deep sigh of satisfaction and opened her eyes.

Epilogue

December 1826

Catherine sat in the parlor of Leed Manor, her six-month-old baby boy perched comfortably in her lap. Andrew James Bradford was a beautiful baby, his round head already covered with silky black curls. Catherine dropped a kiss on her son's chubby cheek, urging a happy gurgle from the child's mouth. She hugged him close and let her mind drift for a moment.

Much had happened in the months since her rescue from the dank room at the waterfront. Waltham was dead. He was found so in his cell at Newgate Prison before he could stand trial for his foul deeds against both Joan and Diane, let alone for her abduction. The guards insisted the man had killed himself and no one was of a mind to investigate the matter further. Catherine prayed that Joan and Beatrice would be able to find peace with that hateful man gone from God's earth. Diane Plymouth was on the mend. And with her friends and family more than willing to help her and keep her story safe, she'd no doubt make her reemergence into society when the Season resumed in a few months.

Catherine kissed the baby once more and shook off her mind's wanderings. She looked over at her sister-in-law and smiled. Michelle shakily returned her smile, her eyes nervously following Rose as she scampered about the room. The little girl was nearly three years old now and kept her parents and an endless string of nannies on their toes. Even now, as the ladies watched her so closely, the child managed to wiggle her way into the ashbin near the fireplace.

"Rose!" Michelle exclaimed, jumping to her feet.

Clicking her tongue, Michelle brushed the ashes from Rose's hands. The child merely shrugged, a big grin on her sweet face.

Catherine laughed. "I'm most pleased that Andrew is still content to sit in my lap."

Michelle rolled her eyes, finally returning her smile. It was Christmas Eve, and the family was gathered at the manor once again. Paul and Michelle would host a ball the next evening, continuing the tradition begun the previous year. Catherine was quite looking forward to spending the holiday in such familiar company. She happily anticipated the pleasant conversation coupled with the opportunity to twirl about the room held closely in her husband's arms.

Paul and James returned from their ride, invigorated from the brisk air. Both the Earl of Talbot and James's father had ridden with them, the latter nearly himself again. When the older gentlemen went upstairs to clean themselves up, James and Paul entered the parlor in search of their wives. Catherine looked up as James appeared in the doorway of the parlor, a smile curving her lips.

James returned the expression and crossed to where his wife and child sat. The baby squealed happily and waved his arms at the sight of his father.

"Hello, love," he said to Catherine, kissing her lightly.

"Darling," she answered, a warm look in her violet eyes.

He bent down and tickled the baby under his chin, staring into the gray eyes so like his own. "Hello, little mite." James scooped the baby up in his arms, all but throwing him up into the air. The baby let out a squeal of delight.

"James!" Catherine chided, shaking her head.

James laughed and cradled the boy in the crook of his arm. He turned to face her once more. "Did you pass the afternoon in a pleasant manner?"

"Very," she returned. "I do so love to see you holding him, James. He's your very likeness."

He caught the moment when her thoughts turned from their child to himself. "Catherine," he said, his voice a promise.

When heat flared in her eyes, he knew he'd guessed correctly.

Paul's voice broke through their reverie, causing James to straighten and Catherine to blush lightly.

"Tomorrow's bash should prove quite enjoyable," Paul said with a grin. "Elizabeth's betrothed will be joining us, the poor sod."

"Paul!" Michelle admonished. "I like Lord Palmer very much, as do you."

"He's a pleasant fellow," Paul allowed.

James and Catherine voiced their agreement to Paul's assessment of the gentleman. He was a good sort, and quite smitten with Elizabeth who had quite matured since the entire episode with Waltham. She had spent several weeks with Diane and the two had grown closer. It was at Lord Henry's country estate that she'd met Lord Palmer, a cousin of Diane's who'd been abroad for several years and had only just returned. From what he'd learned from Catherine, that devil Waltham hadn't ruined Elizabeth's chances at her own happy future.

"It's a pity Kane and Rebecca can't join us," James said.

"Oh, I received a note from Rebecca just the other day," Michelle said. "She's quite large with child now and Kane will scarcely allow her out of the house to walk the grounds."

"She must be going mad," Catherine said in sympathy. "I do look forward to seeing Chester and Constance."

"Oh, yes," Michelle put in. "I wish they were bringing the baby, however. We haven't seen her since she was but a few weeks old."

"She's grown even prettier, Michelle," Catherine told her. "She's the very image of Constance."

"That's a very good thing," James cut in.

Catherine swatted his arm, at which he pulled away sharply, jostling the baby. Little Andrew giggled excitedly at the play.

Paul chuckled and walked over to his wife. "Have you discussed tonight's repast with the cook, love?" Paul asked. At her nod, he turned back to James and Catherine and rubbed his hands together in anticipation. "We'll be quite stuffed this evening, I tell you."

"Ah," James said with a grin. "If your cook prepares half of what she did last Christmas Eve, I'll scarcely be able to climb the stairs to our guest room. Why, the lamb was scrumptious. The gravy was thick and—"

Michelle groaned, stopping James in mid sentence. She held her hand over her mouth and ran from the room, leaving Catherine and James staring after her in alarm. James turned back to Paul, disconcerted to find him wearing a silly smile.

"Leed, what's wrong with you?" James asked. "Michelle is obviously ill. Shouldn't you go and see to her?"

"She isn't ill, Roberts," Paul said easily. "It appears little Rose will have a brother or sister come the summer."

"Oh, Paul!" Catherine exclaimed, throwing her arms around her brother. "That's simply wonderful news!"

"Yes," James added. "I daresay what with Rebecca and Michelle on the nest, not to mention our own little addition, we're well on our way to populating half of England."

Michelle returned to the room just in time to overhear James's comment. "You and Catherine may have the next one, Roberts," she put in, recovering her good humor. Her eyes darted to where her daughter stood near an ornately-carved side table. "Rose, don't touch that vase," she began worriedly. "Rose, put that down. No, no! Don't—"

Paul quickly caught the vase from the little girl's hands before she could drop it to the floor. He set it back on the table and looked down at her.

"There now, little love," he said to his daughter. "I fear you'll drive your mother quite mad. Isn't it time for your nap?"

Rose shook her head emphatically. "No nap! No nap!"

Michelle bent down to hug the child. She shot a meaningful glance at Catherine as she ran her fingers through Rose's tousled red curls. "It's time for Andrew to take his nap, sweetheart," Michelle cajoled. "Perhaps Aunt Catherine will let you go upstairs with her to the nursery?"

James knew Catherine caught on to Michelle's ploy when she nodded her assent.

"Come, Rose," she said, holding her hand to the child. "Uncle James and I would much appreciate your help getting Andrew down for his nap."

A big smile spread across Rose's face as she straightened her tiny shoulders. "I'm a big girl, Aunt Catherine," she insisted. "I'll help you."

James nodded solemnly, hiding his own smile. The little girl kissed her mother and father. Catherine held Rose's hand as she led her out of the parlor, James and

Andrew bringing up the rear.

They entered the nursery and Rose quickly explained to her nurse that the baby was sorely in need of a nap. “He’s quite done in,” she said with a nod that caused her red curls to bounce.

The woman nodded sagely and asked the child if perhaps she herself didn’t wish to rest a bit on her bed. Rose placed a noisy kiss on Andrew’s cheek and hopped onto her bed. Placing her thumb in her mouth, she was asleep almost before her head hit the pillow.

Smiling, Catherine took the baby from James and laid him in a crib set in the corner of the large room. James followed her and the two of them stared down at their son, quiet for the moment. Catherine reached down and tickled the baby’s belly, at which he smiled up at her winningly. A dimple showed in his little cheek, his mother’s only visible contribution to his looks.

“My, he’s a handsome little fellow,” James remarked with pride.

Catherine nodded her agreement. “I daresay he’ll be a charming rogue like his father before him,” she said, leaning over the rail to drop a kiss on his silken curls.

The baby yawned and closed his eyes, snuggling into the covers. After a moment, James took Catherine’s hand and led her from the room.

They entered the chamber set aside for their use and James closed the door tightly behind him. He watched Catherine as she walked further into the room.

“We should ready for tea, husband,” she said, bound for the dressing room.

Something troubled him. Something Catherine had said in the nursery. “Wait a moment, love,” he said softly.

Catherine sensed his hesitation and turned toward him. “James, what is it?”

“Do you see me as a charming rogue, Catherine?”

Smiling sweetly, she shook her head at him. She returned to him, reaching up to place her hands on his shoulders. "You're more than charming, James," she said, removing his jacket. She began to unbutton his waistcoat. "So much more."

James untied his cravat as she opened his shirt. She bent her head and placed little kisses on his chest.

"More?" he asked, reaching behind her to unfasten the hooks of her dress.

"Yes," she answered, her lips trailing over him. "You're my husband. My friend. My lover." She kissed his throat, his chin. "You're the man who gave me my son, the man who rescued me, the man who—"

James placed his finger on her mouth to still her. She stared up at him, her eyes dark.

"The man who loves you beyond reason, darling," he finished.

Catherine gave him a slow nod.

His fingers tunneled through her loose curls as he pulled her closer. "I love you, Catherine," he rasped, settling his mouth on hers.

She sighed into his mouth. "You're everything to me, James." She breathed. "Everything and more."

With that, he swept her up into his arms and carried her to the bed. There he loved her thoroughly, drawing gasps of sheer pleasure from her lips.

Afterward, while they lazily summoned the energy to rouse themselves for tea, James marveled at the wonder of his life. He'd discovered this girl, this violet-eyed angel, directly beneath his nose. Before he'd found her, he'd been content to charm his way through society, never letting any one woman touch his heart. He knew now that it had taken more than charm to win Catherine's heart.

Happily, he found he was more than up to the challenge.

About the Author

JoMarie DeGioia has been making up stories for as long as she can remember and has spent years giving voice to the characters in her head. She's known Mickey Mouse from the "inside," has been a copyeditor for her town's newspaper, and currently works as a bookseller. She writes Historical Romances with a touch of mystery and Contemporary Romances with a touch of home. She divides her time between Central Florida and New England, and you may contact her at JoMarie@JoMarieDeGioia.com

www.ingramcontent.com/pod-product-compliance
Lightning Source LLC
Chambersburg PA
CBHW060307260626
47160CB00007B/2529

* 9 7 8 1 9 2 7 5 5 5 1 3 2 *